DEVON C. FORD
ADAPTATION

TOY SOLDIERS

AETHON BOOKS

ADAPTATION

©2019 DEVON C. FORD

For their time spent finding obscure translations for me.

ALSO IN THE SERIES

Toy Soldiers:

Apocalypse

Aftermath

Abandoned

Adversity

Adaptation

Book six yet to be named (coming 2020)

PREFACE

All spelling and grammar in this book is UK English except for proper nouns and those American terms which just don't anglicize.

PROLOGUE

"Absolutely not, Professor," said the man in the grey suit, with a cold finality to his words. He didn't raise his voice, but the intensity was there. "No way. No how. No chance whatsoever." He stabbed an index finger onto the desk to underline his point in case he hadn't been heard clearly. "*No.*"

"But," Professor Sunil Grewal whined, annoyed that the bureaucrats lacked the ability to comprehend that what he was asking for was vital, "without subjects to conduct the research on, Professor Chambers and I simply won't be able to confirm whether or not the serum works, let alone what side-effects it might have on—"

"He's right," Chambers agreed reluctantly from the only other chair in the room, which he'd occupied without offering to his colleague. The two men hated one another, or at least Chambers despised Grewal, as he'd been personally responsible for creating the unnatural abomination which had wiped out what he guessed would be more than half of the world, by that point. "Without a test subject, a series of test subjects ideally, we can't be certain of anything."

"I'm confused," said the suit who called himself Agent

Fisher, as he leaned back at his desk and steepled his fingers. "You assured me that the recipe you cooked up in the lab killed the virus ten times out of ten. Explain to me how that's now wrong."

"It's not *wrong*," Grewal snapped petulantly. "Tests in a petri dish are very different from tests in live host subjects. Already there have been reports of… *variations* in the behaviour of some infected subjects, and we aren't even close to beginning to understand or explain why that is. If you'd simply allow us to study a series of captured specimens a—"

"*Study?*" the CIA man enunciated coldly. "*Captured Specimens?* Professor Asshole, I'm not sure you fully understand the ramifications of those words, so let me lay it out for you." He whipped a hand up and snapped his forefinger and thumb together, indicating to Grewal that he should keep his lips firmly together while the man spoke.

"Studying a captured specimen means constructing a purpose-built lab with strict control and containment procedures. That holds significant risk to the United States Armed Forces personnel involved in every aspect. *Furthermore*," he said loudly, repeating the gesture with his fingers to stop Grewal from interrupting when he saw the opportunity. "Capturing those specimens would require missions in hostile territory to return an infectious *host subject* to US soil and jeopardise those personnel on the mission. Moreover, we would threaten the safety and security of the *entire* United States by bringing even one of those *things* back here, so no, Professor, you can't ha—"

"What if we don't have to bring them back here?" Chambers asked quietly from across the office, his eyes staring upwards at the ornate patterns chasing themselves over the ceiling. Grewal and the suit looked in his direction, waiting for the rest of his thought. Chambers leaned forwards in his chair, eyes back on the two men and his hands moving with the words he used to air the idea out loud.

"There's a secure, military-run base in Britain, right?" he said, waiting for a reluctant nod from the CIA man, who wondered which one of the people at the facility had been talking too much. "So we task their military to capture the specimens and we do the testing over there. That way the whole Atlantic sits between them and home."

The suit sat back, watching Grewal out of the corner of his eye before turning to fix him with a direct stare and a crooked smile.

"I'll run it up the chain of command," he said, pretending that he wasn't a very senior shot-caller and not convincing either of the scientists, "but I'd say you two need to pack up and get ready to fly to Scotland."

ONE

Squadron Sergeant Major Dean Johnson couldn't sleep. He didn't sleep much at all anymore. He stood in the morning air, the pre-dawn chill tightening his skin and reminding him that he was alive, sipping from a mug of tea as he thought about the day's work to come. Exchanging a curt nod of greeting with the evidently cold man standing guard and eagerly awaiting the arrival of his relief, he stared out over the low, rolling landscape looking inland over the half-hidden profile of the Warrior emplaced to guard the single approach road.

Leaving the Hilltop wasn't an issue for him as the place had never even remotely been home; home was with his squadron and what he had learned via radio from one of the few people of his former life still alive made him feel like a nomad.

The crunch of feet on gravel made him stiffen, until he reminded himself that he wasn't in danger, wasn't out in the battleground that was anywhere not protected or fortified against the remnants of the population who had died yet continued to walk the Earth. Turning, he saw the expected sight of Peter stepping in his direction; his small feet treading lightly, as if suggesting the boy had evolved and adapted to this new and brutal world as much as the faster type of Screechers had. He gave his young companion a nod, warmer than the one he'd given the sentry, and softened his usually harsh features with a small smile.

"Can't sleep either?" he muttered in a low voice, sympathetic to the fact that almost everyone else there was still slept.

"Never do," Peter answered in a tone of voice that made him sound forty years older than his mere decade. His brow furrowed slightly as he thought about it. "Didn't before, not really, and finding out about…"

He trailed off as though saying the words out loud would make the knowledge of his sister's survival and subsequent disappearance all too real. Johnson reached out his huge left hand and rested it gently on the nape of the boy's neck, giving him a light squeeze of reassurance in an attempt to convey how he felt.

So many emotions ran through him at that moment. He felt a heavy loss for the boy and, if he were honest, for himself. He felt a burning and fierce pride for the sacrifice of the two Royal Marines who had held their own long enough to allow him to drive the box van away from their small sanctuary and save the lives of the two children and the others, and that pride swelled inside him when he learned from Daniels that they had made it out alive somehow.

"I know, lad," he said, feeling the words to be wholly inadequate but needing to voice his understanding. "I know. We won't give up yet, though." He looked down to meet Peter's eyes with his own. "You believe me?"

Peter gave a sad smile which seemed to say that he knew Johnson meant the words but he was just too pessimistic, too broken by the events of the last months, and indeed all of his life before, to allow himself to believe anything good could ever happen again. He let out a long, resigned sigh.

"If she's survived this long," the boy said as he shrugged his shoulders to hide his neck from the cold air, "then I'm sure she'll manage a little while longer."

Johnson felt a wave of sadness at his words because he realised they were given to reassure the old soldier and not to provide the child beside him with any form of comfort.

The boy's resilience and maturity humbled Johnson. He'd seen more good sense and practicality from him than from many soldiers he'd commanded in his years, and could only imagine what Peter would have become if he'd had a better start in life. If he'd had the opportunities and education which had been wasted on Oliver Palmer, he'd have quite likely become an intelligent and capable leader, like the infuriatingly arrogant second lieutenant's older brother was.

Both of those men were gone now; travelled north to Scotland, according to Daniels. He let out his own sigh and wondered if he'd ever meet up with them and the other members of the squadron again.

"I'm sure she will," he said quietly, bringing his attention back to the world and the boy's words. "I'm sure she will."

Peter seemed to shake his own dark mood off in the same moment and rolled his shoulders to stand taller, as though he'd banished the frightened child inside him to his room without dinner.

"When do we go?" he asked the squadron sergeant major with no squadron.

"We?"

Peter smirked playfully. "You grown-ups wouldn't last five minutes without me and Amber to look after you." Johnson laughed in spite of his own dark mood and the early hour.

"Oh, if I'd had a squadron of Peters... we'll go soon," he said as he extended a finger towards the partially hidden light armour, "and we're taking that to be on the safe side."

It was Peter's turn to smile. Despite the collapse of their world, despite the fact that they had been cut off and abandoned, he was still a ten year old boy, and what ten year old boy didn't want to ride in a tank?

Pauline, the apparent leader of the Hilltop survivors, wasn't surprised when Johnson had told her they would be leaving soon. She didn't expect such rough soldiery types to sit back and settle, not when there was a war to fight, and the news that they would be setting off to link up with their own people and search for Amber's mother and Peter's sister was expected.

In some bizarre parody of loved ones setting off for a day's work, she brought them all sandwiches made with thick, fresh bread to sustain them on their search, along with a few insulated flasks of strong, sugary tea. The flasks, arrayed inside the Warrior side by side, their tartan decorations looking like some new type of ammunition for the 30mm main gun, provided Johnson with a curious amusement as he maneuvered the big, tracked vehicle out of the widened ditch it had occupied to hide the hull from any approaching enemy.

Michaels, one of his former troop sergeants turned Hilltop dictator by all accounts, had still retained enough sanity to ensure the Warrior had a full tank of diesel and was loaded with both blue and yellow-tipped ammunition for the autocannon. Johnson sneered suspiciously at the controls for the chain gun which was widely rumoured to be a poor upgrade for their tried and tested general purpose machine guns firing the same ammunition.

Still, he told himself, beggars couldn't afford to be choosers, especially when he felt the grunt of the engine through the controls and it bucked free of the ditch which would've stranded even the most capable off-road truck for an eternity.

Being the only man among them accustomed to operating and living inside an armoured fighting vehicle, he was forced from his rightful place in the turret and took up residence in the forward hull to drive. Peter, much to his absolute delight, was offered a spot inside the turret alongside Bufford, who Johnson had trained in the basic use of the chain gun.

"What about the big bastard?" Buffs asked him as they sat in intimately close proximity as the commander and gunner would. Johnson patted the breech of the 30mm and shook his head sadly at the sergeant of the Special Boat Service.

"You expect me to be able to teach a frogman how to hand-crank an HE round into this and follow up with a clip so as not to get a stoppage and have to start over?" Bufford gave him a withering look, secretly pleased that the comfortable inter-services rivalry had begun to reassert itself. "Just stick to the chain gun," he told him. "You still probably fuck it up, so pay attention. And no coffee breaks," he grumbled as he fought to maintain a straight face, "I don't want to have to retrain you when you forget it all."

Astrid Larsen and Kimberley Perkins stepped inside the dark confines of the troop-carrying section comprising the rear of the Warrior, their arms loaded with bags of supplies and weapons. Amber followed, her own backpack stuffed with her favourite things, along with water and food should she need it. The top of that bag sprouted a threadbare and tired-looking stuffed lamb which had previously been Peter's sister's and had been one of his only comforts from the place where he used to live—not that he called it home even in his head. It had become Amber's prized possession not long after he had found her alone and frightened and she had carried it with her ever since. She also carried Peter's creation, his 'sticker' as he called it, fashioned originally from a pitchfork and modified for small hands to wield against the shambling corpses still wandering the landscape.

"Zero-Bravo, Zero-Bravo," Johnson said into the radio after they'd said their farewells to the civilians who had shown them kindness, "this is Foxtrot-Three-Three-Alpha."

He waited a beat before the excited voice of corporal

Charlie Daniels came back to him, his usual calm radio demeanour chipped away to release the emotion he felt.

"Three-Three-Alpha, Zero-Bravo," he replied in quick words, using the out of date rotated callsigns which were the last they had been issued.

Johnson pressed the button to transmit but took his finger away again.

"Fuck it," he said aloud to himself, unheard by the other two members of their little band inside the tank over the noise of the engine. He pressed to transmit again, this time abandoning the protocols he had spent a lifetime drilling others to adhere to.

"Charlie, we're on our way to you now. Get the kettle on, lad. Out."

TWO

"What the *bally hell* do you mean?" Second Lieutenant Oliver Simpkins-Palmer shrieked obnoxiously at the uniformed but hatless man standing safely on the bow of a ferry twenty paces from land. "I order you to dock that boat, *immediately*, and allow my men and these civilians to board." The soldier, wearing no obvious badge of rank or indication of his unit, could be heard laughing by everyone on the empty concrete of the Mallaig ferry port.

"Who's *actually* in charge?" he yelled back.

"Now you look here," Palmer erupted, his face turning crimson and spittle launching from his mouth on a trajectory like heavy artillery. His finger was extended, wagging furiously as though the mere threat of the digit would enforce his weak words. "I'll have you court-martialled an—"

"What seems to be the problem?" a voice asked from behind him, cutting him off and making him suddenly aware of his self-inflicted embarrassment, not only at being denied after a life of entitled ease, but by the shame of losing control of himself.

"Major," Palmer said, composing himself and greeting the

man with the genteel nod of an aristocratic bow. He stepped aside for the tall, bearded Special Air Service officer to lay eyes on his enemy, "this…" he waved a frustrated hand in the general direction of the small car ferry, "*man*, is refusing my orders to dock and allow us to board. I must insist that y—"

"That you, Tip?" Major Downes called out.

"It is," replied the man testily in a broad Newcastle accent. "I'll leave you to have a word, Boss." He turned away, stepping down from whatever he had stood on to call out his instructions to the officer.

"Lieutenant," Downes said, "perhaps you need to take a minute?"

The order was made in a polite, suggestive way which Palmer's education and breeding should have picked up on instantly, but the exhaustion and stress of their long journey by road had robbed him of his decorum.

"Major, I really must insis—"

"Oliver," Downes interrupted him angrily, "you really must *stop* insisting. In fact, bugger off out of my sight while I talk to a *real* soldier." Palmer looked ashen, as if he'd been struck in the face with a dead fish. In truth, he was not the only one to be so exhausted by days of travel under constant threat, and Downes' uncharacteristic outburst served to underline just how strung out they all were. He watched as the young officer moved off, uncertainly at first, but building up to a stomping march, no doubt to find his older brother and make the man's life harder. Downes sighed, wondering how one family could produce two so incredibly different sons. He turned back to the man on the bow of the ferry sitting low in the water.

"How've you been, Tip?" he asked corporal Stanley Tipuric of 'B' squadron, SAS.

"Not too bad an'all, considerin'," he responded dolorously. "Good to see you made it."

"Tell me about it," Downes agreed. "And you too."

"Still got your boys?"

"I do," Downes called back, "it'll take more than this shit to kill off Mac," he added, knowing that a jibe at the hard Scotsman's expense would serve to break whatever ice there was between them.

"I'll need yous all to follow the instructions to the letter," Tip said in a more professional tone now that the brief pleasantries were out of the way.

"Containment and quarantine?"

"Aye," Tip shouted back, waving an arm behind him to some unseen person controlling the boat. "The Colonel'll fill you in later."

"Colonel?" Downes asked. "I thought Major Kelly was in charge here."

"Aye, only it's *Colonel* Kelly now."

———

"Honestly, the man *laughed* when I gave him an order! Laughed! And the Major added insult to injury by banishing me so he could speak to—"

"Olly," Captain Palmer interrupted tiredly as he rubbed both hands over his stubbled cheeks, "did it occur to you who the man might be if the Major knew him on sight?" His younger brother recoiled as he always did when he had missed the obvious, his chin retracting so much that it all but disappeared until he regained his composure.

"I don't give a good God damn who he is," the younger brother blurted out, albeit with less gusto than his original complaint. He further betrayed his anxiety when he glanced surreptitiously over both shoulders before continuing his rant in a softer tone. "I don't care if the man sprouted wings and was anointed by Her Majesty the bloody Queen; he's a rank and file man and he failed to observe the ru—"

He stopped talking, mouth hanging open in confusion as his older brother simply walked away with an exasperated shake of his head.

Palmer senior arrived at the edge of the docks just as his German counterpart did. Hauptman Wolff, as characteristically pleased to be alive as he was every day, looked just as tired as Palmer felt, although he somehow made his tiredness seem far more precise, as he did with everything. The two officers fell in step as they approached the SAS Major.

"I rather fear we'll find ourselves interned in some kind of concentration ca…" Palmer began, his words trailing off as he realised too late the insensitivity of them.

"I suspect," Wolff replied without any trace of anger or upset, "that you are correct." A smirk began at one corner of his mouth before it spread uncontrollably. "And you should not fear saying such things to a German, Captain. We are just as appalled as you are about the history of our armies, as I think that you are of your own histories, no?"

Palmer was saved from having to respond and defend the proud honour of the British Empire, as the major heard their approach and turned to fill them in on developments.

"Small contingent of police, civilian and military, but mostly it's our boys," he informed the two captains. "Pretty much all of B squadron were home when it kicked off; on standby for the terrorism thing and all that."

"Am I to presume that they will want us quarantined?" Palmer asked him.

"Yes," Downes said, "civvies first. They want three loads so we don't inundate them."

"Inundate?" Wolff enquired politely but uncertainly.

"The boys on the island don't want too many of us at once," Palmer explained. "Rather than be overwhelmed in quarantine, they prefer that we stay here until they can process us in a more controlled manner, I presume."

Downes nodded, taking charge for the first time in the months he and Palmer had known one another.

"Captain Wolff," he said, earning a click of the man's boot heels to indicate his undivided attention. "Can you maintain watch on the road and come over on the last boat with my boys and me?" The German tank commander's head nodded in a short, sharp bow.

"Of course, but I do not see how these," he held his left arm out, ramrod straight and palm held vertically flat, to point at the small civilian car ferries, "will possibly transport the weight of our tanks."

"And you'd be absolutely right," Downes responded, which is why we're all dismounting and going over on foot. Vehicles stay on this side of the water. Infection risk."

Palmer swore that he could have detected the slightest gasp of shock and loss from their ally, and he knew only too keenly how the loss of a man's mount affected him, as he had been forced to leave his own Chieftain behind many months before.

"I must protest this," Wolff said, unknowingly repeating the words of the younger Palmer which had so recently earned him a humiliating retort. "What infection can a machine have? It cannot catch a virus! Why must we leave our tanks…" He trailed off as his eyes followed the outstretched hand of Downes and took in the sight of a matted, crushed slab of blackened meat on the front of the nearest vehicle. White bone jutted out of the mess of gore and rags as an unidentifiable chunk slid slowly away from the metal to hit the ground and make them all grimace at the soft slapping sound it made.

"I understand, Major," Wolff said quietly.

"They'll still be here," Downes reassured the man. "No Screecher I've seen yet can figure out the controls on a Leopard…"

"But," Wolff answered softly, "I do not like the thought of leaving *Edda* alone here among the enemy."

Palmer and Downes exchanged a look, both men fighting down the urge to laugh. Palmer's tank had been called *Annabelle*, and as much as he'd enjoyed the bond with the machine, he hadn't felt the same heartbreak that their friend was evidently feeling.

"Edda?" Downes asked quietly, unable to resist.

"Ja," Wolff shot back with a look of challenge in his eyes, "this is the name of my grandmother. It means maiden of battle, like the Valkyries of the Norse." His impassioned defence of the name of a tank left both British officers silent for a moment until Palmer placed a gentle hand on Wolff's shoulder.

"Edda will be here when we need her again," he reassured him. They were saved any further awkwardness as the ferry bumped into the dock gently, emitting a clanging sound loud enough to remind all of them that they weren't exactly safe until they got off the mainland.

"Julian," Downes said as he turned to Palmer, "if you could organise the civilians? Send as many of your chaps with them as you can and the rest are to take the second boat."

Palmer nodded. "What about Mister Lloyd?" Downes glanced up, taking in their theatre and scanning the assembled mix of people for the marine officer. Spotting him adjusting a defensive position of a pair of surviving marines, he satisfied himself that the job of their defence was adequately taken care of.

"If you could inform the Royal Marines that they will be taking the second transport. The *Hauptmann* and I will fill the last one." He turned away but snapped his fingers as a thought struck him.

"Actually," he said carefully, "if you wouldn't mind being on the first one? Perhaps your, err, perhaps the Second Lieu-tenant can accompany the remainder of the men?" Palmer swallowed and gave a weak smile of understanding. The shame of his brother's poor attitude and ineptitude at all things soldiering was a blemish on his reputation, but blood was blood and privately he couldn't stand to hear his brother maligned by so many people.

"I'll let him know, Major," he said tonelessly.

"All aboard," came a soft and distinctively Geordie shout from the sloping dock into the icy water. "One at a time, if you don't mind," Tipuric said to the nervous civilians as they stretched cramped limbs and stiff backs on the short walk towards the boat. "This way to safety, folks."

THREE

"What the bleedin'ell is she doing?" Sergeant Bill Hampton asked as he looked out of the window. Marine Enfield, a man who had been unnervingly quiet and still, even before the world burned down and he lost his best friend in a helicopter crash, appeared beside his sergeant soundlessly. Hampton flinched in fright before covering his shock with a string of expletives.

"Shouldn't be out there by herself," Hampton complained, "not even wearing a proper coat…"

Enfield stared out of the window of the room they shared, the only sound he made a low whistle of breath through his nose. He watched the girl for a few moments longer, before shrugging and turning away. Neither of them had spoken to the only other people to have arrived separately, apart from themselves that was, and neither knew how they were so intrinsically linked to one another through their associations.

Hampton continued to watch the girl, seeing her breath mist and linger in the heavy, cold air, like miniature clouds which hung to mark her progress towards the frosted-over hull of the tracked vehicle. Seeing her bang on the side of it and step back, he allowed himself a private smile as the squadron's surviving radio man popped out of the hatch to lean way over to accept whatever hot beverage she'd brought him.

———

Charlie Daniels, shivering inside the empty interior of his Sultan command vehicle as the heater powered by the small external generator struggled to fight off the cold, jumped when he heard two bangs on the hull directly behind his head. Too often he'd experienced and subsequently relived the sounds of so many undead hands clawing at the armour like a frustrated cat attacking a sealed tin of tuna, knowing that something tasty hid inside.

Taking a few breaths to relax and compose himself, he stood and spun the handle to open the hatch before poking his head and shoulders out.

"Down here," said a small voice. Daniels leaned over to take in the smiling face of the teenage girl cupping a tin mug in both hands. The contents steamed tantalisingly, which told Charlie all he needed to know. Reaching out with a broad smile, he took the drink and thanked her, bringing it to his face to inhale the sweet steam. He wrapped his hands around the mug, his gloves protecting him from the heat of it; at least, protecting all but two of his fingers, since he'd cut those two from his glove so he could still manipulate the radio dials.

Hot chocolate. With a sigh of satisfaction, he gingerly touched his lips to the drink, only to recoil as the liquid was hotter than lava.

"What you up to?" the girl asked.

"Just waiting for my friend to call up on the radio," he told her, forgetting his very recent injury and foolishly trying the drink again to see if it had cooled down in the last second.

"Can I help?"

Daniels opened his mouth to answer, recognising that he would actually be glad o the company of someone interested in his secondary profession. But a nagging doubt plucked at the back of his mind.

"Do you want to bring someone else to keep you company?" he asked her awkwardly.

"Like who?"

"Like, err, like that woman you turned up with?" he tried, listing the only person he knew that she knew, bar the now-absent SAS patrol who had found them. Their arrival had sparked another, more concerning fear about their security, causing them to face the prospect of risk coming from other people for the first time since the virus had swept over the country.

"She's been in bed for over a week," the girl answered, reaching up to grasp the cold metal and placing a boot on it, ready to haul herself up.

"Hold on," Daniels said, suddenly seeming worried that the girl was coming aboard regardless of the need for a chaperone.

"What?" she said, ceasing her climb as she saw no way to scale the high side.

"It's…"

"You're worried what people will think if you hang around with a girl my age?" Daniels looked shocked but swallowed and nodded.

"Don't be so silly," she told him dismissively and resumed her climbing.

"Go 'round the front," he told her, "you'll never get up this way." He waited as she dropped back down, heard her boots shuffling towards the lower section at the nose of the vehicle until she reappeared on the hull.

"Move over."

He did, ducking back inside and moving away from the

hatch as she lowered herself inside, flailing for purchase with her feet. Eventually spilling into the Sultan's interior, she straightened her clothing and grinned at Daniels.

"Easy," she said, her smile wavering as her teeth chattered.

Daniels frowned, glancing around and resting his eyes on a tattered, green army smock that he snatched up and went to drape around her shoulders. He froze, leaving the jacket resting over her slim frame as he backed off.

"Relax," the girl said, "I know you don't have any funny ideas." Daniels relaxed but couldn't help maintaining the frown.

"How do you know? I mean," he added hurriedly, "I *don't*, but still... how do you know?"

The girl shrugged. "I don't really," she admitted, reaching down to slip a sharpened slither of metal from her right boot and twirl it before her face to catch the dull light from the open hatch. "But if you did have, you'd only have them once, know what I mean?"

Daniels knew precisely what she meant.

"So, who's your friend and where is he?" the girl asked. Daniels slid back into the seat in front of the radio as his fingers went to work on the switches and dials.

"He's my boss, actually, and he's on his way here."

"He's in the army too?"

"Yeah. He's my Squadron Sergeant Major," he said, investing the title with all the grandeur he felt for it.

"So?"

"Sooo... so he's my SSM." He shrugged as if to indicate that the matter was dealt with. "That's it. We got separated after the island—that was the last place we were before here—and everyone thought he was gone, but I wouldn't take those odds..." he glanced at her to see her confusion and rephrased. "He never made it out on a helicopter when some of the boys and the civvies were knee-deep in a hell of a fight. Well, he did make it out, only the helicopter went down, which we'd never have known about if they hadn't survived the crash and the winter." The girl looked at him with a curious eyebrow raised.

"You're really confusing," she said. "You know that?"

"Sorry," Daniels said, sipping the drink again and wincing as it was still unnaturally close to boiling. "My boss was missing in action, and everyone thought he was a goner. I stayed behind in case he popped back up, still believed you see, and he did. Not long after everyone went, as it happened…"

"Went where?" she asked, picking up a new avenue of questioning but intending to circle back around to her original lines of enquiry.

"Scotland. Or at least a big island just off the coast of Scotland."

"And what are they doing there?"

Daniels shrugged, not entirely sure how to answer the question with anything meaningful.

"Not worrying about zombies. I thought you knew all of this. Didn't you get the option to go with them?"

"They said something about going," she answered with a shrug of disinterest. "My brother's still here, so I'll stay." Daniels' face dropped. He stopped tweaking the dials on the radio and sucked in a breath ready to be the voice of reason. Turning to face her, he started to speak as gently as he could.

"Liste—"

"Don't," she snapped at him. "I'm sick of people telling me that he *probably* didn't make it or that he *probably* got evacuated or anything else like that. Unless you've seen Peter walking around as one of those… *things*, then you can save your breath."

Daniels shut his mouth and turned back to the radio. The two sat in silence for a long time before she broke the spell, and it started with a conversation about music. She couldn't understand that for a car, as that was essentially how she saw the tracked command vehicle, it didn't have a radio or cassette player. When Daniels pointed out the radio, she laughed at him and explained it as though the corporal was a little slow.

Her laugh wasn't cruel. It wasn't unkind or hurtful but more that her default setting was one of defensive aggression; as though she was a much older woman who had been bitten hard by life and chose to get her digs in first.

The two unlikely companions talked for a while as they grew more comfortable around one another, never straying far from the safe topics of conversation so as not to scratch any surface too deeply and risk unveiling their darker thoughts beneath.

"I heard you mention…" Daniels began, shaking his head slightly as he decided to just come straight out with what he meant. "Someone said you had a brother." She glared at him, her nostrils flaring once and her eyes glazing over with a coldness that spoke volumes about how fast the girl could erect a defensive wall. Daniels saw that and spoke more quickly to prevent her closing down completely. With his eyes cast down to stare through the thick metal beneath his boots, he muttered the words through a tightening throat.

"I had a brother," he told her. "My twin brother, actually. He was six minutes older than me, which he loved telling people…" Daniels sucked in a sudden breath through his nose and sat upright, delivering the next sentence as though reporting on the weather. "He moved away a few years back, chasing some promotion. The town where he lived is gone now. One of the swarms—did you ever see one of those?"

She shook her head.

"Those swarms were something else. Not just thousands of people in a crowd, but moving like they all became one and poured over things like water." His face contorted slightly out of anger or repulsion before he mastered his emotions and physically shook the feelings away. "Well, one of those swarms went through where he lived, according to the reports. I have to accept that he's either one of them, in which case he probably went down in the fight at the island, or he never came back as one of them and is just... *dead*."

He gave another simple shrug, as if to indicate that it was just one of those things. It was what it was and shit happens and *c'est la vie* and any other worthless platitude he could think of to try and feel less wretched about everything. Finally sniffing and looking up through wet eyes at her, he saw his gaze mirrored almost identically.

She gave him a small, sad smile.

"I'm sorry about your brother," she told him softly. "But mine isn't dead and he isn't one of them. I *know it*." Daniels gave her the same pitying smile and opened his mouth to respond before the radio headset crackled in time to stop him. He snatched it up and turned up the volume.

"Zero-Bravo, Zero-Bravo, this is Foxtrot-Three-Three-Alpha."

"Three-Three-Alpha, Zero-Bravo," Daniels answered almost breathlessly, agonising his way through the pause that followed.

"Charlie, we're on our way to you now. Get the kettle on, lad. Out."

Daniels smiled broadly, a warming feeling of happiness and satisfaction radiating through his body as he turned to regard the girl again. He realised in that moment, even though common sense had told him that his brother was almost certainly gone, his faith that Johnson was still out there had paid off, so her faith that her brother was still out there couldn't be dismissed just yet.

FOUR

"A few shufflers starting to head our way," Mac reported to Downes and Lieutenant Lloyd, who were organising the loading of the second ferry.

"Any Limas?" Lloyd asked. The dour-faced Scot shook his head slowly, but the negative reply didn't offer any hint of optimism.

"Not yet," he intoned ominously.

It had been that way ever since the cold weather had shown the first signs of moving on. Throughout the coldest time, they had seen far fewer of the Screechers, the shuffling corpses slowed by the unspeakable damage wrought upon their bodies by the elements and other factors. They held no regard for one another, and many were found dragging themselves along roads on worn stubs of fingers, their legs having been crushed into ruin by the trampling feet of their undead comrades.

Since the days became less bitterly freezing cold, the shuffling type of zombie had begun to re-emerge, or at least had started to move enough to catch up with them wherever they were and stagger into sight, like the most catastrophically hungover people; their clothes rotting and falling off them in strips to expose the pale, dead, emaciated flesh underneath.

"How far out?" Downes asked, his undivided attention on his sergeant.

"Few hundred yards and closing. All coming straight up the road."

"Tell Smiffy he has the green light to start popping them," Downes instructed, "but nobody else is to fire unless they get in close." Mac nodded his understanding of the simple orders and turned away to see them fulfilled without another word. Smiffy, the SAS patrol's Londoner, was still in possession of the suppressed stolen Soviet VAL sniper rifle and had proved his ability to hit undead heads from distance with very little noise, in comparison to the loud reports of other weapons.

"It's only a matter of time," Lloyd warned the SAS major, meaning that the one kind of enemy invariably led to the other making an appearance. The addition of a few Limas would complicate their evacuation no end, not to mention run the risk of losing men and bringing the contagion to the safety of the island stronghold.

"Isn't it always?"

Lloyd smiled back at the taller man, silently acknowledging his point that they were only ever moments away from total disaster.

As the second ferry, loaded with a mixture of bedraggled squadron men and royal marines, chugged slowly backwards to boil a wash of white water against the sloping dock, a raised voice from behind turned Downes' attention. Eyes darting left and right, he saw in an instant what was happening.

"Limas!" cried Dezzy, left hand cupping his mouth as his right gripped the stock of the dismounted machine gun which he had a worryingly intimate relationship with. His suppressed MP5 bounced against his waist as he jogged back, abandoning the frontal position to move and cover their left flank, where a more pressing danger had presented itself.

Downes glanced over his shoulder, seeing that their ride off the mainland was still blocked from docking by the slow moving second vessel. Gunfire broke out; not the subtle, focused coughs of his team's weapons as they lined up careful head shots, but the heavy clattering bursts of the MG3 machine guns mounted on the German tanks. The very fact that they were forced to use them conveyed enough of a threat to cause Downes significant concern, and his orders reflected that.

"Recall everyone on foot," he bawled, "to my position *NOW.*"

His orders were relayed, only half heard by some in between the chattering bursts of heavy gunfire. Mac reached him first with Smiffy close behind, the long barrel of his sniper rifle jutting over one shoulder as the automatic shotgun appeared in his hands. Downes saw it and followed suit without hesitation, dropping his MP5 on its sling to retrieve Dezzy's shotgun, which he still carried after their demolitions man refused to part company with his acquired GPMG.

No sense in wasting 9-mil bullets and blowing out the baffles on the MP5s, his mind reasoned. *Plus, 12-bore cartridges are a lot easier to come by than bullets.*

His uncharacteristic loss of concentration was shattered by Dezzy stitching three short bursts from his belt-fed gun at a shape appearing between two buildings.

"*Rückzug! Alle Mann zu mir!*" Wolff bawled to his men, who responded immediately by stopping their onslaught with the mounted guns and closing hatches to drop to the ground and run towards the dock.

Lighter gunfire, rapid and staccato, added to the din as the dismounted troopers added fire to the approaching mob with their Uzi submachine guns. A knot of men formed, all facing outwards and cutting down anyone, any*thing*, appearing between the vehicles and around nearby buildings. They weren't in any immediate danger of being overrun, but their position was undefendable in the long term and they all knew it.

"Fast fucker!" Mac yelled. "Eyes left!"

Downes turned, his eyes passing over the prone form of Dezzy, who was working his machine gun alone like a stone-cold professional, searching for the subject of Mac's warning.

Then he saw it. Jumping, no, *flying* through the air like no human body had the right to do. It must have flanked their position, creeping close before leaping from the roof of an abandoned car to attack Dezzy from outside his field of fire. The implications for what Downes saw didn't even register as he brought up the barrel of the wicked shotgun and fully depressed the trigger, while holding on as tightly as possible with his left hand. The gun bucked, shaking his entire body violently as it spat the contents of half a dozen heavy cartridges in the direction of Dezzy's impending death.

He fired on instinct, not properly aiming the gun or even holding it, so that it couldn't do him damage, but every shot seemed to spit from the barrel in a gout of flame so slowly that he began to fear he would fail his man.

The fourth shot blew away the lower part of the creature's extended left arm, the inertia of the lead spinning the body slightly as physics did what it did best. The fifth shot seemed to hit nothing, but the sixth caught the Lima's spinning skull to blast away the top of the dome like a boiled egg being expertly opened.

Time seemed to return to normal speed as the ruined attacker slammed onto Dezzy's back and forced the air from his lungs with a pained *oompff*.

"Dez!" Smiffy screamed, running towards the intertwined bodies and lining up a kick to the jaw of the zombie. Downes saw that his shot hadn't killed it at all, merely stunned it, and watched in utter horror as he tried to raise his gun again, only to realise that any shot would invariably pepper the SAS.

Smiffy's kick connected directly under the jaw, which was already beginning to open in anticipation of a bite of warm flesh. The open maw snapped shut with a sound louder than a pistol shot as Downes saw two small, white projectiles fly out of the thing's mouth in opposing directions. The force of the kick was so great that it took Smiffy off his feet to land on Dez's back and force another grunt of breathless pain from him. Downes looked at what was half of his patrol vulnerable on the ground, taking the initiative and raising the brutal shotgun as the filthy creature was just clear of them.

But he didn't fire. Seeing the Lima rocked back on its knees, upper body arched backwards at a grotesquely unnatural angle, Downes lowered the shotgun and fought against the spasms in his stomach as he took in the sight.

With his last shot, which had opened up the top of the skull, combined with the savage force of the kick, the thing's brain had leapt up and out to hang in gory ruin over the right side of its face. Milky eyes fluttered as the damage wasn't quite enough to end the creature, and the sight of that fluttering involuntarily tightened Downes' finger around the trigger for him to destroy the pulpy mess.

"Fuck's sake!" Dezzy groaned as he rolled out from under Smiffy, who was cursing and clutching his right ankle.

"We must be leaving, Major!" Wolff shouted, tugging at his shoulder. He nodded, helping Mac drag the other two troopers to their feet to half carry them to the last ferry, which was finally approaching the dock. Downes looked around, seeing a few zombies but marking all of them as the faster type from their easily recognisable movements. Gunfire continued all around him, but without him and his team adding to it, the encroaching enemy were making concerning progress.

"Into the water," he shouted, repeating himself louder until Wolf shouted the translation in German. Louder cracks of gunfire sounded then, making the major look up to search for the source as his legs felt the savage cold of the water he'd stepped into. The second ferry, stopped just out of the way of their own, sprouted all of their marines pouring volleys of shots into the approaching enemy to buy them the time they needed to escape.

The water went suddenly deep, submerging many of them as they paddled desperately towards the low hull of the ferry and the safety it promised. Hands reached down to grasp at Downes' soaked jacket and haul him aboard, in turn dragging Dezzy with him, as he wouldn't release the winded soldier.

The two men were dumped on the deck unceremoniously and lay on their backs side by side.

"Did you see that?" Dezzy asked through gasps. "The fucking thing... *flanked* me..."

"I saw it," Downes told him, saying nothing more as he didn't like to share his darker thoughts.

———

Downes, in spite of being intimately acquainted with hardship and twin concepts of cold and wet, was shivering uncontrollably by the time their boat docked on the picturesque Isle of Skye.

Low cloud shrouded the towering rock crags to their left, obscuring the true height of the cliff face, but to their front the small port was anything but idyllic.

Soldiers in full NBC suits, *Noddy suits* as his men called them, stared anonymously at them as the circular holes showed only their eyes inside their respirators. It was less the way they looked at the bedraggled men and women arriving and more the emplaced gun positions that caused the greatest concern.

The dock had evidently been prepared to perform the task of quarantine admission, given that metal mesh grids had been hastily welded together to form a sealed walkway for them to pass through. The men from the island piloting the boats remained onboard, staying to the upper decks where they didn't come into contact with anyone representing a potential infection risk.

"All weapons and equipment into the buckets," shouted a voice muffled by a respirator and dulled by repetitive boredom. "Keep moving forwards... All weapons and equipment into the buckets..."

Recovered from the impacts during their brief crossing, Dezzy stiffened beside his officer.

"Are these Green Army muppets?" he grumbled, worrying that their more exotic arsenal would be seen as novelty toys by men unaccustomed to more than a few weapons.

"Not all of them," Mac answered from behind them. "Look at the rooftops." Both Downes and Dezzy looked up, spotting the shape of a rifle held by one man and recognising it as a Colt. "Got to be our lot mixed in among them."

"Classic, *aashi*–" Smiffy said, gasping in pain as he put too much weight on his injured ankle. The shouted instructions continued to be repeated as they dutifully shuffled forwards. When it came to their turn at the cut-out section of heavy mesh to deposit their trade tools into what looked like hastily repurposed plastic fish tubs, the man calling out the orders stopped to stare as the four men spent longer than everyone else removing everything from their persons that could be classed as lethal. Smiffy hesitated, the liberated Soviet rifle clutched in both hands as he fought with every fibre of his body, not wanting to let it go.

"Put it down," Mac said unkindly. "It's just a gun."

"It's bloody not!" Smiffy protested. "It's mine, an—"

He stopped talking as Downes' bearded face spun to fix his

eyes with a shadowed look. Wordlessly, he placed the VAL into the bucket as though laying a beloved pet to rest, before standing tall and limping onwards without a second glance.

They deposited next to no spare ammunition for any of their weapons, having expended most of their rounds since getting back to the UK so long ago and starting the roller-coaster ride they'd been on ever since.

"One at a time," came the next shouted orders, "step through and remove all items of clothing..." the enclosed walkway split into two lanes, both intermittently opening up and sealing again as solid metal sheets slid open and closed to admit one person at a time.

The backlog of civilians, understandably hesitant about that phase, though unconcerned about relinquishing their weapons—the reversal of the soldiers' concerns— passed more slowly, as the military personnel were oddly more accustomed to getting naked in front of strangers.

The enclosed sections were lit by bright yellow lamps which forced Downes to shield his eyes as he went through to receive more instructions from another suited soldier.

"All your clothes off," he said with as little effort as was required, "into the bag."

Downes stripped, feeling the soreness of wet clothes already so uncomfortable through travel and sweat. He still shivered and his skin was cold to the touch, which caused him concern; he was well trained enough and experienced enough to recognise the early signs of exposure and hypothermia, but explaining that right then would have delayed the process so he kept his mouth shut. He was struggling to take his boots off, so the soldier passed him a short-bladed knife to cut the laces. His feet were in shit state. Pale, translucent skin peeled off in large patches to expose the sore pink beneath. No deployment he'd ever been on had left so little time to maintain himself.

"Arms up," the speaker waited until Downes had complied.

"Spin around." Again a pause. "Okay, put this on and keep moving through."

Downes accepted a plastic packet containing a dark blue boiler suit with a chunky zip so awkward for his numb fingers to operate that it smacked of a government bulk buy from the lowest bidder. The boiler suit was accessorised with a pair of wellington boots after he had been asked his size.

"T…Ten…" he stammered through chattering teeth.

He was handed a pair with a large '12' stamped on the sole but he didn't care.

The separation ahead of him slid back, forcing him to squint again from the harsh daylight obscured by the clouds, and he shuffled forwards keeping his hands wrapped around himself.

The next station in the conveyor system where he was instructed to stop required him to place a thermometer under his tongue and wait in silence until the hands of a cheap, plastic clock ticked around and a thickly gloved hand reached out to take the instrument and inspect it. Satisfied that he wasn't running a fever—as would have been evident to anyone bothering to look at how close to hypothermia he was—he was waved through the final obstacle of a heavy, rubber curtain and into a tented area where the noise of so many people talking at once assaulted his senses like a flashbang.

His nose directed him through the crowd of civilians and squadron men and marines to where he detected the origin of the coffee aroma, but his uncontrollably shaking hands couldn't manage to manipulate the tap on the urn. Panic rose inside him, so uncommon for a man who had fought through lethal warzones for the last year of his life, not to mention all of the trials he had faced before.

The simple fact that he couldn't manage to pour himself a cup of coffee threatened such a debilitating wave of anxiety that he almost dropped the mug as his knees gave out on him.

Before he could hit the ground, strong hands grasped his upper arms and held him up to pull him back to his feet.

"Allow me, Major," captain Palmer's impeccably mannered and cultured voice sounded softly in his ear. The cup was taken from his unresisting hand as the major fought a wave of dizziness which forced him to grip the edge of the flimsy trestle table for balance.

"Sugar? Milk?" Palmer enquired.

"He'll take both," Mac's gruff voice announced as the Scottish sergeant shouldered his way through the crowd to appraise his officer with a practised eye.

"Grab a couple, if you don't mind, Captain," Mac told him, still not taking his eyes off Downes before grabbing the nearest civilian by the sleeve and pulling him towards him. "You, go get me three blankets." The man nodded, his eyes wide, and disappeared to comply.

"We need to get you sat down," Mac said in a tone that was probably intended to be soothing but still sounded like a threat to anyone who didn't know him. He walked the major towards the small gas-bottle heater which was the focal point for so many cold people, and his loud voice cleared a path like Moses.

"Move your arses!" he bawled. "You! Clear out of the way." This last was aimed at a young man who fled from his choice position in front of the glowing bars radiating heat, just in time before Downes was deposited directly in front of the heater and Palmer arrived to thrust the cup containing hot, sugary liquid into his hands. Before Mac could say or do anything else, a speaker erupted inside the fenced shelter.

"Commanding officers report to quarantine exit. I repeat, commanding officers to quarantine exit."

Mac looked up, meeting Palmer's eyes and nodding to convey that the tank captain had to speak for them all. Maxwell, filling the boots of his predecessor perfectly, appeared behind the captain's right shoulder. Mac's eyebrows met in the middle, not hiding his response to the other arrival as Palmer Senior turned to find his younger brother had fallen in with them, somehow making his bland boiler suit look like the high fashion he was born to parade.

Captain Palmer, too exhausted to be careful with his words, elected to give his instructions to his younger brother under the guise of speaking to the NCOs. He spoke, fixing his brother with a direct stare that made it obvious he was talking to him.

"Leave the talking to me," he said quietly. "I rather suspect we aren't as welcome as one would hope."

FIVE

EIGHT DAYS PRIOR

The US Air Force C-130 transport plane banged hard onto the tarmac as the engine shrieked and roared in full reverse, with a juddering running throughout the airframe which threatened to break it apart. The pilot's warning to brace for a 'combat landing' meant nothing to Professor Grewal, serving only to panic him into believing they were dropping down into a war zone. So when the wheels hit the ground hard and bounced the heavy cargo plane back up into the air, to reverse his body's grip on gravity so suddenly and sickeningly, he cried out in panic, thinking that they were crashing.

His hearth thumped in his chest almost as hard as the screeching tyres did as they hit the tarmac a second time and let out a tortured noise before the plane rose into the air again. The fuselage skewed sideways, like a powerful car would do when the driver floored the throttle from a standing start, only with the sensations being reversed so that forwards was backwards and up was down. It simply overwhelmed him, forcing from him another yell of panic.

On the fourth or fifth impact, punctuated by the tortured, muted sounds of rubber on tarmac, his body tried to tell his mind that they were slowing down even if he wouldn't believe it. When his brainstem overrode his choice to hold his breath and he gasped in a deep lungful, he finally understood what the pilot meant by the term 'combat landing'.

The headphones he forgot he was wearing crackled into life and played a short burst of static before the pilot's muffled voice filled his ears.

"Thank you for flying zombie airways. We know you have no choice, so we don't really care if you enjoyed your flight. Be sure to take all of your shit with you when you leave."

The plane turned a slow circle on the spot, so close to the end of the runway, which fortunately Grewal didn't have a forward view of, as one of the uniformed soldiers nearby unstrapped and stood up to stretch. The man was average height with a stocky build but other than the fearsome beard and a stare that could penetrate steel, he seemed entirely... *average*. The other men on his team seemed similarly fit, as if they could swim five miles of open ocean before breakfast each day, and all of them were equally as dismissive of the two scientists and their small staff.

They didn't exactly get off on the right foot when the Brit assumed they were there to carry his research equipment, which had been dumped on the tarmac at the airport near Langley. He hadn't seen the team come in via chopper from Little Creek, so he'd had no idea who or what they were when he'd given them instructions on carrying the crates onto the plane.

Grewal neither knew nor cared that the US Air Force pilots were acting on behalf of the CIA, nor did he care that the men and women providing their security were part of the US Army's Medical Research Institute of Infectious Diseases. He knew that some of the staff attached to what he considered to be *his* project were with Chambers and had come direct from the CDC, but with so many different people from various places using a whole raft of acronyms and reporting to different admirals or generals or politicians, he'd lost track and managed to confuse a US Navy Seal team with grunts who were there to carry his boxes.

He still hadn't had the opportunity to make up for his rudeness, not that he ever tried hard to consider the feelings of others, but something about the unsettlingly still man in charge of that team made him feel as though he'd committed a grave error that he needed to rectify soon.

"Come on, Doc," Agent Fisher said as he moved past towards the ramp and broke the eye contact between the tough soldier and the terrified scientist. Fisher had swapped the Langley camouflage of his grey suit for the more practical black military style clothing, bearing no badges of rank or any insignia at all to denote who or what he was.

He wore a black vest over his anonymous-looking uniform and carried weapons, as did the other two men sporting identical haircuts to accompany their outfits, and Grewal tried to recall their names. Wood? Carter? He shook his head as he realised that he didn't care anyway.

"At ease, Master Chief," Fisher said in a tone somewhere between sarcastic and respectful as he passed the staring SEAL. Grewal was forced to follow and pass unnervingly close to the man he was certain hated him; but then again, he had grown accustomed to being hated everywhere he went. Since being rescued by British Special Forces from the London lab which had been the epicentre of the outbreak, he hadn't been many places other than US military bases. Still, everyone there hated him too, even if he had created the virus only by accident while carrying out the orders of both his and the United States governments.

He shuffled along behind the agent, eager to be off the plane which had so recently tried to kill him, and eager too to get away from the malevolence hiding behind the beard that still tracked his movements like a predator.

"Are you Fisher?" a man wearing British army camouflage uniform asked confidently as he and a small entourage approached the rear ramp of the plane. They had disgorged from a pair of dull, green military vehicles parked nearby, and from their physiques and bearing, all had the obvious look of fighting men.

"That's me," the CIA man said, stepping up to greet the speaker.

"Colonel Kelly," the man said, offering a handshake and half crushing the agent's hand with enough force to push a vein out in the side of his own neck. Grewal shot a quick look at Fisher, who still maintained the poker face he wore permanently, even if one eyelid did flicker a tiny bit. The Colonel offered no other information, and Grewal guessed that was either because the agent knew who he was or else the man just enjoyed secrecy. He turned, pacing away and expecting to be followed as he continued to talk.

"We've arranged a facility for you to use," he explained. "It's basic, hardly the standard I imagine you're accustomed to, but needs must." Fisher ignored the jibe at him needing a five star hotel.

"Have the requirements been met?"

"Isolated location, secure perimeter, given that three sides of it are the Atlantic, and a power supply," Kelly responded. "Like I said, it's basic." He reached the driver's side of the vehicle he'd arrived in and opened it, pausing before climbing back in and peering down the short runway towards the sight of three transport trucks lumbering towards them.

"You'll be taken directly there," he told the visitors. "I have a small force in place to ensure you aren't disturbed." Something about the way he narrowed his eyes when he said that made Fisher think he meant that they weren't to leave their basic facility. "And other than that, I expect you to conduct all of your *experiments* without affecting the population here." He climbed behind the wheel without another word, the three other soldiers doing the same before the engine barked into life. It rattled away under the kind of acceleration a person might use when the maintenance of the vehicle wasn't his or her personal concern. This left the gaggle of Americans alone and waiting for their convoy to arrive.

"I think we can safely assume they aren't exactly pleased to see us," Fisher opined to the others, his gaze resting finally on Professor Grewal, who was transfixed by the look that implied he was solely responsible for that, too. Movement directly beside him made him jump and move away, to find that the leader of the US Navy SEAL team had appeared at his side without Grewal being aware in the slightest of his approach.

"Master Chief," Fisher said, "I trust you and your team can be ready for an excursion by sixteen hundred?" The man nodded, still not saying a word, and turned to requisition one of the approaching trucks for his team and their gear.

Grewal walked back to the plane, hurrying with his hands out in front of him saying, "No, no, no!" as he rushed to stop one of the uniformed US Army soldiers from handling a piece of equipment too roughly. The man from the MRIID put it down carefully and stepped back, leaving Grewal to protect the sensitive centrifuge and oversee the rest of the equipment getting loaded onto the transport.

"Bloody ham-fisted buffoo—"

"Everything okay, Doc?" Fisher's voice startled him and elicited a small yelp from him as he clutched the lab equipment tighter to his chest.

"Yes, yes, I err…" Fisher slapped him on the back a little too hard to be entirely friendly.

"Relax," he told him. "A broken test tube ain't exactly the worst thing that could happen, if you catch my drift…"

The term *basic*, was something of an understatement. Their facility, such as it was, was a farm and outbuildings which had been hastily repurposed, and the previous occupants displaced to God only knew where. It was chosen for location, not that Grewal understood that. Situated on the south-western tip of the craggy, mountainous island they now inhabited, the narrow approach to what was now their base could be cut off by a small force to minimise the risk of anything getting loose. When that was explained to him, he nodded sagely and offered his opinion.

"Like Leonidas' defence of Thermopylae?"

"Interesting that you choose a reference where all the good guys died," Fisher said, a mirthful smirk adorning his face.

The rooms of the main house and other buildings were portioned out, with the main, high-ceilinged shed being the main attraction. Judging by the smell, it had previously housed livestock, but the hint of recent blacksmithing hung in the air to mingle with the residual aroma of shit. That metalwork had been the construction of a series of small, steel mesh cubes, evidently the holding cages for what would be their test subjects.

Test subjects, he thought sourly, huffing to himself and earning a mild look of query from Fisher. He shook his head to deflect any questions, and instead began organising where he wanted the equipment unpacked.

"When can you start collecting specimens?" Chambers asked, standing near to Grewal but wearing an expression of distaste to make it clear that their being on the same side wasn't by choice on his part.

"This evening," Fisher answered simply. "You'll have something to work with tomorrow. The MRIID guys will run the security side of this facility and they have orders to put down anything not under direct and total control. That understood?"

The two scientists caught each other's eye for a fleeting second, then both nodded, sharing an understanding in that moment that they were on the threshold of something either very important or else very dangerous.

The plan was simple. They would take samples from infected hosts and run the same tests that they had against the pure viral strain back in the labs on the other side of the Atlantic. Those updated samples, or 'real world' samples as Grewal called them, could throw up any number of complications to spoil their perfect world lab results. Numerous factors could affect the viability or severity of the infection, making it more or less resilient to any possible 'cure' they could devise. As if reading his thoughts, Fisher asked them both a question.

"Don't give me long answers," he warned them, "but can you make a cure we can use?" Chambers and Grewal looked at one another

'Cure' was a subjective word, given that those infected would be killed off, but technically speaking it could cure the rest of the world by killing the infection in the hosts. Chambers sucked in a breath and pursed his lips, radiating anger that his years of experience and research were treated like everything was a yes or no answer when it came to anyone from the military or the government. Grewal adopted a different approach.

"If our compounds work the same in the field as they did in the lab, then yes," he told the agent simply, having gone over this very subject with the man more than once already.

"*If*," Fisher answered. "Lot of ifs involved with things nowadays…"

"Well," Grewal said in a tone of voice designed to end the conversation, "*if* we don't get any test subjects, there will be some definite *nos*."

SIX

Johnson was more comfortable driving the Warrior than he expected to be. It was a vast improvement on the previous generation of fighting vehicles he'd driven before, and combined all of the things he liked and added a whole raft of new tricks and gadgetry. He still had that unavoidable fifteen metres of limited vision when he drove closed-down, with the hatches sealed to protect them from anything outside that felt like biting them. He mused that they—the developers of such mighty war machines—would only solve that problem when they gave the drivers television sets with externally mounted cameras, so that they could play the most expensive of arcade games.

"Left at the next T-junction," came Bufford's voice through his earphones. "Left, left."

The repetition was something so familiar to the military men; men who could ill-afford a mistake when half hearing words with a subtle difference such as 'no' and 'go'. Johnson acknowledged the instructions, grateful for them, because he couldn't make out the road signs clearly after such a short time without the routine cutting back of trees and hedges. Even after the bitter winter had forced so much life to retreat in the exceptionally low temperatures, nature was rapidly reclaiming the land.

Another voice cut through to him, this one female and curious in accent and inflection, but the tone of it made things clear to Johnson that the speaker was suffering.

"We have to stop," Astrid Larsen said, her voice sounding thicker and more sluggish than usual.

"Is everything okay back there?" he asked, concerned that something was wrong in the rear troop-carrying section of the armoured beast he was nursing along the relatively smooth roads.

"The fuel tank," Larsen said with evident difficulty. "It is moving and making us all sick."

Immediately Johnson eased up on the controls, more like those of an aeroplane rather than a conventional car, to slow their ride and hopefully reduce the effects they were feeling. He cursed himself for not recalling the rumour around the base when these new vehicles arrived for testing; that their transparent fuel bladder caused seasickness to those sitting next to it in the back.

He paused at the junction, seeing a pub on the opposite side of the road with an almost empty car park and he decided that it was more than open enough to offer them a chance to rest. He called it out to Bufford sitting behind and above him in the commander's position, waiting as the man assessed the ground through his viewport before he agreed.

The Warrior rolled in, turning almost on the spot instead of looping a wide arc to swing around like a car would, and came to a stop in the middle of the open tarmac.

"Is it clear?" Larsen's voice came over the radio. Johnson peered out of his own limited view, seeing nothing to cause him any worry, and waited for the SBS man to give the word.

"Looks good," Bufford declared. "Let's take ten minutes."

Hatches open, rear doors wide, the armoured fighting vehicle looked oddly out of place in the semi-idyllic setting of the country drinking hole. The two abandoned cars sitting on flat tyres, and the overgrown, neglected feel of the building and beer garden spoiled it somewhat, but those in the back didn't seem to care for those small things as they spilled out to steady themselves and gratefully suck in long breaths of chill air.

Johnson and Bufford, both with weapons in hand and eyes constantly roving for threats, didn't ask them such stupid questions like enquiring if they were okay; merely allowed them the time to settle their stomachs after sitting beside a huge, sloshing fuel tank for the past hour. Peter, clambering down the dappled green hull, jogged to Amber and knelt down to her. He asked if she felt sick, but the girl just smirked and shrugged one shoulder up to her ear as if to say that she was fine and couldn't understand why Astrid and Kimberley were so affected.

The sight of the two children interacting, still a welcome novelty that made the adults both happy and at the same time tragically sad to watch, was interrupted by the sound of glass breaking.

It wasn't a smash, not a shattering blow of a window imploding under force, but was more of a ringing, snapping sound, as if someone had leaned on a single pane too hard. All heads whipped towards the source of the noise and saw nothing coming from the building to indicate an immediate threat, but still they readied their weapons as Peter ushered Amber back towards the safety of the vehicle.

Guns up into shoulders, with the exception of Kimberley and Peter, who held their melee weapons with sweating palms and formed the second rank of their small defence, they held their ground to see if anything presented itself.

Nothing happened. The eerie quiet of the car park told them nothing, as sweating hands gripped weapons tighter in preparation for an impending confrontation with the dead, as feet shuffled nervously to adopt the perfect stance in readiness. A gentle change in the breeze pushed the light wind into their faces and carried with it a hint of sweet, necrotic flesh that they recognised all too well.

"What the hell are we doing?" Peter asked in a hushed whisper from the back of their formation. "Why don't we just leave?"

The solution to their peril, so simplistic and easy to recognise for someone so young and logical, stunned the trained soldiers for a heartbeat. Their heads had been filled with angles of fire, approach routes of the enemy and their numbers; with the risk of the faster ones being in play, and all manner of other problems that Peter's mind wasn't encumbered by through an overload of knowledge.

Johnson spoke first, mimicking the same low whisper that Peter had adopted.

"Everyone inside the wagon," he hissed. "Nice and slow."

As they turned to file back inside the safety of so many layers of metal armour, a new noise broke the spell. A loud bang with an accompanying crack, followed quickly by a second with a louder, more worrying sound of smashing glass and the tuneful tinkle of the broken shards hitting the ground below. As one, their eyes roamed slowly upwards to the first-floor window, breath catching in throats as a collective series of gasps fired like a ragged volley.

From that window, only fractionally too small for a fully grown adult to squeeze through, protruded the head and left arm of a Screecher which moaned at them and gnashed white teeth set in receded, black gums.

"Now would be good," Bufford said as his feet propelled him towards the side of the tank. He dropped his weapon to turn and hoist Peter high up to grasp the top of the hull and begin to pour himself through the open hatch. The sound of the rear doors closing came loudly, but not as loudly as the splintering of wood and more breaking glass as the unseen door holding back the hungry monsters gave way.

Johnson, moving lithely for a big man with all the encouragement of a gruesome death at his back, knelt on top of the Warrior and slipped the short-barrelled shotgun from his shoulder to point it in the direction of the building.

His intention was to provide cover, should any of the bastards break ranks and make for one of his group before they were safely ensconced, but if he was honest with himself, he relished the prospect of firing the gun to relieve some of the pent-up rage he had been bottling up inside himself for far too long.

"We're in," Bufford reported. "Let's go!"

"Hold on," Johnson said, telling himself that he was in little danger and that he needed to satisfy a curiosity that had just presented itself to him. He wanted to know, after such a brutal winter, which had followed the hot end to the previous summer and the short, sharp shock of a brief autumn season, how the ones preserved inside had degraded. They'd seen well enough how those zombies stuck in the open had turned out. They were generally ragged, emaciated and pale-to-the-point-of translucent skinned. But his curiosity, mixed with a hint of bloodlust, kept him in position atop the armoured vehicle.

Behind him, on the higher section of the hull, he heard the hatch bang shut and lock to indicate Bufford's escape to safety. His own hatch, to the front and left of the vehicle, was open and inviting for him to step down into, but still he didn't make a move.

"Come on!" Bufford's voice yelled from inside, the sound travelling out through the open hatch to him. He turned to look at the hatch again, only spinning back to face the pub at another, far more insistent noise than the shouting of his comrades. A boot-sole crunching stone—one of those sounds that the mind understood deep down far more quickly than the brain could verbally identify —followed by the desperate sucking inwards of breath in what he knew was preparation for the ungodly shriek the things let out.

It never got the chance to finish the call to arms, as Johnson's blast took it full in the chest to throw it down in broken ruin. He'd loaded the gun with the heaviest of hunting shot, effectively launching a handful of small ball bearings into the body at brutally short range before the pattern of the projectiles had time to spread out. The body hit the ground, landing on its back with a crunch as a second, heavier sound copied it. That sound, Johnson saw with disgust, was the head-first impact of the mindless monster from the upstairs window finally wriggling itself free to plummet the short drop to the car park, where it met an instant end, the inertia of the weight of the body cracking the skull to switch off the lights for good.

More spilled out around the corner of the pub and just as Johnson pumped another cartridge into the chamber on instinct, good sense prevailed as his mind recognised the danger he was putting himself—putting all of them—in, as one of the tightly-packed crowd of overstaying late-night drinkers was leaping over the front ranks with inhuman agility to reach its canned meal first.

Johnson turned, heading for the hatch just as a mechanical whirring sound above his head forced him to duck underneath the swinging barrel of the main gun. Bufford, likely just as eager for some payback as Johnson was, swung the cupola towards the threat just as the SSM threw himself inside and slammed down the hatch.

The deafening, chattering racket of the main coaxial chain gun hammering rounds into the mob blotted out every other sound in the world until the hatch was sealed. That gun, firing at the closest range it could manage with the barrel fully depressed, tore bloody ruin through the pack to turn the previously quiet car park into a butcher's shop in seconds.

Johnson threw on the headset to hear the tail end of Bufford's opinion.

"…oody hell are you playing at? Get us out of here!"

Johnson fired up the massive engine, throwing it into gear and taking off fast enough to buck the Warrior's nose up into the air and force the still-firing gun to tear great chunks of stone out of the building in a sweeping arc as they made their escape.

He didn't let up until they were half a mile down the road, then he realised he'd gone in the wrong direction and slowed to report his error to the others.

"We've gone bloody east," he reported, annoyance heavy in his words of self-criticism. "I need to turn us around and go back past the pub. Buffs?"

"Oh," the SBS man chuckled, "I'm ready for another pass. Still not letting me use the artillery?"

Johnson ignored the quip, only giving a low growl in response, not wanting to expend a valuable piece of ordnance by sending a high explosive shell into a pub housing a few Screechers and a now-deceased Lima.

"Give them another pass with the co-axial," he said. "I'll stick to the far right of the road to give you space; make sure none of them gets near us."

"My bloody pleasure," Bufford responded.

The pub came into his limited field of view in under a minute, and he didn't slow to allow his gunner the time to enjoy himself, but blasted past at close to their top speed amid a roar of diesel engine revs. The gun began barking and burping its rounds at the strung-out crowd milling about in search of the promised meal that had vanished before their eyes. Johnson steered to the furthest side of the road away from the building to keep his distance, but was still forced to line up two of them to be crushed under his right side tracks.

In a fleeting moment, they were past, and even though the cupola had swung all the way around to continue firing on the move, the gun quickly fell silent.

Johnson took a few deep breaths, settling himself back into a more sedate cruising speed, and let out a sigh. In his earphones, he heard amused chuckling rising into uncontrollable laughter which went on for slightly longer than he wanted to tolerate.

"What's so bloody funny?" he snapped at Bufford.

"I… I was just thinking…" Bufford replied in a voice that implied he was wiping tears from his eyes. "That's probably got to be the longest pub lock-in of all time…"

SEVEN

Professor Grewal, along with Professor Chambers and his small team, set up the lab equipment in readiness for having something to work with. As per their requests, banks of fridges and freezers filled one wall of the former livestock barn under bright lights and their samples of potential vaccine cultures had been painstakingly transferred to the freezers from mobile cold storage, using liquid nitrogen.

Grewal, finding himself at a momentary loss for useful activity, wandered over to where the stainless-steel urn bubbled away keeping the water warm for their drinks. He used a plastic spoon to shovel a decidedly unmeasured amount of instant coffee into a polystyrene cup, before splashing the almost-boiling water in. He looked around for sugar and fresh milk to accompany it, instead finding only an off-brand powdered creamer. He picked it up, inspecting it as he might a particularly virulent strain of bacteria, and decided against contaminating the drink with lumps of the stuff.

"Yo, Doc," barked a loud voice from behind him, forcing a small yelp from his lips as he jumped and turned around to face one of the men from the US Army department responsible for all matters regarding infectious diseases.

Grewal opened his mouth to explain for the thousandth time that he was a professor, and hadn't been a mere doctorate holder for well in excess of a decade, when he saw the inane look on the man's face and decided not to waste his breath.

"Yes?"

"The frogmen are on the horn, saying they're coming in hot with a couple of new buddies for you."

———

Master Chief Petty Officer Ryan Miller was unhappy about his orders. He made representations about those orders, even so far as requesting a meeting with the base commander prior to shipping out, only to arrive at the commander's office to find the man's desk chair occupied by a guy in a grey suit that screamed 'Langley' directly into his brain.

As soon as he met the man, Fisher, he claimed to be called, although Miller always knew his type to have forgettable fake names, he also knew that arguing was pointless. Orders were orders, and it looked like his orders came directly from the CIA.

He'd changed his approach then, and instead of standing to attention and addressing a senior officer as he had planned to do, he removed his headgear and flopped into a seat without asking for permission. Treating the man like an equal, even if the son of a bitch was technically in charge, set Miller's stall out plain as day.

"So,' he mused in a tone of obvious annoyance. "You want us to fly to butt-fuck nowhere, England—"

"Scotland," Fisher interrupted annoyingly.

"—butt-fuck nowhere, *Scotland*, and take a boat to the

mainland where we'll be *capturing live specimens* of infected humans. I got that right?"

"In a nutshell," Fisher told him, politician's smile not wavering.

"And your intel package is complete and up to date?" Miller went on.

"Count on it."

"And how do you propose we go about securing said infected assholes?"

Fisher leaned back in his chair and smiled. It was the smile of a man who knew he had already won, because unless the SEAL wanted to commit mutiny and refuse to carry out his orders, he was stuck with them.

"Master Chief," he said smoothly. "I'll leave the finer details of that matter to you entirely. Just get it done." Miller banged his clenched fist hard on the top of the oak desk, knocking down a framed picture of a square-jawed man in an officer's uniform shaking hands with a man who looked remarkably like Reagan, and he snarled at the CIA agent.

"Easy for you to say, four thousand miles away in your office." Fisher's smile evaporated and he leaned forwards to look directly into the eyes of the soldier.

"I'll be there with you, Miller," he said quietly. "And just because I wear a suit now, don't think I didn't get my hands dirty. I've seen shit all over South America and the Persian Gulf, and that's got me where I am. You don't like your orders? Tough shit. I'd prefer you to be a willing participant in this, but I asked the president for a team of elite operators and he sent me you. If you're not up to the job, I can request the US Army or the Marine Cor—"

"We'll do it," Miller interrupted before Fisher went on to commit further blasphemy. "Just don't think we agree on everything." He stood and replaced his headgear before fixing Fisher with a hard look. "You got that?"

———

"Got it!" Miller's man, Hernandez, called from behind him after Miller had pointed out the low section of rocky beach he wanted to land at. The six SEALs had enough time to stow their gear and tool up for the immediate mission, as Miller reminded them that the sooner they got it out of the way, the sooner they could rest up in safety.

They had met as a team and thrown ideas out together after reading the briefing dossier on their newest enemy. It was simpler than understanding the fighting capabilities of a foreign power, because these things only had one tactic, and that tactic would be the same the world over.

They swarmed en masse, and they tried to eat you.

Miller had told them, over and over, that they would only engage small groups and lure them in ones and twos into their cargo net trap. Then, with their 'volunteers' snagged in the nets, they would drag them directly back to the facility on the island just off the mainland, without coming into contact with them and risking any of them catching a bite. Sure enough, those 'volunteers' would be wet through from being dragged along a small stretch of icy water, but he passed that off as a tactical choice, given that the reports from the British claimed that low temperatures slowed their movements.

What bothered him most of all was the reports of some of the infected displaying increased physical and mental abilities over the horde. As much as Grewal and Chambers wanted one of those, Miller was reluctant to make it his priority until he'd had his own boots on the ground and seen how badly the shit had really hit the fan.

Hernandez cut the engine before they neared the shore, floating in as silently as possible to bump and scrape the boat onto the rocks in the shallows before the others jumped out to drag it ashore. The bundled cargo net was carried out from the prow of their small, black inflatable and they patrolled fast up the shore to get away from their infiltration method just like they had drilled to do.

The fact that they were fighting a new kind of enemy didn't register, but Miller wasn't completely ignorant of having to adapt their tactics, which is why he assessed the narrow street of what appeared to have been a small coastal village and formulated the execution of his plan.

"Shepherd, Coleman," he hissed in a low voice designed to carry only as far as it needed to. "Take the north and south rooftops over that chokepoint." He indicated the empty street ahead with a bladed hand. "Hernandez, ready on the boat. Jackson, on me with the cargo net."

"Where do you need me?" the youngest and newest member of their elite team asked. Miller smiled at the kid in the dark, not that he saw it.

"You're the bait, Willy."

———

"I'd like to formally lodge my complaint about this mission, Master Chief," Walt Wilson complained quietly as he stood alone in the street. He didn't mind being called Kid or Willy, hell he enjoyed the hazing as it meant the SEALs must have liked him to some degree, even if they hadn't gone to war as a team until then. But what he didn't like was being bait.

"Shut up," one of the two Daves hissed from the low rooftop to his left. Miller and Jackson were out of sight too, keeping watch over their area of operations, leaving only Hernandez a few paces out to sea with the boat's engine ticking over, ready to open the throttle wide.

"You're doing fine," Miller's voice sounded low and reassuring, before he raised it slightly to encompass the whole team within earshot. "Flare out."

A pop and a whooshing, hissing noise seared along the street, bathing the quaint abandoned houses in a fiery red glow. They stayed at high alert, every sense dialled way up in anticipation of their first encounter with the enemy. The flare burned fiercely ahead of their position, giving off more noise than they'd expected, but the sheer emptiness of the world, devoid of any trace of life, seemed to amplify any disruption to the silent dark.

As the glow began to fade and the noise abated, Miller's nerves began to increase as he considered their next move.

Should he fire another flare and double-down on a tactic that might not work? Should he relocate his team and try the same thing further inland?

As he was weighing up the options, a voice cut through to focus him completely.

"Contacts. Three, approaching from the east." Miller slowly inched his head around the side of the rough surface of the bricks to see three dark shapes silhouetted against the fading red light.

"Hold position," he told his men. "Kid? Make a noise."

"Make a…?" Wilson started to say before trailing off. He drew himself up, feeling alien as he stood tall out of cover, and cleared his throat.

"Yo!" he yelled, leaving the single syllable to echo down the artificial canyon of the terraced buildings.

"Yo?" Miller asked, chuckling. "First contact with the enemy and you decide to lead with 'yo'?"

"Well," Wilson shrugged, "you kinda put me on the spot… I didn't know wh—"

"Look alive!" Coleman snapped from above them. They all snapped their focus back to their front, where the shouted word had sparked a slow, cumbersome approach to their position.

"I, er," Wilson said. "I don't like this…"

Miller ignored him. He carefully watched the three figures

shambling closer through the red, smoky haze of the dying backlight. He was certain that none of them was the reported faster type, the ones who had been seen running and jumping instead of walking like drunks, but he also knew that they didn't exactly have a mastery of their chosen battlefield.

"Master Chi—" Wilson began, before the words were drowned out by a tortured, ripping, gasping shriek in stereo from the advancing pair.

Gloved hands instinctively gripped weapons tighter as brains fought against the body's natural urge to defend itself; to kill the *Screechers* before they got close.

Wilson's nerve threatened to break first as he raised the butt of the sub machine gun into his shoulder and took a bead on the closest zombie. Before Miller could stop him from pulling the trigger, he abruptly lowered the weapon a fraction and stood a little straighter but remained ready to drill rounds into it.

"Back up now," Miller told him, his breath catching in his throat as the kid stumbled on the heavy knotted rope of the cargo net when his boot heel caught it. He righted himself, stumbling backwards a little faster until he was clear of their rudimentary trap.

Nobody spoke. Nobody opened fire. The only sounds were the ripping, gasping shrieks of the monsters and the dying fizzle of the flare as it sputtered and flashed darkness over the red-bathed street. Just as the leading zombie stepped a halting, bare foot onto the edge of the cargo net, the flare died completely and plunged them all into darkness.

The absence of the flare's light wasn't a true darkness; even with the total absence of any light pollution, the night sky held a few twinkling stars and a dull wash of moonlight. Red light didn't obliterate a person's night vision like the white beam of a light bulb would, but still the panic of losing their sight was enough to trigger fear to rule over their bodies.

Wilson turned and ran, adding a, "Fuck, fuck, *fuuuck*," to keep the undead attackers zeroed in on their meal. Miller held his nerve, closed his eyes to imagine how the scene was playing out without the distractions his eyes would give him, and gauged how fast they were moving.

"Hernandez!" He bawled, "Now!" Sparking multiple things to happen at once.

Hernandez, out of sight but connected to them by a long, heavy rope, gunned the throttle of the inflatable boat to snap that line taught and snag the two creatures in the net as it folded up around them to drag them towards the stony beach.

Miller and his team abandoned their positions to retreat, now that their mission objectives were bagged, and he jogged forwards to make out the shape of their youngest team member scrambling backwards on the ground to get his legs away from the writhing, shrieking mess tangled inside the heavy net.

"On your feet, kid," he snapped, keeping his own very wary eyes on the dangerous cargo. "Everyone onboard and let's get the hell off this island."

EIGHT

"Be advised," the tinny-sounding, far away American voice said, "significant infected event travelling south to north close to your bearing. Expect contact to the east as early as seventeen-hundred, over."

"Acknowledged," Daniels said into the radio with a resigned tone laced with fear. "Thanks for the heads-up. Out."

"What is it?" the girl, Jessica, asked from the front of the cramped Sultan as she mimed the actions of driving the tracked vehicle, complete with engine noises. Daniels swallowed, not sure how to answer the question. He was accustomed to living his life surrounded by other hardened men and not a young girl with a blunt and forthright manner. He paused, long enough for her to turn around and give him a stern look, before deciding to just tell her.

"AWACS reporting another swarm," he said, opening his mouth again to explain his use of military jargon.

"The Americans are still flying over us then?" she asked, betraying the fact that she listened a lot more than she spoke. "They haven't entirely abandoned us?"

"Who knows what they're doing up there... spying on

something, no doubt," Daniels answered, leaning back in the narrow seat and laying out his small pouch of dry tobacco scraps to try and force enough together with his fingertips to be worth the effort. Jessica abandoned her pretend driving position, stepping towards him and noticing his shaking fingers were making a mess of the task requiring fine motor skills. Wordlessly, she took the thin strip of paper from his sweaty fingers and gently sprinkled the tobacco evenly along the crease down its centre. Her own small fingers deftly rolled it into a smooth tube better than Daniels' usual efforts, before she licked the gummed edge and passed it to him. He thanked her with a mumble and lit it, sucking hard to get a lungful of stale smoke, before letting it out with his eyes closed.

"Where'd you learn to do that?" he asked, eyes open again as he regarded the well-rolled cigarette.

"Swarm warning?" she asked, ignoring his question.

"Yeah," Daniels answered, pausing to draw on the rolled smoke again before his eyes went wide. "Shit, we need to warn the SSM!" He snatched up the radio set and turned dials before calling out a repeated phrase over and over, with no reply.

"Is it close?" she asked quietly in a lull between his hails.

"Yes," he said, not turning to look at her. "It's coming from the island—the place we were before here. They must've got off at low tide somehow and back on the mainland."

"Is it heading here?"

"They're not sure. Last reported direction of travel was just 'north', which puts them heading right to left off to our east going past." She frowned, evidently thinking the problem through geographically.

"So they'll miss us?"

"Foxtrot-three-three-Alpha, Foxtrot-three-three-Alpha this is Zero-Bravo, come in, over…" he said into the radio, ignoring her question.

"Oi," she said, jabbing him in the upper arm with an extended index finger. "They'll miss us, right, Charlie?" He dropped his head, mouth open ready to try and call his SSM again.

"Maybe," he said quietly. "But the others are heading this way right into their path."

———

"Getting something garbled over the radio," Bufford said to Johnson over their link inside the Warrior. They'd driven hard for ten miles before they were forced to stop and deal with the scraping noise directly above the driver's hatch. With that lucky hitchhiker removed and half decapitated by Bufford's shiny pioneer's axe, they had resumed their journey, heading north and west over the low, rolling countryside, which was beginning to show the earliest hints of spring.

"What is it?" Johnson asked, his eyes narrowed as he focused forward on the small slice of road he could see through his viewing slit.

"Well, if I knew that…"

"I think they're saying 'Foxtrot'," Peter said confidently. "That's you, isn't it?" Johnson opened his mouth to reply with the long version, stopping before he wasted his breath.

"It might be," he answered. "Keep listening. It's probably just Daniels seeing where we've got to."

Forty minutes of steady driving later, Johnson stopped the Warrior abruptly. Noises of complaint came through his headphones as the uncomfortably seasick passengers in the rear section would have been banged around with the suddenness of their halt. Johnson ignored those complaints and stared ahead.

"What do you make of that?" he asked, prompting silence in his ears. The question was intended for Bufford, who remained quiet as he stared through the optics to their front.

"Nothing good," he finally answered.

"What is going on?" Astrid's voice sounded in their ears.

"How far does it extend?" Johnson asked.

"Left to right… as far as I can see with the topography. No way around."

"What is happening, Johnson?" Larsen demanded in a tone that betrayed her former seniority among the Special Forces of her native country. A pause hung heavy on their communication channel before Johnson broke it with the sobering news.

"There's a smear on the horizon to our front," he said in a flat, almost emotionless voice. "Buffs, the toggle on the fire controls, zoom in." Bufford found the controls and used the magnification to full effect before a hiss of breath filled their ears.

"*Shhhhit…*"

"Be specific, Sergeant," Larsen admonished from the back, where she couldn't see what they were talking about.

"It's a swarm," he said, mirroring the same toneless vocal attitude of their driver, "and it's directly in our way."

———

"Zero-Bravo," Daniels said with evident relief in his voice. "Be advised there's a reported swarm in the area."

"We know, lad," Johnson said, no longer concerned with correct radio protocol. "We were driving straight towards it until we saw it."

"Send grid-reference and bearing," Daniels instructed. Johnson, anticipating the request, gave the grid from the local map and a compass bearing as best they could ascertain. Silence followed after the brief, "Wait one," reply as Johnson imagined his corporal checking the location and direction against his own position.

Knowing the man was competent at reading a map, Johnson grew annoyed and then concerned as the silence stretched longer than expected.

"Daniels," he called into the radio, "bearing isn't towards your location. They'll bypass and head north." The logic was sound, as the things rarely deviated from an easy route when they gathered in numbers, unless something grabbed the attention of the Limas.

"Negative," Daniels' voice came back in a hoarse whisper. "Bridge on that road is out. Collapsed last summer. They'll be forced down the lower ground directly to our location."

The transmission had been cut shortly after that, when Johnson's questions had been answered and he was unnervingly in agreement with the corporal's assessment. He prayed he was wrong, prayed that the swarm—even if it was miniscule compared to the ones they'd encountered before—would ignore their comfortable country residence and carry on up the country.

They were stuck, with no way to cross through the flowing river of dead meat and reach the others, and knowing now that the bridge north of them was destroyed, they had no way to get ahead of the shambling procession in time. As the light began to fade, Johnson reluctantly turned their big tracked vehicle around to find somewhere safe to spend the night.

Peter's heart raced as he peeked out of the open hatch to see a large farm building ahead of him. Memories of his previous life came back in an unbidden rush that made his body react to the influx of adrenaline he experienced. Calming his breath as he focused hard on climbing out without falling, he forced away the images that came to his mind.

The poor cows, unable to outpace their hungry attackers, being pulled down and devoured.

His father's dog opened up like it had exploded, to soak the rough carpet, a white shard of rib bone protruding at an odd angle as hands clawed at the insides.

His mother, smeared with gore, trying to bite him through the dirty glass of the patio doors.

Hundreds upon hundreds of pairs of feet passing by only inches from his face as he tried to stay still and not breathe in case the horde detected him.

"You okay, son?" Johnson asked him quietly, seeing the odd look in his eyes and voicing his concern.

"Yeah," he replied between rapid breaths. "Fine." He hefted his sticker—the pitchfork he had adapted for his size to make it the best weapon for killing zombies—which seemed to signal the end of their conversation; he was ready to work.

"Clear that barn," Bufford announced firmly but quietly, "secure all the exits and back the tank in. That's our emergency exit if we need one."

Nobody disagreed with the plan, nor did anything need adding to it. They formed up, going about their work as required. Johnson thought of asking Peter to guard the rear of their Warrior with Kimberley, but decided that he wanted to keep the boy close, given his uncertain mood.

The two Special Forces trained soldiers moved in, fanning left and right through the wide entrance to the dry, musty barn to clear every corner of it and search every nook and cranny that could hide a human of any size.

They swept the lower floor, finding it clear of other exits or entrances and blessedly free of Screechers.

"Upstairs," Bufford called out, indicating the narrow wooden stairs leading up to a timber mezzanine with a low head clearance. Johnson raised the muzzle of his suppressed MP5, a gift from Larsen with the ominous words that it had belonged to a friend of hers, but Peter placed a small hand on his arm. He looked down at the boy, who shook his head.

He followed Peter's gaze and saw how thin and fragile the dry wooden slats of the steps seemed, and understood. Johnson nodded back, lowering his gun and holding out a green torch to the boy, who accepted it and slipped his slender shoulders out of the straps of his bag to do a swap with the big man.

Johnson watched him go up, red glow of the torch radiating out ahead of him as he advanced up the stairs, the point of his pitchfork held ready. He felt no shame at letting a child face danger in his stead, he realised. That in itself was bizarre, but not as abnormal as the fact that the kid had seen the danger and offered to face it as the best weapon their group had in that situation. His own small weight bowed the steps dangerously, so much so that Johnson was certain he'd have fallen through them before he'd even reached halfway to the mezzanine. When Peter went out of sight at the top and the only indication of his safety was the red glow from the torch sweeping left and right, he held his breath until a little voice called down to them with all the military gusto his declaration deserved.

"Clear," he said, letting them all relax as he clicked off the light and carefully climbed back down.

Johnson quickly backed the Warrior inside, and then it took all of them to force the seized runners of the heavy wooden doors to move. Eventually, after much swearing and grunting, the two doors almost met in the middle and were secured with a loop of heavy chain.

The barn, judging by the oily smell of old spilled diesel, had been used as a tractor shed to save the valuable machine from braving the worst of any seasonal weather outside. Now, the mighty machine replacing the tractor's parking spot was opened up as they spread out and got comfortable for the night.

Larsen ignored the priority of food and drink, instead

searching the shed until she found a tub of thick paint and a stiff brush, which earned her a quizzical look from Kimberley.

"What's that for?" she asked.

"I swear," Astrid told her, "if I have to watch that fuel moving around like the waves of the ocean for even one more kilometre, I will be sick all over the other people."

"Oh," Johnson said, shocked by the quiet woman's outburst. "Not very comfortable, then?"

"It is the right fucking bastard," she snapped back, betraying how much the motion sickness had affected her, and also how much time she'd spent in the company of the men of Her Majesty's armed forces.

Johnson, after ten minutes of trying, finally got Daniels back on the radio. His face when he returned to the others told the story before any of them had the opportunity to ask.

"They've been forced to abandon the place they were living in," he said quietly. "They're on their own now, just like we are."

"Your man Daniels tell you that himself?" Bufford asked. Johnson shook his head.

"He was driving. Looks like he's trained himself a young apprentice." At those words he couldn't help but feel his eyes drawn to Peter.

NINE

"They don't believe us," Daniels half screamed with the sheer frustration of it all.

"None of them?" Jessica asked him as she looked up from the bag she was re-packing on the hull of the Sultan. "Not even the army ones?"

"Some of them do," Daniels admitted as he checked over both shoulders to see if anyone could see how much ammunition he'd swiped from the room designated as an armoury, after collecting his Sterling. "But even those who *do* believe us don't think we should follow the others. They probably don't want to be back under orders. Makes you wonder what kind of people chose to stay…"

Jessica acknowledged that with a grunt, stopping what she was doing to look up at an approaching figure. It was Ellie, the young woman she had run from their hilltop prison with. The two were locked to one another, intertwined by shared experiences and by similar losses in their lives. She was hurrying over carrying a large bag, but her face registered more anger than fear. She threw the bag up at the girl ten years her junior and stormed to the front of the vehicle to clamber up.

"You're sure?" she snapped, sounding annoyed with the girl.

"Don't ask me," she answered with a shrug, nodding her head down at Daniels.

"You're sure?" Ellie asked again, directing her question at the soldier juggling an armful of loaded magazines.

"Yes," he told her, "I'm bloody certain of it. Which means we need to be gone from here, either east or west but preferably west, sometime in the next ten minutes."

"Hold on," Jessica asked as she stood up from her packing as if struck by a thought. "Are they going to just *let* you take this?"

"Not exactly."

"What does 'not exactly' mean?" Ellie grilled him.

"It means there's nobody left to ask. Not really."

"Not really?" Jessica needled him, knowing him well enough by now to know he wasn't being entirely truthful.

"It means that I'm technically the highest ranking soldier here, and I'm just a Corporal."

"But there are more of…" Ellie waved her hand irritably towards the house behind him. "…*them* than you, and they might not like the idea of you taking your tank away."

"Armoured vehicle," Daniels corrected her peevishly. Ellie ignored the comment.

As if to underline the point she'd just made, two people came from the house and headed in their direction, one clearly carrying the unmistakable profile of a shotgun.

"Look alive," Daniels told them, as if either understood what he expected of them. He let out a sigh of exasperation and turned to face the approaching men as he held the sub machine gun casually in his right hand.

"Fellers," he said as they approached.

"You ain't fucking taking that," one of them said, the one

not holding the shotgun, before Daniels could say anything else. "It doesn't belong to you."

"No?" Daniels asked, still keeping his hand holding the gun very still, but his eyes focused on the twitching man behind the speaker. The man was shifting his grip on the shotgun nervously, as though his palms were slick with sweat that was preventing him from holding it steady. Daniels recognised that as a bad sign.

"Who does it belong to then?"

"Her Majesty the Queen," the speaker sneered with sarcastic nastiness at him, as though invoking royalty made his point any more valid.

"Whom I serve," Daniels answered calmly. "Do you?" The man bristled, nostrils flaring as his own argument was turned on him in an instant.

"I've paid taxes all my life," he snarled. "What about you, Mal?"

"Yep," croaked shotgun man from over his right shoulder.

"So, we've probably paid for that over the years, along with whatever pittance you earned driving it."

"First off," Daniels said as a flutter of movement caught his peripheral vision. The two men saw his reaction and began to turn to look, so he spoke louder to get their attention back.

"First off," he said louder, earning stares from both of them, "I've paid more tax than they've paid me." That was a clear lie, but it never helped to let on how much his second career was worth back in the world. "So, I've paid for it too, if that's your way of thinking."

"Pfft," the speaker scoffed at him, as though the childish dismissal of his logic would win the argument. "You're not taking it, anyway."

"Yes, we are," Daniels said, still cool. Shotgun man, his nerve breaking as his minute vocabulary was already exhausted, growled and raised the gun to point it at him.

Daniels smiled and took a pace to his right, putting the speaker directly in between him and the gun. Both men opened their eyes wide in surprise at being so easily thwarted, and both recognised that they were in water beyond their depth.

Shotgun man was saved from having to make any decision by the hollow, sickeningly solid-sounding *clunk* of wood striking bone. Daniels leaned past speaker man, who had whipped around at the alien sound, seeing the shotgun fall to the grass as his bodyguard's eyes rolled back in his head. Toppling like a felled tree to thump into the damp earth at his feet, he dropped to reveal an angry and impatient Ellie, who appreciatively weighed the pick-axe handle in her hand, suggesting that she could get used to the feel of it. Her eyes snapped up to offer speaker man a slow, wicked smile.

Daniels tapped him on the shoulder and cleared his throat, asking him if he wouldn't mind awfully fucking off.

Two minutes later, long enough to retrieve the shotgun and the belt of cartridges to accompany it, the corporal and his two young female companions rolled towards the exit of their country house and towards the lonely sentry who faced a choice of whether to attempt to accost them or not.

He evidently decided against it, instead choosing to melt away into the shadows, no doubt to claim that he hadn't seen them leave. Daniels drove, seeing as the teenage girl would never be let loose on the controls for anything other than pretend, and the scowling young woman, Ellie, showed no inclination to do anything other than sit in a canvas seat and wait.

"Stop," Jessica yelled over the sound of the barking, whistling engine. She repeated it, louder this time, until Daniels heard her and eased off the throttle. What she'd seen from her elevated position behind him, with an infinitely wider field of view than his own, was obviously beyond his vision and he trusted her enough to slow to a dead crawl.

Over the quieter sound of the vehicle rolling forwards, he heard a new voice shouting.

"Wait!" it yelled; desperation conveyed through the single, shouted word. Unable to see clearly to the right side of the Sultan, he popped open the forward hatch and tried to lean out enough to see a young man running towards them with his arms full of clothing and possessions which he was trying and failing to shove into a backpack affixed to a metal frame. Jessica, self-appointed as the gatekeeper for their escape, called down to him.

"Who are you?" the words sounded blunt and judgemental, hasher than Daniels knew was actually the girl's personality.

"I'm coming with you," the man said, running towards the front of the rolling vehicle and shouting at the driver.

"Charlie, stop for fuck's sake!" At the use of his first name, Daniels hit the brakes to bring the Sultan to a creaking stop.

"Who's that?"

"It's Steve! Steve Duncan," the man yelled back, lobbing his half-packed bag up on the front of the vehicle and clambering up behind it. Daniels hadn't worked with the man directly, but he knew him well enough. He was originally from the admin troop of their now scattered squadron, and hadn't been with them long, having only recently come through the basic training courses to be attached to their reserve unit.

"Where's your weapon?" Daniels asked him, seeing the man was wearing his webbing over civilian clothes but not finding the shape of the sterling sub machine gun he should be in possession of.

"Still in the armoury," he answered. "Some wanker's there blocking the door and mouthing off about having you arrested for assaulting someone." He dropped inside the hatch to follow his mess of kit and seemed shocked to see the two female occupants. He nodded and smiled at Jessica, who smiled back and waved. Then he turned to do a double-take at Ellie, colouring up slightly as he mumbled something which was drowned out by the revs building back up to lurch them onwards away from the house.

Duncan sat at Daniels' usual seat, lifting the headset to speak more clearly to him.

"Getting clear and heading west?" he asked.

"I reckon so," Daniels answered. "No chance of getting west ahead of them with the bridge out. And besides, I wouldn't be surprised if they were already this side of the main road."

"Exactly," Duncan answered, "why the hell didn't anyone else believe the report?" Daniels' reply made him tick off the reasons in his head, which all made sense.

"Because it came from me," Daniels told him. "Because it was based on a report from the Yanks, and because people are comfortable so they don't *want* to believe it."

"What's *that* got to do with it?" Jessica's voice cut in on their conversation. Duncan spun to look at her, seeing her holding the large earphones over her head and her eyes burning into him for an answer. He opened his mouth to speak, feeling more than a little nailed to the spot by the forthright girl, but Daniels saved him from responding.

"They don't *want* to believe they aren't safe there," he explained. "They like their little slice of freedom and they don't want the status quo to change."

"Status Quo? What's the band got to d—" Jessica began, stopping herself before she asked the embarrassing question.

"The people who stayed," Ellie explained, her own ears covered with the headset normally reserved for the vehicle commander, "were the ones who didn't want to leave with the army. They don't like other people making rules for them to follow, so they're not going to give up their new life now."

"Even with the chance of a horde of those things bearing

down on them," Duncan added, glancing at the woman and locking eyes with her to show he understood her perfectly.

"So they don't want to believe they're in danger because it doesn't fit in?" Jessica asked.

"Yeah," Duncan said. "I tried to tell them, even the other lads," he said to mean the few remaining squadron men who hadn't left under orders, "but nobody wanted to listen."

Silence filled their earphones as all four of them were left in quiet contemplation.

"Speaking of listening," Daniels said as he turned the nose of the Sultan to head north up a farm track, instead of driving towards the main road where he half expected to see the leading ranks of a detachment from the dead army approaching, "get on that radio and call up the SSM."

"I can do it," Jessica said excitedly, clawing her way through the interior to get to the seat beside their newest crew member, "Charlie taught me how it works."

"Foxtrot-three-three-Alpha," she said into the radio, her lips forming the words in their uncommon combination with concentration.

———

As the sun began to sink to their left, the leading edge of the swarm found themselves suddenly dropping from their path as the roadway under their shambling feet fell away to nothingness.

The rubble below in the narrow, muddy creek bed was rapidly added to with the writhing mess of twitching, moaning bodies, and the inexorable flow of dead followed the precise course of action that corporal Daniels had predicted. Even though they were dead, they still followed the same generic behaviour of living humans and inevitably followed the path of least resistance. Much in the same way that water always flowed in the easiest direction to follow the unbreakable laws of physics, they spilled out of the small riverbed and poured down the slope in the general direction of the low rise hiding the large country house from sight.

Nothing from that direction overtly attracted them; there were no smells or sounds that could carry that far to serve as a lure. But the swarm was so inexorable, such a self-perpetuating phenomenon, and the noise the leading rank made attracted more behind them. This pushed them onwards, making more noise which, in turn, brought on more from the creek bed and road, the slowest of which were in danger of being left behind, without a reason to go on. These stragglers were abandoned to wander in response to the flutter of a bird's wings or a gust of wind rustling the first early leaves on a tree.

That momentum gathered, sparking the small percentage of Limas in their midst to surge ahead, to leap and climb over the slower-moving bodies of their subordinates and force their way to the front where new sensations piqued their primal instincts.

Smells, brought like the ghost of a whisper on the wind, turned their heads to the large buildings on the lower ground. Their direction of movement was followed when the rest of the swarm, as if sensing the excitement of their front runners, sped up their own advance and began to moan and issue occasional shrieks. Those noises quickened the pace of those behind, setting off the chain reaction that would whip the thousand former people into a frenzy which the unprepared and hopelessly under-equipped residents of the big house could never hope to defeat. Vehicles fled not long after the first ranks appeared on the horizon, but the exodus was too little, too late. Some of those vehicles caused a large mob of the main assault to break away and follow the sounds of revving engines north, sparking off another chain of events that would prove catastrophic.

The unorthodox crews of two armoured vehicles settled in for the night; one fully closed down in the open and the other shut inside a large farm shed. They all heard the faint sounds of heavy gunfire in the distance, denoting a desperate defence which they all hoped would be successful, even if they knew deep down it would not be.

TEN

"Oh, dear God!" Professor Grewal cried as the contents of the cargo net thrashed and hissed and shrieked at him and his small team. "What are we supposed to do with these?"

"Not my problem," Miller answered flatly, hiding the enjoyment he was lapping up from frightening the British scientist. With a hand signal, he and his team melted away from the makeshift lab, having fulfilled their responsibilities for the night and leaving to get something to eat and some sleep.

Grewal, left with a lethal cargo and no way to control it, turned desperately with pleading eyes aimed at the man from the US army's infectious diseases department. The man, a sergeant as far as Grewal could make out from the multiple stripes on his sleeve, smirked.

"Alright, boys," he said, "suit up. Doc, you might wanna get yourself clear for this part…"

Four of the soldiers, all wearing heavily padded suits with an outer layer of thick, rubbery material and plastic visors covering their faces, approached the cargo net which had been dragged into a large caged area. The taut ropes keeping the mouth of the net closed were loosened, and the suited soldiers stepped forwards with long poles complete with loops of heavy wire sprouting from the ends. Grewal recognised them as the kind of thing used to secure and control dangerous dogs, and he had to admit that the principle was an easily transferrable one.

With a lot of yelling and a few tense moments when one of the soldiers was forced onto his back by the attacks of the soaked and shrieking beasts, eventually both of them were secured, each with two poles looped around their neck. The difficulty came then when they couldn't figure out how to drag them out of the larger cage and into the smaller ones where they could be used as lab rats.

"Fuck this shit," the sergeant said, reaching up to strip off his own helmet and rummage in his removed equipment to retrieve a cigarette and lighter. He struck flame to the end of a smoke and inhaled deeply, his eyes closed, before he stepped forwards and opened the cage.

"Alright, assholes," he announced, gaining the instant and undivided attention of the thrashing corpses. He blew smoke at them and brought up both hands to gesture them forward. "If you'll step right this way, thaaat's it, keep following the sound of my voice…" he paced backwards, luring them towards him as both bubbled and tried to shriek at their slowly escaping meal. One by one, they were corralled into individual cages, the loops being removed from their necks before the team took off their suits and began to scrub them down with a strong-smelling bleach solution.

"Draw straws for the next time," their sergeant said, "unless one of you screws up, then being the bait can be your reward. Oh, hey, Docs." This last was aimed at Grewal and Chambers, who had re-entered ahead of their own team. "All yours. I'm sure I don't need to tell you not to stick your fingers through the bars. These animals may bite…"

"No," Grewal answered, "you don't."

"Your team are staying here, though, right?" Chambers added. In answer, the sergeant raised his eyes to a section of the shed elevated about twenty feet from the floor. Up there, just visible in the gloom, was a pair of soldiers sitting behind a heavy machine gun, ready to end the experiment should anything go awry. Chambers nodded his understanding, turning to give his orders.

"Full tissue samples," he ordered them. "Run everything from the beginning. Blood, DNA, everything. And anyone getting themselves bitten will find themselves instantly dismissed from this team." A heavy clunk of metal sounded from behind him, prompting all of them to turn and look.

"Anyone gets themselves bit," the sergeant said dourly, his hand still resting on the heavy semi-automatic pistol he had produced, "and I'll personally guarantee your dismissal from the human race through the medium of my forty-five." They all stared at him, waiting for his face to crack and betray the fact that he was joking. His face, however, stayed resolute and the awkward silence extended until the lead scientist cleared his throat for their attention.

"Get the samples," Grewal told them, "set up the tests and then we can get some sleep. We'll deal with the results in the morning."

Grewal watched as the grunt work of their scientific mission was undertaken. He hung back, offering such encouragement as he thought fit in the form of loud tutting and the occasional patronising slow shake of his head. Seeing the suspicious and permanently scowling sergeant still sitting cradling the large handgun he'd threatened them with, he drew himself up to his full, if meagre, height and approached him.

"I'd prefer," he began, his courage abandoning him slightly as the sergeant's head turned slowly to glare at him. He made a low noise in his throat, as though he wanted to cough but fought the urge. "I'd prefer it if you weren't quite so… *hostile*, to my staff."

"I'd prefer it if you weren't such an asshole," he replied without a trace of humour. "But we don't often get what we want now, do we?"

"What's your name?" Grewal demanded, as if the implied threat of a complaint could frighten the man.

"Yates. Staff Sergeant Yates."

"Well, *Staff Sergeant Yates*, as I said I'd pref—"

"I heard you," Yates snarled quietly. "I also don't give a shit. You and your little science project set the whole goddam world on fire, and now me and my people are putting our lives at risk so you can do it again. You want a," he sarcastically air-quoted with his finger, "*less hostile work environment*? Don't kill half the people in the goddam world. Period."

Grewal shut his mouth and backed away, watching the sergeant lean back in his uncomfortable chair to resume staring at the two bedraggled creatures in their cages, who had given up their frantic shrieking and were satisfied just to moan and chew at the heavy mesh to try and get to the living.

He waited in the shadows of the barn lab until the samples were taken and placed in the chillers to await the response to the serum he and Chambers had developed.

Finding a way to attack the virus had been a simple thing to approach, but a very difficult one to refine. Using highly infectious host carriers to deliver it, as he had with the original disease, was his first and only thought on the matter, but he was anxious to see how the tests fared in a real-world experiment. Using something aggressive had been automatic for him, and he toyed with a few possibilities.

He experimented with the world's newest killer virus on professor Chambers' insistence: HIV; despite his concerns that the rate of degradation would be too slow for his style. The biggest problem with that disease was that it killed its human hosts by attacking their natural ability to defend themselves through their immune system. Given that the infected didn't respond with their immune system, the early tests had failed to give them any kind of positive results.

After two weeks of failed lab experiments using anti-viral medication, Grewal turned back to what he did best and began messing with nature on a cellular level. He attacked the deadly zombie virus samples with Dengue fever, hoping that he could cause some kind of catastrophic body shutdown in the infected humans, but while on the cellular level it did indeed attack the virus, the delivery method still escaped them.

That's when he circled back around to the only aggressive virus he knew well, and one that boasted a one hundred percent mortality rate if untreated. Trying to combine Dengue fever with rabies was impossible, given that the lyssavirus was just so incompatible with the haemorrhagic fever, and he was forced back to the metaphorical drawing board.

A wasted week of working alone followed in the gloom of their subterranean lab. In a rare moment of reflection, he realised he didn't even know which state it was in. This period of solitary labour saw him combine the samples at his disposal and utilise the aggressive nature of rabies to deliver the haemorrhagic properties of Dengue fever.

Eventually, working through the samples of every infectious disease known to mankind, courtesy of the US Army MRIID and combined CDC freezers, he stumbled on a rare example of virus he'd never even considered using, until he saw the four letters stencilled on the glass vial. IHNV. Infectious haematopoietic necrosis virus; a form of flesh-eating infection seen in certain fish.

The destructive properties of the virus, those which effectively turned the insides of an infected host to gloop, fit his requirements perfectly.

Infected tissue, when treated with this serum, haemorrhaged and effectively died at the cellular level in every single test they conducted. When the plain suits who deflected attention whenever they were asked if they were CIA heard the explanation, it became clear to Grewal that they had very different expectations about the work.

"So you've developed a cure?" they had been asked. Grewal turned to Chambers, the two men locking eyes and hoping that the other would answer. Chambers stayed quiet so Grewal let out a sigh.

"There is no *cure* as such," he explained. "Not unless you change the parameters of *cure* to include the destruction of an infected host." He'd seen the annoyance on the man's face and went on to explain further.

"The virus destroys the brain function, effectively killing the host anyway. Even if we could somehow find a way to purge it from their bodies, they'd be left a brain-dead vessel, capable of barely remaining alive at absolute best. More likely, from what we've been told, they'd have acquired injuries or simply rotted away so that there would be very little left, physically. So no, we can't bring anyone back, but we *do* think we can kill them off a second, more *permanent*, time."

That conversation led them to where they were, on a cold and windswept Scottish island with two former human beings in cages, minus chunks of their mottled flesh which were sitting in glass dishes, waiting to see if the theory worked in the real world, instead of just in a laboratory.

———

The following morning, after a short and uncomfortable sleep, Grewal returned to their lab wrapped in multiple layers of clothing in an attempt to keep the biting wind from seeking out any gap it could find to chill him to the bone. He poured coffee, shuddering at the sachets of foul-looking powder the Americans called 'creamer', and hugged the cup in both hands, before making his way towards the sample fridges and the start of their real work.

The discovery they made, the one that would change the fate of the world's survivors, wasn't due to any of the complex biological work, but due instead to the most random of occurrences.

Grewal walked past the position where he had suffered the conversation with Yates only hours before, glancing down at the soldier fiddling with the dials of a radio to fill the space with the hissing crackle of static.

"Cut it out, Mancini," another uniformed man chided him. "You ain't gonna find anyone playing songs anymore."

"Oh, ye of little faith, Corporal," the man evidently named Mancini retorted, just as the feedback from the speakers shrieked and hissed, before emitting a low hum that barely registered in the ears of the humans.

Grewal froze, glued to the spot as his chest heaved in animalistic terror at the sounds coming from his right. Mancini carried on spinning the dial and the two caged zombies stopped shrieking and launching themselves at the bars, to lapse back into their slower state of animation.

"Do that again, Private," he said, with a finger pointed at Mancini.

"Specialist," the man muttered back, turning the dial as instructed. When the sound dipped back into the low, barely audible hum again, the two corpses wailed and attacked the heavy mesh to get to them.

No, Grewal though, *not us; the radio.*

"Take it back again and leave it there." The soldier did as he was told, his wide eyes fixed firmly on the two occupied cages. When the hiss and whistle of static gave way to the low frequency sound once more, the dead went into a state of savage behaviour, trying to force their faces through the wide mesh to reach for the source of their excitement.

"Oh, Jesus," one of the American lab assistants cried, seeing what the smaller of their two test subjects was doing. All eyes turned to it, many turning away in repulsion as it—*she*–forced her face through the small gap in the mesh to strip the mottled skin away, like a potato being peeled, to expose a bright slash of white cheek bone beneath. Someone vomited noisily, the meagre breakfast of toast and coffee splattering onto the concrete floor of the shed. From behind them, a wavering voice wailed, "Oh, dear God!" before a single, booming noise made them all flinch in fright and sudden deafness.

The half-peeled face snapped back, the contents of the skull fountaining outwards where the back of the head had been ejected in bloody chunks of bone and scalp. The half-headless body slumped slowly, mouth closing as it sank down to its knees to rest against the mesh.

"Shut that shit off, Mancini," Yates barked, weapon trained on the head of the second zombie, in case that one tried to pour itself out of the cage like the other. The radio clicked off and everyone relaxed.

"Sergeant," Grewal began, seeing the solider whirl on him and holster the heavy pistol.

"*Staff* Sergeant," Yates snapped. "You don't hear me going around calling you the wrong thing, Doc." Grewal opened his mouth to correct him but thought better of it.

"You didn't have to kill the subj—" he began.

"You do science," Yates interrupted him, "I'll do security. You rile 'em up again and run the risk of one breaking out, you'll see me do that again. And now I've got to explain to a bunch of Navy SEALs that they have to risk their lives, *again*, to fetch you another lab rat…"

Grewal ignored his words, turning to look at the shocked

young man still sitting by the radio he'd been playing with in the vain hope of finding some entertainment.

"Specialist," Grewal said, the word unfamiliar to him as something he would call another person, "could you take that very far away from here and find out *exactly* what frequency that was?" Mancini looked up to Yates, who nodded. "And someone find Agent Fisher urgently."

ELEVEN

"Major?" Mac said gently, still managing to sound almost angry at everything as he spoke. If not angry, then very disappointed at the least. Downes opened one eye, then the other, groaning and moving to sit up, like he had the mother of all hangovers. His body ached all over, worse than after any PT session he'd ever experienced, but nobody told him to stay flat on his back or rushed to help him up; perhaps because they knew he'd just shrug them off anyway.

"How long?" he croaked.

"About eighteen hours," Mac answered, sounding jealous.

"Jesus," Downes swore as he rubbed the heels of both hands into his sunken and dark eye sockets. "What's the gen?"

The 'gen', according to Mac at least, was that they'd been better off down south, but he didn't want to give that opinion to his major just yet.

"Best you get your strength up and meet the Colonel yourself," he answered cryptically, the absence of facts speaking volumes. With more groaning, swearing and a liberal amount of blasphemy, Downes stood unsteadily and took a moment to acclimatise to being upright. Blinking open his eyes again to aid his balance, his vision cleared to take in the form of the tank captain, smiling and offering him a bone china cup on a saucer.

"Always trust an officer of Her Majesty's armed forces to bring the good china on a campaign," he joked weakly, with slowly formed words. A crooked smile joined his jest, which Palmer acknowledged with one of his own.

"Quite right, Major," he said. "Although I'm ashamed to admit that all the good brandy and cigars have perished; casualties of war, I'm afraid. And I've misplaced my backgammon board." Downes accepted the tea, taking in a long gulp of it, despite the heat, and letting the sugary goodness coat his throat as the strong aroma filled his sinuses and worked to wake his brain up the rest of the way. With an almost ungentlemanly *aaah*, he replaced the delicate cup on the matching saucer and regarded the young officer.

"I trust you handled everything in your stride while I was incapacitated?" he asked with an apologetic edge to his words.

"Not much to handle, truth be told. The Royal Marines' medic declared you unfit on account of exposure." He held up a hand to ward off the protests and explain more. "A combination of the cold water, a lack of rations and exhaustion. In his words," he pulled an amused face and attempted to affect the accent of the Midlander.

"There weren't enough heat left in the coals to revive the fire!"

Downes smiled at the terrible impression but recognised it for what it was; an attempt to alleviate the stress and embarrassment with a little weak humour, much as he had done when he first woke. He gulped the remainder of the tea, his thirst intensifying, as if the small cup he'd just finished had awoken his senses. He turned wordlessly to Mac, wearing a look one could only call 'hopeful', and the dour Scot took the cup and left the room, muttering to himself.

"Something of a character, your Mister Kelly..." Palmer

said when the two officers were alone. Downes' expression darkened at the second intimation that things weren't as rosy as they should be.

"Tell me," he said.

Palmer shifted in his seat, his exquisite manners fighting against his tiredness and natural urge to be blunt. Eventually, after a stern and quizzical look from the SAS major, tiredness won through.

"I never expected a military dictatorship to be this…"

"This what?"

"Well, it's not quite as enjoyable as one would imagine."

Downes hmmm'd in response but was saved from making any immediate reply as the door banged open and Mac reappeared arse-first to spin in the doorway, revealing a tray with a pot of tea, more cups and the most welcome sight of thickly sliced bread bearing the unmistakable smell of fried sausages. Mac put the tray down with as much care as he would a sack of potatoes and shoved a plate towards the major.

"Had them put a snotty egg in yours," he said. "Just how you like it."

Downes, had he been able to, would've thanked his NCO profusely. He said nothing, instead nodded in wide-eyed thanks as he'd just crammed the biggest bite of the greasy sandwich as possible into his mouth quicker than he could reload his MP5.

Palmer, less driven by crippling hunger, reached for the tea pot.

"Shall I be mother?" he asked, the words an automatic reaction to the task. With obvious care, he poured the aromatic, dark liquid into three cups and offered one to Mac, who grunted in thanks and sloshed in an unmeasured amount of milk, before heaping sugar into it and banging the teaspoon around like he was ringing a dinner gong.

Palmer, ignoring the lack of manners as an irrelevance, deftly scooped sugar onto his own spoon and cascaded it into the liquid, then added milk with such precision that he didn't spill a drop. He finished his ritual by swirling the liquid and gently running the edge of the spoon on the lip of the cup, to then place it down without a sound. He offered that cup to Downes and repeated the ritual as the man chewed desperately, before swallowing large mouthfuls of bread, pork and egg.

When Downes had finished, gently thumping one fist into his chest as though he could force down the food, he nodded his thanks and took a long gulp of tea, only to pull a face and squeeze his eyes shut, forcing that swallow down. He opened his eyes to regard the tray and saw Mac snatch up his own sandwich in case it was picked off by enemy fire. Palmer gently pushed his own towards him.

"This would be my second of the day," he admitted, "and I also ate yesterday. I insist, Sir."

Downes offered no resistance and gladly ate a second sandwich as the three sat in silence, waiting for him to regain his strength. Palmer made him another cup from the pot and waited patiently.

"So," Downes said as he leaned back and hid an uncomfortable burp behind his hand, "Kelly has adopted the strongarm approach to matters?"

Mac and Palmer exchanged a look before the captain picked up his cup and lifted one leg over the other as he sat back.

"Perhaps I should start from the beginning?"

———

Downes' collapse caused more than a little hysteria among the civilians of their convoy to have witnessed it. Their medic, a man inclined towards sounding at the same time both bored and annoyed, if only because of his accent, had rushed in to take over and deal with the major. This was a condition his training and experience made him far more comfortable to treat than the uncertain arena of infected human bites.

"Commanding officers report to quarantine exit. I repeat, commanding officers to quarantine exit," the speaker announced insistently. The younger Palmer appeared, his boiler suit somehow fitting him, whereas everyone else's only seemed to fit where they touched. He ignored the obvious look of hostility from the rough SAS soldier and smiled at his older brother in the hope that he could convey his support without words.

"Leave the talking to me," Palmer Senior said with a quiet forcefulness. "I rather suspect we aren't as welcome as one would hope."

The two officers and the NCO met up with Lloyd and the German, Wolff, as the hastily built shelter was unlocked and the five men slipped out amid the shouted questions and protests of the civilians. Three uniformed men, all wearing respirators and carrying automatic rifles, led the way up the slope away from the ferry dock. They were ushered into the rear of a military Land Rover, climbing up to sit under the canvas back that kept the persistent drizzle from their cold bodies. The ride was blessedly short, given that they bounced around on the cold, hard metal interior over the bumpy roads, all the while feeling the chill of the brisk Atlantic wind as it found every gap in the flapping canvas cover.

With a metallic squeal of protesting brakes, the vehicle pulled to a stop and the sound of the driver banging his flat hand on his own door prompted them to shuffle awkwardly to the back and climb down. A two-storey stone cottage was before them, with a single soldier standing sentry at the door, so low that they were forced to duck under the lintel to escape the rain.

The cottage, a modest dwelling which had evidently been

repurposed very recently, opened up into what would have been the sitting room and which now played host to the dining table, covered in paperwork. The five newcomers stepped inside, filling all the available space in seconds to somehow reduce the air in the room.

A whistling sound came from the next room, prompting Palmer to step towards the threshold of the doorway and clear his throat politely.

"With you in a minute," came a strong reply. Palmer stepped back delicately, as though chastened by a teacher at the expensive boarding school of his youth, to wait as the sounds of china clanking together drifted out to them. Moments later, a man of remarkably average height and build walked in bearing a tray loaded with mugs piled on top of one another precariously and a large pot venting steam from the spout. He cleared a section of paperwork from the table by shoving it along and slid the tray onto the wood. Letting out a breath which spoke of relief at his success in not dropping the precious cargo onto the floor, he turned to regard them before snapping his fingers in front of his face.

"Biscuits," he said, turning his face towards the kitchen and bellowing the word for the attention of someone they had yet to see. A man wearing the uniform of the Grenadier Guards, adorned with a captain's insignia, stepped into the room with a handful of the small, wrapped parcels they recognised from their ration packs. The biscuits were added to the tray and the two men turned in the small room to regard their visitors.

"Kelly," the first man said by way of introduction before gesturing at the younger man. "Barton."

Barton nodded his greeting and ducked out of the room again, evidently not needed for whatever conversation was about to take place.

"Colonel," Palmer Senior began, one flat hand on his chest

as he prepared to launch into a short speech of gratitude for their hospitality.

"And you are?" Kelly asked in a brief bark.

"Palmer, Sir. Household Cavalry." Kelly nodded once and turned to the next man in line. Wolff's heels snapped together and he opened his mouth to speak, but Kelly lifted a hand dismissively.

"I can guess who you are, Captain Wolff. You?"

"Lloyd, Sir. Royal Marines." Kelly's eyebrow twitched upwards as if to explain that he could damn well tell the difference between the uniforms of the British army and the royal marines, and then his gaze came to rest on the second to last man.

"Lieutenant Palmer," Palmer Junior crooned, dropping the double-barrel as his brother had, so as not to confuse matters unnecessarily, "Yeomanry."

Kelly looked at the last man, meeting Mac's eyes and exchanging a nod with the man who came from the same place he did.

"Am I to assume," the colonel said sombrely, "that Major Downes did not make it here?"

"He's well enough," Mac answered, "suffering from a touch of exposure on account of taking a wee swim as the rear guard." Kelly smiled, genuinely pleased that the other SAS officer had survived.

"Right, well, I shan't keep you long," he said, "I know you'll be anxious to get back to your people. We'll give you a few days to rest, but after that, I'll need every able-bodied man, woman and child to pitch in; things aren't exactly *easy*, isolated up here." He paused to pour tea from the pot into the mugs, beckoning them forward to help themselves and spoke as they waited patiently for their turn at the tray.

"There are a number of farming and fishing tasks in need of more hands—not the deeper water stuff, obviously, just coastal trawling—and a significant amount of work is required to patrol the perimeter here." He took a sip, smiling at the drink as if he were pleased with himself for making it well when it wasn't a task he was remotely accustomed to performing.

"We've got over six hundred square miles of rocky island to keep clear, and you're never more than five miles from the coast at any one point, I'm assured. Lots of places one of the bloated bastards could wash up, and it'll come as no surprise to you that I could do with more trained men. That's where you'll come in, when you're rested, Captains," he said, pointing at Palmer and Wolff. "The men already in place will maintain control of the two open quarantine docks but you'll oblige me by commanding a section of coast for patrols."

Kelly ignored the lieutenant, assuming him to be under the command of the man with the hint of family resemblance who must have been a relation, turning to the royal marine to request of him the same task. He left Mac off the orders list, no doubt intending to catch up with his officer when he was able to.

"And, Sir," Palmer asked as he took half a step forward. "Might I enquire as to the state of things in the wider world?"

"The wider world?"

"Quite. You see, we've been somewhat out of the loop, so to speak…"

"Yes, I imagine you have been. Well, Captain, I'm sorry to say that the European continent is lost; either to atomic bombs or to the enemy." He let the silence hang so that they all understood the finality of his words, noting how stone-faced their German ally was at receiving the confirmation.

"Given that the Americans nuked the Russians as soon as the Russians nuked their European borders, and a good number of their own Soviet States I might add, we can assume that everything to the east is either dead, dying or otherwise shut off. Australia, New Zealand and a handful of other island nations are closed off, although they're still speaking to us, at least..." he trailed off, glancing at the front window as the sound of another vehicle pulled up outside. "Speaking of the outside world," he said with a hint of annoyance as the front door opened and a man walked in, wearing black uniform with a sidearm holstered on his belt. He stopped, taking in the dishevelled men in matching boiler suits before smiling at them in welcome and helping himself to a cup from the table.

"Gentlemen," Kelly said, "Agent Fisher, CIA." Fisher spluttered on his drink.

"Dammit, Colonel. I brought you some coffee..." He turned to face the men again.

"Just Fisher is fine," he said. "And congratulations on surviving this long." He turned to Kelly and raised his eyebrows as if to ask why they weren't already talking in private.

"You'll be given billets after everyone passes quarantine. Take a few days to recuperate and get your equipment back. Good day, gentlemen."

They filed out, finding their uncomfortable ride still in place with the engine running. Climbing back aboard to wait for the bumpy return ride, Palmer had to raise his voice for the others to hear him.

"I'd hazard a guess that we've just discovered where the real power lies."

TWELVE

"Ladies on the left, gents on the right," Daniels announced after tentatively checking outside their armoured vehicle for any signs of unwelcome attention. They'd driven until darkness forced them to stop, and as they were unable to find anywhere enclosed to rest, they'd elected for the most open area where nothing could approach without being noticed.

They went to their respective sides of the Sultan in the early dawn to empty the overnight contents of their bladders; Daniels took his Sterling to their side, insisting that Ellie take their only other weapon, the shotgun, to their female bathroom.

"Try the others?" Jessica asked as they climbed back up to escape the cold outside air for the slightly less cold air inside the Sultan. Duncan checked the maps as Daniels started the engine to get some heat into the interior. He hadn't wanted to leave it running or rig up the external generator.

"Need some bloody fuel soon," he mumbled, earning a demand from Jessica to know what he'd just said.

"Nothing. Did you want to try them?" Jessica didn't

respond to him, but threw herself into the seat by the radio set and began to hail Johnson.

"They're not answering," she yelled after a while, frowning that she hadn't received an answer and clambering up to poke her head out of the hatch. She opened her mouth to repeat herself, but then stopped, seeing the direction they were all facing and hearing the noise that had attracted their collective attention. Her elevated position meant she could identify the source of the noise before they could see it, and the single spoken word sparked a flurry of action.

"Car."

Daniels and Duncan scrambled for the front of the Sultan, making Ellie follow without instruction. Duncan dropped into the driver's hatch as Daniels settled himself in behind the butt of the machine gun mounted on the top, to swing the long barrel towards the direction of the approaching sound. Then they waited.

"Start her up," he instructed. "Just in case."

"In case what?" Jessica asked, remembering only fractionally later than the others that not all people were as welcoming as they would be. Tense seconds ticked by until a dirty brown car rolled over the top of a rolling dip that characterised the roads in the area. Daniels adjusted the aim of the GPMG to meet the sudden intrusion but almost immediately let the barrel of the gun swing up as he relaxed.

"It's the marines," he said, climbing out to meet them as the car pulled up close to them with protesting brakes.

"There's hospitality for you," the thick-set driver complained as he pulled himself out of the car and limped around the front towards them.

"Sorry," Daniels said, gesturing up at the gun. "Can't be too careful…"

"He meant leaving without us, dickhead," the passenger said, having exited the vehicle without being noticed. He cradled a short rifle with a fat barrel across his body and looked so comfortable with it that the weapon seemed like an intimate part of him.

"Sorry," Daniels said again. "Had to move quickly before the locals brought their pitchforks." The two marines, still wearing most of their uniform but with bits of civilian clothing evident on both, gave each other a fleeting look.

"We know what you mean," the older man said. "Ran into some resistance when we were gearing up to leave, ourselves."

"Oh?" Ellie asked from her spot on top of the tracked vehicle.

"Nothing we couldn't handle," the man with the rifle said dismissively. She could imagine one of the self-styled leaders of the people left at the house trying to tell these two what they could and couldn't do, and smiled to herself as she imagined the two Royal Marines doing what they wanted anyway. The smile faded when she thought of all the people left behind.

"Did the swarm come?" she asked quietly.

"Think so," the man with the rifle said. "We saw the faster ones coming over the hill when we took off."

"And there are more than usual out on the road this morning," the driver added, "so we should probably get moving."

"Okay, we keep going north," Daniels said before looking to Jessica. "And keep trying Johnson on the radio."

"Johnson?" the marines chorused in shock.

Daniels frowned, confirming who he was talking about. He hadn't spoken to the two men since they had arrived a few days earlier and they had been resting ever since the ordeal that left them at the house.

"Where are they?" Hampton demanded. "Have they still got the kids with them?"

"Kids?" Ellie asked.

"Boy and a girl," Enfield said quietly. "Peter and Amber."

Ellie gasped, looking at Jessica, who was wearing a look of abject shock that mirrored her own.

"You get on that bloody radio," Ellie hissed, "and you find out where they are."

―――――

The muted crackling of the radio inside the Warrior drifted out into the barn, causing the occupants to stir. Exhaustion and adrenaline had taken their toll. One adult was left on sentry duty and could be forgiven for falling asleep while guarding their location. So when the radio sparked to life and the scratching and moaning answered from outside, they all woke to see a panicked Kimberley looking aghast that she hadn't raised the alarm sooner.

Bufford was up first, weapon in hand as he moved towards the gap in the barn doors and held out a hand towards the frightened woman to try to tell her that it was okay. Larsen joined him, moving her head from side to side as she tried to see through the crack into the dawn and assess the strength and numbers of the enemy, without getting too close.

The radio crackled again, prompting a swelling surge in the intensity of the moaning outside. Bufford turned back to flap a hand at Johnson in the gloomy interior of the building, telling him silently to shut the noise down.

"Shit," he hissed, glancing at Astrid and receiving confirmation of his assessment of the enemy.

"Twenty or more out there," she said quietly. "I would suggest that we go now." In response to her words, the moaning outside swelled and the wooden doors creaked as the combined body weight of so many agitated corpses surged towards the crack. They hastily threw their gear inside as Johnson primed and started the raucous engine. In the confines of the barn, the exhaust note barked louder than any car on the road ever could, to rise and growl with a deafening rumble. Hatches closed just in time as shafts of wan daylight began to appear in the wooden walls as well as the sliding doors, threatening that the structure could not hope to hold back the dead for long.

Johnson slammed down his own hatch just as the left-hand door splintered and fell inwards at an angle to admit a meagre flood of hungry creatures, like water breaking through a child's dam in a stream. The last image he had of the grotesque sight was of a Lima crouching to leap onto the front of the tracked vehicle, to shriek as it beat bloody fists into a ruin of broken bones and torn fingernails as if, with the sheer force of its malevolence, it could break through.

As his hands and feet manipulated the controls, Johnson realised the horrific sight wasn't the only assault on his senses in their rude awakening, because some of the stench that followed the former humans had crept inside before he had safely sealed the hatch.

The Warrior bucked, pitching the Lima forward to break its nose and knock its remaining teeth out on the metal, before tumbling it back into the slower ones in its wake; just in time for the heavy tracks to crush and crunch them into the straw-strewn dirt. The weak barrier of wooden doors didn't slow their escape for even a second, as the dry timber exploded outwards in far less spectacular fashion than in any action movie.

Accelerating away and flattening the rearmost stragglers, Johnson saw a flash of bodies through his viewport until the road ahead was clear of obstructions. It was like a snapshot his mind took, which didn't even allow him the time for the image to develop. He thought fleetingly of the instant cameras he'd seen which could do this. His snapshot revealed to him some explanation for why the last few were late to their surprise breakfast meeting.

A woman, age unfathomable given the decaying ruin of her face and sagging, emaciated body, stumped towards them with both arms reaching out as if begging for their help. She had an exaggerated, lop-sided limp due to the fact that her right foot was missing from mid-shin. The thing beside her, two heads shorter and destroyed to the point of appearing androgynous, walked with a wobbling gait as the broken bones of its legs threatened to give way with each step.

Twitching the controls fractionally to his left, Johnson made sure to put both of them under the tracks to save them the trouble of having to walk any longer.

"We're clear," he announced. Over the headset he'd hastily thrown over his ears, he could hear heavy breathing but no panic or distress. "Peter, was that Daniels calling us?"

There was no reply.

"Peter?"

"He's not here," Bufford said breathlessly, with more than a hint of panic in his quiet words. In response, their forward momentum was cut violently enough for shouts to come through as those in the rear section were slammed into the separation. He began to turn the vehicle around, spinning it on the spot, with the tracks churning the ground up in opposing directions, just as a loud thud sounded on their roof. That thud was accompanied by a second, slightly louder, and two sections above their heads were being scratched and clawed at in animalistic desperation by what could only have been the faster ones; the ones who still retained just enough cognitive ability to understand where their quarry had gone to ground, and who were now trying to dig them out.

"Larsen, is he there with you?" Bufford asked. A pause hung heavy with hesitation before any reply came.

"He is not," Astrid answered, her own voice sounding broken by the stupidity of their unforgiveable mistake. Two of them were Special Forces soldiers, trained to a staggeringly high level and accustomed to working in small teams. The very core of their ethos was to always work as one and never leave anyone behind. More thuds and shrieks sounded as their Warrior was swarmed by the remains of the crowd, which had swelled to a far larger number than they had originally thought.

"We're going back," Johnson announced, delivering the statement as if daring anyone to countermand his decision. They rolled forwards, not even feeling the bumps of those undead bodies crushed under the weight of their wagon, until Johnson stopped and stared forwards through the limited view he was afforded. He swallowed, feeling a lump in his throat he hadn't experienced for a long time, as he saw the hundreds of Screechers flow around the barn with the ruined door and head directly towards them.

Bufford saw it too, wishing he could reach out and squeeze the sergeant major's shoulder to reassure him with the words he carefully chose.

"Going back for him signs his death warrant, Dean," he said. "We need to lead the rest of these rotten bastards away and come back for him. We've got to trust he'll know to keep his head down, and that we'll come back for him."

Johnson said and did nothing for a long time, but simply stared ahead. He couldn't see the dead ground in front of them, but it was filling up with the tightly packed undead, who pawed impotently at their armoured skin like a cat scratching at a patio door in the rain.

"Sit tight, lad," Johnson said with a wavering voice. "I'm coming back for you."

The revs rose aggressively as the Warrior shot backwards and slewed left, before loud clunking noises indicated their switch of gears to launch them forwards and down a tree-lined single-track road, away from the farm.

"Light those fuckers up, Buffs," Johnson snarled, no longer

able to hide the sound of his sniffing nose betraying the fact that he was crying for the first time in as long as he could recall. "Let 'em have it and don't bloody stop until they're all done for."

———

Peter couldn't sleep during the night. Almost everyone else was so exhausted that sleep wasn't something they had to find, merely submit to. He was tired too, only something about their location set his nerves on edge and prevented his heartrate from slowing enough to even consider slumber.

Sleeping in a barn made him reminisce the early days of being all alone, and the logical train of thought took him back further to the arrival of the first Screechers he'd seen and the subsequent interactions with his mother.

It wasn't the horror of what he had seen that put him on edge. It wasn't the immediate loss of his childhood—what little there had been of one—or any other such self-absorbed sorrow; it was more a reminder of the existence he'd suffered and survived *before* the dead came back to life and tried to tear the living apart.

He finally began to understand that it was his fear of those living people from whom he'd been unable to escape in what he considered to be his former life. With this thought came the further realisation that he genuinely preferred his current existence, and all that it had given him, to everything prior. This realisation brought on a wave of nausea so profound that he had to stand upright and lean against the side of their small tank to steady himself.

That nausea turned to a grumble in his stomach, so threatening it couldn't be ignored. His eyes adjusted slowly to the gloom inside the barn, showing him a slither of silhouette and the barest of reflections of light from the axe head in the hands of the person taking their turn to keep watch.

He remained still, hoping that he hadn't disturbed Kimberley and taken her concentration away from her task. Reaching down slowly for what had been his pillow, he scooped up his battered backpack by the loop on the top and carried it with him as he tiptoed towards the creaking stairs leading up to the mezzanine level. He had to move so slowly, taking each step with infinite care and precision so as not to wake them all up. But the only alternatives were to go outside—not high on his to-do list—or else perform the basic bodily function that was nagging at him in front of the others. Given the option of climbing the rickety stairs and doing what he needed to do in private, he elected for that choice.

Reaching the dusty, dark privacy of the upper level, which looked as if it had been abandoned for its original purpose many years before, he used the precious possession of the green metal torch and its red-filtered lens to bathe an eerie glow on his task.

Reaching into his bag and working by feel, he pulled out the item he needed and used the sensitive tips of his fingers to locate the edge of the cellophane wrap and stretch out a length of it, then he used his teeth to cut the plastic and pull away a square to lay it on the ground. Carefully unfastening his belt, he lowered himself into position with the empty plastic bottle held in place for the secondary function, and tried to stay silent while he did what he needed to do. When he'd finished, he used some of the precious toilet paper flattened inside the top pocket of his pack. Wrapping the unpleasant bundle to seal the odour inside, so as not to attract the unwelcome attention of anything less than alive, he added a second layer of plastic wrap to the package and settled it neatly in a crevice far away from anywhere it could be found, allowing himself a smirk that perhaps one day, when their country was reclaimed, someone would find the preserved remains and open it for an unpleasant surprise.

Feeling much lighter and less uncomfortable, he settled himself against a pile of old, dusty sacks and found the spot more comfortable than he had been at ground level with the others. Despite the scratchy feel of the old, rat-eaten material, he found his eyelids getting heavier by the second as the crack of starlit blackness through the doors grew ever so slightly grey, until he drifted off into a light sleep that would last for barely an hour.

The dull crackle of a radio speaker tickled his consciousness, making him think that he hadn't tuned his clock radio properly to one of the four stations he could get from his room. He reached out with his right hand, expecting to find the long, rectangular button that would allow him just a few more minutes of sleep before he really had to get up or face the consequences of having to be told to do something twice by either of his parents.

He groaned as he stretched, reaching out further to find his school clothes to pull them towards him and slip them on under his covers, but his hand didn't touch folded cloth like he'd expected. Instead, it found the worn-down grip of the sawn off shotgun resting on top of the rough material of his pack. His small fingers explored it as his eyes stayed closed, finding the metal of the trigger guard cold to the touch, which served to send a bolt through him, like it was electrified.

His eyes flew open as the shouts of alarm from below cut through his reverie. Grabbing his bag with a gasp of panic— because any one of his companions shouting meant that there was imminent danger—he leapt up to join them, totally forgetting his environment and slamming his forehead hard into an exposed wooden beam of rough wood.

The blow didn't knock him out, not out cold anyway, but it

dealt enough of a blow to stun him sufficiently that he could only watch through a wide crack in the warped floorboards. He saw the rear end of their Warrior surging out of the barn in a cloud of thick exhaust smoke, to rip the doors off and let in a wash of dawn light. It also exposed the invading crowd of Screechers left moaning and following their escape to step and stumble over their crushed and partly destroyed comrades alike.

Peter didn't move. He hoped they wouldn't be able to detect him where he was, relying on the smells of so many warm-blooded people there, mixed with the thick fumes from the Warrior in the confined space, to sufficiently confuse the ones who remained there.

He watched, still face down on the exposed boards of the treacherous mezzanine, as the few who lacked the sense to follow the mobile can of zombie spam milled about beneath him like lost souls;

He didn't panic, at least not at first, but instead watched one Screecher with fascinated interest as it moved uncertainly beneath him. It took three or four staggering steps in one direction, before stopping and throwing its head wildly from left to right in search of something, only to repeat the process over and over.

Inside the safety of his head, Peter gave a commentary to the Screecher's behaviour, chuckling to himself as it amused him to imagine what it was thinking, if it could think. He watched it fly forwards again, knocking over his sticker—his modified pitchfork that had seen him through a number of sticky situations—as it froze and looked about, bewildered.

What the bloody hell did I come in here for? He heard in his head. The thought spoke in his mother's voice, which didn't bother him at first, but when the confused zombie repeated its behaviour, he heard the words spoken again with more venom, as if it was *his* fault that his mother had walked into a room without knowing why; blaming her only son instead of her alcoholism or her sick mind.

He scoffed involuntarily, and through the wide split between the two wooden boards where his right eye had a clear view of the ground below, he saw the confused zombie freeze and crane its neck awkwardly upwards until it stared straight at him. He didn't breathe, waiting for the awful, ripping noise of the shriek he fully expected at any second. That shriek, he knew, would attract more of them. He could see it playing out from start to finish in his mind with brutal clarity. They would try to climb the old stairs, collapsing them and trapping him on the upper level. Even if any of them made it close enough to reach him without falling, he knew he could defend that narrow staircase until the end of time with nothing but a plank of wood.

If he had an endless supply of water and food, that was.

He knew he only carried enough water for a day or two, but after that he would be too weak to make any attempt at escape with a chance of survival above zero.

In a moment of realisation so sudden and overwhelming, he knew he had to escape now or else be trapped to die of dehydration over days of agony, when he would grow weaker and more delusional by the second.

Snatching up his backpack, he stood, not rising to his full height as the drying blood on his forehead, leaking from just inside his hairline, served as a harsh reminder, and he made for the stairs just as the noise hit him.

It wasn't the noise of a shriek. Wasn't the battle cry of a Screecher calling out the location of food to every other undead bugger in earshot. Instead, it was the very loud and oddly reassuring sound of heavy machine gun fire barking out big bullets a way down the road from him. He watched through the gaps in the floor again as the handful of confused undead still stuck in a time loop inside the barn made directly for the exit to follow the sounds of gunfire.

Granted the slightest of reprieves, Peter threw himself down the stairs as fast as he could, to break through a broken board five steps from ground level. He thumped down hard, banging his face painfully into the dirt, to be rewarded instantly with the taste of blood in his mouth. He scrambled to his feet, his fumbling right hand grasping desperately for the shaft of the pitchfork, to throw himself from the barn and turn instinctively in the direction where he saw the fewest undead shambling towards the building.

He ran, stopping and slipping in a painful slide that left him on his back as his feet backpedalled desperately to avoid another group rounding a corner further ahead. He got back to his feet, diverting his route towards a ladder set against the side of a large, low building and he attacked the rungs with as much speed as he could muster. Reaching a flat roof larger than the barn three times over, he lay on his back and listened to the sounds of gunfire getting further away with each echoing burst.

"They're leading the herd away," he told himself in a quivering whisper. "Then they'll come back for me." His eyes screwed shut and his mouth contorted as his body betrayed him and he began to break out in tears. He forced it away, managing to keep it at bay for a few seconds but then the tears came in a flood that he was unable to stop.

He cried angrily and silently to himself as he lay flat on his back on the roof, his chest heaving and his diaphragm spasming like an inconsolable toddler, all the while hearing the sounds of the engine and the gunfire fade away, as the only people he'd ever trusted since his sister was taken from him left him all alone.

THIRTEEN

"In English, Doc," Fisher said with a smirk that Grewal guessed was intended to make him seem confident. It didn't, instead lending the American an added air of arrogance that made him marginally less likeable than he had previously been. Grewal sighed, not in an exhausted way in spite of the few hours' uncomfortable sleep he'd had, but in a mentally tired way that conveyed just how much he enjoyed explaining complex matters to his intellectual inferiors. He sat, sucked in a breath and looked the CIA man in the eyes.

"The serum works within the very small and confined tests we've conducted. There is still a very long way to go to ensure that its lethality is fine-tuned sufficiently, bu—"

"That's getting away from English again…" Grewal swallowed down the retort he knew his tiredness threatened to unleash, before answering in a measured tone.

"Stage one looks good," he said in a strained voice that bordered dangerously on being too sarcastic. "Stages two to four need to go just as well before we can say we have a cure. What I really wan—"

"You dragged me all the way down here to tell me that you'd what? Got a gold star in a third grade math test?"

"I'd have come to you, only I'm not permitted to leave the *facility*," he answered through gritted teeth, continuing before Fisher could interrupt again. "That's not the breakthrough we've made, however."

At the mention of the word 'breakthrough', Fisher shut his mouth and shot an expectant look at the scientist. Taking his uncharacteristic silence as permission to continue, Grewal spoke.

"I won't bore you with the details," he said sarcastically. "However, we made an unexpected discovery during testing yesterday."

"This is how one of your lab rats ended up with a forty-five through the dome?" Grewal ignored the interruption, knowing Fisher's silence was too good to be true.

"The subject became so animated that it literally broke itself apart trying desperately to get to the source of a simple noise." Grewal held up both hands to keep Fisher quiet long enough to complete the report. "A soldier was trying to tune a radio set and stumbled on a patch of static that was barely audible to us. That frequency sent the subjects quite literally wild. It was like a feeding frenzy; like the phenomenon of sharks sensing blood in the water and becoming almost mindless with bloodlust. We need to harness that sound and utilise it to draw all of the infected into central locations where we can re-infect them with the completed serum."

Fisher sat still, eyebrows almost meeting in the middle as he processed what he'd just been told.

"Sooo," he answered, "you're telling me you know their personal phone number? Their magic frequency? You know the sound that drives them wild and you want to use it as a lure?"

"The sound itself isn't necessarily the real trigger, probably more likely that it simply simulates one of them, getting it agitated as it hunts or kills an uninfected host... like I said: blood in the water."

"Huh," Fisher answered, not bothering to explain his views any further.

"I thought that, perhaps, you could develop something that could deliver this frequency somehow," Grewal tried hopefully.

"What?" Fisher said, seeming to reconnect with the conversation suddenly and recall the few words he'd missed. "Oh, we, er... we actually *have* something already for that. Just needs a few minor adjustments, I reckon."

It was Grewal's turn to look confused, which seemed to delight Fisher, who sat upright and glanced over the Professor's shoulder towards the partially open door of the room he'd commandeered as his office. This he'd achieved by summarily ordering the two US army personnel resting there to find somewhere else to be.

"This is classified," he began, then shrugged as though it didn't really matter if he divulged the secret, as the enemy it had been designed to be deployed against no longer existed. "You've heard the term 'Psy-Ops'?"

"Psychological warfare?" Grewal asked, his mind racing ahead to the conclusion but not saying it out loud in case he deflated the CIA man too much, given how excited he seemed to be by divulging state secrets.

'Uh huh. See, we had this idea way back—like Vietnam way back—and we'd developed a battlefield sound emitter designed to degrade an entrenched enemy and force them to surrender or abandon a position that would otherwise be too costly in servicemen's lives to take conventionally." Grewal sat back and casually raised one knee over the other. He did it naturally, seeing nothing wrong with the gesture, but Fisher was distracted by it as he found it unnervingly effeminate. He shook his head slightly and carried on.

"It's like a bomb," he explained, moving his hands through the air as they described the smooth shape of the projectile. "Only there's no warhead—no explosive charge—instead, this thing hits the dirt after being dropped from pretty much any altitude and cracks open like a nut. When the housing comes off... *pow*! The device inside activates and gives you eighteen to twenty-four hours of the worst high-pitched screaming and white noise you could imagine."

"Why don't they just blow it up?"

"What?"

"The device," Grewal asked. "Why wouldn't the enemy just destroy it?"

Fisher hesitated. "It, er… it should be too painful to get near for starters. Like, *agony*, to be anywhere near it."

"Irrelevant," Grewal said half to himself. "The infected subjects would just try to eat it, I imagine. So, how soon can we have a few and how quickly can they be retrofitted to emit the low frequency sound?"

"Hold up there, Doc," Fisher said defensively and leaned away as though warding off his enthusiasm. "I mean, there are channels to go through here. I can't just call up Langley and say, "Hey, remember those weapons we have mothballed in the basement? The ones that were probably war crimes waiting to happen? Yeah, I'll take four to go. With mustard. Can you deliver?"

Grewal stared back at him, not finding the sarcasm amusing in the slightest. Fisher deflated, his shoulders sagging as his fingertips rubbed the skin at his temples to distort the shape of his eyes.

"I'll place a call," he said, "see if I still have any sway back home." He nodded his chin to the doorway, which Grewal took, with awkward grace, as his dismissal. Fisher stooped to pick up a heavy plastic case from the threadbare carpet and set it on the small desk in the room as Grewal stepped outside, pausing at the top of the stairs to peer back through the gap and eavesdrop on the one-sided conversation.

———

Fisher went through the laborious process of setting up the satellite phone and dialling the correct sequence of digits to reach his superiors at Langley. The call bounced around through a couple of extensions until the right people were located, and a glance at his watch made him curse his own stupidity as he realised he'd called the Pentagon at a little before eight a.m. their time.

"Hellard here," came the gruff, almost fatherly voice from the other side of the Atlantic.

"Sir, it's Fisher. With the science team sent to Scotl—"

"I'm well aware of who and *where* you are, Agent Fisher," the older man interrupted, belying the kindly tone he usually employed to be his professional front. "Have you found a cure to the 'problem' yet?"

"We're working on that, Sir," Fisher stammered quickly before getting directly to the point of his call. "Sir, we've made a discovery here that would make a number of options more viable if it worked…"

"Well, spit it out, Son!"

"I—we—need as many of the prototype TSE devices and some engineers to re-tune them as you can muster. Long story real short, Sir, we think we can attract them into forming large groups which, as I said, will make more than one of our tactical solutions much simpler and more effective."

"Wait a minute," Bob Hellard, deputy director of the CIA, said coldly. "The United States is currently expending significant energy and resources in monitoring the behaviour of those infected in the UK." His words sounded as though he was standing before a closed meeting of the senate asking for budgetary increases. "And now you want to use a prototype device to *intentionally* draw them into herds or whatever?"

"Sir," Fisher said flatly, as if he was dropping the bullshit. "If this project doesn't work out, then I don't need to explain it to you that having them concentrated in the major cities will make it much easier to wipe the slate clean again so we can repopulate."

There was a long pause on the other end of the line, during which Fisher didn't speak. He barely even breathed. In his mind, the next person to speak and fill the void in the conversation was the one to lose, and his career was staked on the mission being a success. Many had simply wanted to nuke Britain and seal off Europe, especially now that the news out of their west coast was just as bleak. He knew their maritime forces were stretched thin enough maintaining constant coastal patrols, not to mention the concerns of many that a horde would walk over the frozen expanses from Russia to Canada with the next winter. But if he could provide the solution to controlling the movements of the infected until they could be purged, either by napalm or whatever artificial virus-killing virus the scientist was cooking up, then the people of America could sleep soundly thanks to him.

That was why his explanation featured the word 'we' so heavily.

"You'll get your toys, Fisher," Hellard said finally. "And an air crew to deliver them. But I expect results by the end of the week." The connection was cut before Fisher could respond, but the abruptness of the call ending did nothing to stifle his sense of achievement.

Outside the door, still and silent, Professor Grewal fought down the urge to storm back into the room and demand an explanation for the terms, 'wipe the slate clean' and 'repopulate'. Instead, he melted away, returning to his foul-smelling cow shed lab to continue working on one of the few things on the planet he could actually affect.

———

The transport plane arrived the following morning, banging down onto the runway in a similarly uncomfortable and reckless fashion as the one which had brought the science team and their minders. Three crates were unloaded with a forklift truck and placed on the back of the dull green trucks the British military favoured so much, before being driven a short distance to where the helicopters operated on a makeshift patch of flattened land adjacent to the main runway.

That rotary wing staging area, filled with very bored personnel, including one royal navy Sea King crew, was stirred into activity when the recognisable noise of incoming helicopters thrummed the mist-filled air and set them all to looking around to be the first to detect and correctly identify the aircraft.

"Sounds big," Lieutenant Commander Barrett opined as he craned his neck upwards and shielded his face with his left hand to block out the meagre light of the sun behind the dense clouds. His right hand cupped a tin mug and the fingers of that hand sprouted a cigarette, a habit he had been drawn back into through long days of inactivity.

"More than one," James Morris, Barrett's younger co-pilot answered. For once he didn't add a vague reference of either song lyrics or a film quote, which Barrett usually failed to recognise.

"Twin rotary," Gary Brinklow, the crew's loadmaster said confidently, without looking up from the dog-eared Jilly Cooper he was reading. He'd served in the Royal Navy longer than either officer, and had enjoyed a relaxed position of authority even before the world had ended.

"Chinook!" Morris exclaimed as he pointed west at a dark shape surging through the low-lying cloud cover.

"Almost," Brinklow corrected him nonchalantly. "That's a CH-Forty-Six. It's just closer."

The two pilots stared at the approaching helicopter, seeing that their NCO was absolutely right and this bulbous, unnatural-looking flying machine was indeed much smaller than the larger Chinook helicopters designed and built by the same company.

"Well," Barrett exclaimed with a chuckle, "*that* didn't make it across the Atlantic all by itself, did it now?"

Neither of his companions answered. The fact that there was at least one aircraft carrier out in deeper water beyond their sight and reach made them feel even more trapped as they were forced to sit and watch their own helicopter gather dust without the fuel allocation to operate it. The realisation dawned on them all at the same time that if the Americans—it could only be them operating such a large machine off their coast—could keep a large twin-rotor machine in the air, then they could surely spare a tank of aviation fuel to allow them to retrieve more survivors.

The large beast banked to loop their small heliport once, before levelling out to set its wheels onto the flattened area. Immediately, the screaming sound of its engines being cut lowered the noise level and the three men of the Sea King that had seen so much action already watched as the rear ramp lowered to reveal an empty cargo hold and the exiting flight crew. There were six of them, indicating that they had sent a maintenance team to accompany the aircraft, and their path would lead them past the British crew to reach the buildings.

"Welcome to Skye," Barrett said, smiling and extending a hand to the pilot in the lead. The man took it suspiciously, not offering his own name in response to Barrett's introductions, but smiled weakly as though to end the conversation without confrontation. Then he just walked away.

"What the hell was that all about?" Morris asked the senior pilot quietly.

"Not sure," Barret answered as he lifted a hand to point at an arriving convoy of Bedford trucks coming from the direction of the newly arrived cargo plane. "But it's more than likely got something to do with that."

FOURTEEN

The argument that flared briefly around the stationary hulk of the Sultan burned out slowly like a dying flare. The strenuous protestations of Duncan were met with blank faces of refusal at best, and a threat of bloody violence from the one member of their party he least expected it from.

The girl, Jessica, pulled a blade from her right boot, and held it low beside her, which seemed to signify her potential use of it wasn't a mere threat. Duncan held up his hands and backed up a pace.

"Whoa, hold on a minute," he laughed, hoping to lower the temperature by lightening the mood. Daniels flicked out a hand to clip Jessica's right sleeve, which caught her attention enough to see his head shake. Sighing, she replaced the blade in her boot but kept her look of target analysis fixed firmly on the man she didn't know.

One of the men, she corrected herself as one of the newcomers spoke. He made words like any other person, only to her ears the sound came with a quiet force to them, like the man didn't need to raise his voice. She was already wary of him from the way he moved, seemingly without making a sound, but his words added a gravity in support of her own wants, which raised his standing with the girl.

"We go back for them," he said simply. No justification. No swaying argument or impassioned speech about why; merely a statement of fact as though any other path simply wasn't an option.

"Agreed," Daniels said, glancing at Ellie, who had her face buried in her hands as her body was racked with sobs she tried her hardest to keep silent. "But we don't have an up-to-date location, bearing or RV point set up…" The two marines glanced at one another to convey a silent opinion about the lack of operational awareness. The taller of them, the man who had simply identified himself as Enfield, reached into the door pocket of the passenger side and produced a map, which he proceeded to spread out on the front of their ugly car.

"What *do* we know?" the heavier-set marine, sergeant Hampton, asked.

"We know they were down on the coast and heading north west towards the house," Daniels explained. "We know they saw the swarm travelling north and they intersected their path. They holed up on a farm somewhere overnight."

"A farm somewhere," Hampton repeated matter-of-factly, looking again at the quiet man cradling the rifle. "Shouldn't be too hard to find around here." He glanced with theatrical exaggeration over both shoulders to take in the open, rolling landscape dotted with a few farms as far as the eye could see.

"Point taken," Daniels said, "but that doesn't explain why they aren't answering their radio."

"No," Hampton mused distractedly as he ran a thick, sausage-like finger over the map to trace the major roads. Silence hung for a while until Daniels leaned in to look at the map to circle his pointed finger in the air before stabbing it down.

"That's where we were," he said, snaking the finger north

to tap on a vague area, "and this is where we are now." The finger lifted up again to hover until it traced the red line indicating a wider road. "Best guess is that they were heading this way—no sense in using the smaller roads when there wasn't enough traffic around here to block the main roads—and the swarm would've come though... *here*... ish."

He gestured a wider track with two fingers to show a roughly south to north direction that passed very close by their residence of yesterday.

"Meaning they'll still be on that side of the line and not answering us," Hampton said. "Anyone want to state the obvious?"

"They were in a Warrior with a full armament," Daniels said firmly, refusing to accept that they had been overwhelmed by unarmed zombies. Thousands of zombies, granted, but still none that could bite through armour.

"And two of them are ninjas," Enfield chimed in helpfully.

"And two of them are Special Forces," Hampton agreed without breaking verbal stride. "What was the plan?" he asked Daniels.

"The plan?"

"Yes," the marine sergeant asked him with exaggerated slow speech. "What was the *plan* for when you met up?"

"Erm, head to the north west coast of Scotland where the others went... We didn't set an RV because we were in radio contact."

"So, assuming we don't find them and can't raise them, would they go there under their own steam?" Enfield asked. Daniels shrugged, admitting the obvious logic.

"No," snapped Ellie as she advanced on the huddled men. "No way. We're not leaving. Not if Amber and Peter are with them." She shouldered her way in between them, dwarfed by their height and size, to stab her own slender digit onto the map. The gesture was intended to make her point but instead it served only to draw the attention of the three soldiers to where her fingertip landed, which was about forty miles away from the places they had been discussing.

"I'm not suggesting we do that," Hampton said angrily. "These people are... these people are our friends. We've spent a god-awful winter with them and both of us were prepared to..." he sucked in a calming breath and closed his eyes briefly before speaking more calmly. "Both of us stayed behind so they could get away." That piece of information silenced the small, fierce woman and her face softened. Hampton took his gaze away from hers to regard Johnson's former radio man.

"We move from here to their last known position. Keep trying the radio and we'll follow in the turd-mobile." He nodded back to the tired-looking ride they'd turned up in, unable to keep the derision from his face as he regarded the Ford Sierra. The vehicle had adopted no fewer than three different shades of metallic brown, despite being only six years old, going by the 'B' registration on the plate.

"Look alive!" Duncan shouted from his position half out of the Sultan's hatch. As one, they all moved with purpose, Enfield spinning to bring the rifle scope up to his eye to scan the road in the direction they had come from.

"How many?" he asked loudly, eye still glued to the optic and guessing correctly that the elevated position afforded a better view of the threat.

"Dozen," Duncan shot back. "Maybe more."

"Any fast fuckers?" Hampton growled as he limped fast for the driver's door of the Sierra.

"Well... oh *shi*–" His curse was interrupted by a coughing twang which Hampton knew was his marine rendering something safe. A second and third shot sounded, both at even intervals, which told the sergeant that the threat was imminent, if Enfield was picking them off at a steady rate.

"Too many," Daniels called out from atop the Sultan.

"Grab your gear and squeeze in here." Hampton hesitated for a second and a half before swearing foully at the awkward lever to tip the front seat forwards and retrieve their bags. All the while, Enfield took steady, measured shots at the heads appearing over the low rise until a noise behind and above him paused the rhythm. The noise was Duncan pulling back the cocking handle on the big machine gun in preparation to fire.

"Don't," Enfield shouted up, "you'll just bring more our way." Hampton emerged from the car, still muttering as he manhandled two large packs and his own weapon.

"And the boot, Sarge," Enfield chided his NCO in between two shots.

"Crap," Hampton cursed, stomping back to fight with the keys and open the boot. "I fully expect you to keep the bastards off me, Enfield," he reminded the marine in a conversational tone. "If you don't, rest assured that I'll make it my afterlife's work to personally eat you, should I become the enemy." He spoke as though there weren't murderous former humans bearing down on his exposed back, as he retrieved a cardboard box with a few holes stabbed through it. The box shook in his hands and he muttered to it as he limped towards the Sultan and handed it up with a warning not to open the lid.

They clambered up the front of the tracked vehicle to bottleneck at the hatch before Enfield took three more rapid shots to expend the remainder of his magazine and then he too dropped inside. The interior, as cramped as it was with the four of them previously, now seemed uncomfortably claustrophobic. Duncan had abandoned his position at the pintle-mounted gun to settle himself behind the driving controls and to fill the empty air around them with the sudden bark of their loud exhaust.

They rolled away, abandoning the car with the doors open in the centre of the road.

"Where did they come from?" Duncan shouted back from

the forward section. "We haven't seen any for days—weeks even—why now?"

"Stragglers from that swarm is my guess," Hampton yelled back before asking the next logical question. "So where did the bloody swarm come from?"

FIFTEEN

For all their secrecy, for all their 'need to know' attitudes, the CIA put things in place with such rapid efficiency that the time from theoretical concept to practical application elapsed in under forty-eight hours.

The cargo plane that brought the experimental Psy-Ops weapons had been loaded almost immediately after Fisher's phone call back to Langley, and the engineers required to reprogram the devices had taken only six hours longer to locate. The helicopter and crews assigned the task of delivering the payloads were already in-theatre, so weren't difficult to find, but the clandestine feel of their orders to land on the Isle of Skye, where they would be briefed in person, rippled around the crew of the US aircraft carrier like a rumour.

The chief engineer, a sullen man with drooping cheeks and permanent bags under his eyes, neither offered his name nor did he engage any of the scientists or soldiers when he was escorted to the facility to test a scaled-down version of what he had created. Staff sergeant Yates, rivalling the engineer for the title of world's most annoyed man, cleared the area and stood his team on alert with express orders not to fire unless he gave the order.

Standing in front of the four occupied cages—with three more subjects brought in during daylight, courtesy of the unfriendly SEAL team—the engineer flipped a switch on the briefcase-sized contraption he had brought with him. As the almost imperceptible, low hum filled the air, all four zombies went apoplectic with an insane rage that caused the living people to take involuntary steps backwards.

"That's enough," Yates growled, just as the engineer had evidently reached the same conclusion and killed the device.

"What's the range on it?" Professor Grewal demanded, haranguing the engineer before he had even closed the lid on his case.

"On this?" he glanced at Yates, who sighed and gestured towards the exit. He took the case a full fifty paces to the house, where he flipped open the lid and activated it again. Almost immediately, Yates began hollering for him to shut it off. They tested it out to a range of almost two hundred paces before the results diminished even slightly. The engineer walked back; eyes cast down as his lips moved in silent calculations.

"Power on this is about one percent of the main device," he explained. "Assuming the same rate of fall-off, you're looking at around eleven miles minimum." Grewal nodded, turning to catch the eye of the quiet and unnerving leader of the team assigned to risk their lives and bring him test subjects.

"Mister Miller?" he said, hoping the man wouldn't berate him for not using his correct military rank as Yates had. He spoke fast to fill the pause that could be filled with derision and abuse. "Would this device be useful to you? A means of attracting them perhaps?" Miller smirked and shot a sideways glance at one of his team, who looked embarrassed. He turned back to the engineer and raised his eyebrows as if to ask his permission. The engineer shrugged as if it was no matter to him.

"I only threw that together to test the frequency," he said. "You'll need batteries for it but I'm sure you'll manage just fine."

"We will," Miller said with a nod, accepting the case and handing it off to one of his men. "We'll call it the 'Yo'." Sniggers rippled out of the shadows where the rest of the bearded men lingered. Miller offered no further explanation and led his men out of the building.

"Before you go, Mister Miller?"

"It's 'Master Chief' to you," one of the other SEALs said with evident hostility.

"Master Chief Miller," Grewal said in an apologetic tone, "I appreciate that your job is a very dangerous one and we appreciate everythi—"

"Get to the point, Professor," Miller interrupted. "I don't need my ass kissed before someone gives me shitty detail." Grewal straightened and cleared his throat.

"Very well, we need one of the faster ones for testing. I need to see how—*why*—the virus has produced different results in them…" Miller kept his cold stare firmly fixed on Grewal for a few seconds past the point of it being uncomfortable. He let his breath out through his nose, before nodding once and turning away. Grewal watched them go, stifling the shudder he could feel threatening to travel down his spine like electricity, before turning back to the engineer.

"How long before you can have the bigger device ready for testing?" The engineer frowned at him and took a step away towards the door.

"Last I checked, I didn't work for you," he answered. "I only came to make sure it made those… *things* pay attention. You stick to your job and I'll stick to mine." He left, not giving anyone there a second glance in his haste to be far away from the infected, who gnashed and snapped their teeth at him from inside their cages.

A loud, slow, almost sarcastic clapping began from the upper level, where the big machine gun was set up pointing at the cages. All eyes turned to see Fisher smiling down at them, a heavy black coat zipped up tight under his chin. He stopped clapping after a few seconds and spoke loudly as he also turned to leave.

"Couldn't have put it better myself. Where's our *cure*, professor?"

———

Grewal mulled over the best delivery method for the serum. Chambers had shown him how all of the lab tests had been successful, in that the chunks of infected flesh cut from their subjects had all haemorrhaged their fluids to leave a gelatinous mess in the sealed dishes.

He had opened his mouth to say that the serum might work on necrotic flesh samples, but it couldn't be certain to work on a live subject, before he shut his mouth, recalling that the subjects *weren't* 'live' and were essentially also necrotic flesh. A thought hit him and he turned to find the man he needed.

"Sergeant Yates?" Yates looked up and pursed his lips at the annoying interruption to the nothing he was doing before. "Sergeant, what would be the best way to infect people with a virus? Militarily speaking, I mean." Yates seemed to consider his question for a few beats before deciding to give him the sensible answer.

"I'm not sure I know about that," he said carefully, "perhaps your CIA man could answer better. The scenario we most suspected the Russians would use against us was a liquid, spread through either a direct attack on our water sources, or an airburst device if the attack was overt." He stared at

Grewal, sighing when the man showed no obvious signs of having understood him. "A bomb," he explained. "One that scatters the infectious substance in the air over a large area."

Grewal tapped the tip of the pen he'd been holding against his teeth as he thought, surprising the few people close by when he launched himself from the seat he was occupying to march to the fridge and pull out a vial of clear liquid. Then he shrugged off the coat he was wearing to begin fighting his way into a hazardous material suit.

"Clear the room," Yates barked, looking up to shoot a few hand signals at his people on duty behind the safe end of the machine gun, before climbing into a suit himself. Grewal said nothing, correctly assuming that the man wanted to keep a close eye on what he was doing.

Suited, he used his ungainly gloved hands to pour the contents of the vial into a contraption that resembled something a person would use to spray water on a plant. He approached the nearest cage, glancing at Yates with a look that seemed to convey a, 'Here goes nothing' attitude, and stepped closer to the cage to spray the zombie in the face twice. He sidestepped to the next cage and repeated the process before backing off.

Neither zombie showed any signs of having been affected by the light mist falling on its dead face and both continued to rage at the mesh which denied them the warm, fresh meat that came so tantalisingly close. Grewal stripped off the mask of his suit and turned to Yates with a smile. He saw that the sergeant had the heavy pistol still gripped in his right hand and was keeping one wary eye on the cages.

"What now?" he asked after nothing happened.

"Now we wait."

They didn't have to wait as long as Grewal had thought. He'd taken himself back to the house to wash and eat something, realising he'd gone straight through lunchtime without noticing. He was therefore understandably annoyed that he didn't even get to take a bite of the sandwich he'd made for himself when the door burst open and one of the soldiers told him with wide eyes that he had to come quick.

His annoyance evaporated when his mind caught up with *why* his presence might be required in such a hurry. He ran the short distance to the makeshift lab, slipping on the smooth stones twice and cursing the infernal Scottish weather for raining almost constantly. When he arrived in the large shed, the noise assaulted his ears painfully. It was the same ungodly shriek they let out when sensing an imminent meal, only somehow different; as though the shriek was their only medium of communication, like a baby crying, and right then, they were trying to communicate fear and pain.

He ignored the offer of the rubberised suit thrust out towards him, walking towards the cages where two of the zombies were moaning and pressing their faces into the metal to get to him. The others... weren't. They were standing and swaying, staggering even as their raw vocal cords played a tortured symphony of uncomprehending pain. One turned towards him, dark, almost black blood leaking from the eye sockets around the blind, milky orbs that seemed to stare at him pleadingly. It opened its mouth again to gargle another hideous sound, but viscera poured from its open maw as it pitched forward to slam its face off the mesh and leave a streak of gore on the metal. It sank to the hard ground to convulse and jerk like an eel, blood beginning to ooze from every visible patch of exposed skin. Before his eyes, the active and very lethal infected person became increasingly still as the vile puddle it converted itself into grew outwards and threatened to touch the toes of his boots. He stepped back in a daze, looking to his left as the second subject fell backwards like a felled tree, gagging and gargling. As both creatures treated with the serum grew still and silent, the absence of their sound was replaced by a ragged cheering and applause from soldiers and scientists alike.

"You think this solves anything?" Grewal roared, turning to stare down everyone in the room and silencing them in a second. "You think this undoes *any* of the damage we've done to humanity? This solves *nothing!*" He paused, breathing hard as even he was surprised by his outburst. He continued in a quieter but still angry tone. "Even if this works on a massive scale... even if we kill every one of the infected, that's still a human life lost. You think we're winning?" He scoffed, "We'll be lucky to scrape our way out of this shit as a *species*."

Pausing only long enough to eyeball all of them in turn, he fought down his body's treacherous urges to cry in response to the surge of adrenaline and the sinking feelings of guilt he suppressed so well every day, and he stormed out of the building.

He found Fisher leaning against the wall by the back door to the house they had commandeered. The man was smoking, still huddled inside his large waterproof jacket, and seemed to find the agitated state of the scientist amusing. Grewal was spared having to either appear rude or attempt small talk.

"The engineer's just gone," Fisher said as he dropped the butt to grind it out on the wet cobblestones with the toe of his boot. "Reckon we'll be good to go tomorrow."

"Good to go on *what*, precisely?" came the retort in a voice that still shook with guilt and anger.

"The testing phase of the lure device." Grewal relaxed slightly.

"For a terrible moment there, I thought you were going to say you wanted to deploy the serum."

"It works, doesn't it?" Fisher asked with raised eyebrows. "What else would you have to cheer about?"

"It worked on them," Grewal answered sourly, jerking his head back over his shoulder towards their makeshift lab. "There's nothing to say it'll work on the adapted strain." At the mention of this, Fisher's eyes seemed to glaze over, just as they did when he was faced with something scientific that he either didn't want to be burdened with or else just felt bored with. Grewal had tried, on more than one occasion, to explain why the variations in behaviour of a small percentage of the infected was so important. Fisher, increasingly under the gun from his masters back in the States, needed answers and solutions instead of more questions and problems.

Fisher watched as Grewal stormed off inside, no doubt to work out his emotions in private, and went back to the room he was using to pick up the radio set and place a call to the other side of the island.

He gave orders for the device to be made ready and deployed as soon as possible, before leaving the house and climbing back into the passenger side of a military off-road vehicle. That was, after first absent-mindedly trying to climb in on top of his driver and muttering angrily about the steering wheel being on the wrong side.

Back at his headquarters, he ordered up some coffee and waited for it, grimacing as all caffeine-addicted professionals did when presented with a beverage they weren't accustomed to. He closed the door to his room and placed another call on the satellite phone to order the AWACS be diverted to monitor the activity of the infected after they had dropped the device, along with the mass production of serum for immediate transportation over the Atlantic.

SIXTEEN

Johnson drove in a noisy stop/start game of Screecher destruction.

The first mile of flight had seen the gun run dry and he couldn't spare the time to stop and reload it, nor could he divert enough concentration to accurately explain to Bufford how to do it. Instead, and much against his better judgement, he grudgingly allowed the SBS man to fire the big 30mm cannon into the largest concentrations of undead.

In the rear section, Kimberley was beside herself with guilt and grief because she had fallen asleep when it was her turn to keep watch. But the real heartbreak came when Amber realised why the adults were so upset. She screamed and pounded her tiny fists against the inside of the armoured door, demanding to be let out and sobbing for the boy who she had grown so attached to, as she screamed his name over and over. The sound of her cries broke their hearts and renewed Johnson's hatred of the creatures for all that they had taken away from so many people.

"Cease fire, cease fire," he growled into the microphone of his headset, using the growing light to line up a knot of approaching Screechers to mow them down under his left-side tracks. Then he crunched into reverse and repeated the process until the road ahead was clear.

The muted banging on the thick armour to his left told him that more had fallen upon their inedible transport from the foliage on their flank, and he calmly reversed the Warrior once more to repeat the process.

"I'll go back for him," Bufford said as he tried to work out the overly complex reloading procedure for the chain gun.

"We don't separate," Johnson answered, still repeating his reverse and advance crushing manoeuvres.

"But the lad's on his own—"

"He was on his own before we showed up," Johnson snapped back, "and he was doing just fine. Don't underestimate him; he's probably safer without us attracting all this attention." He felt callous as soon as he had uttered the words, clamping his mouth shut and concentrating on his task. All around them, more palsied hands clawed at their hull, forcing him to back further away from the farm until he could no longer even see the approach road to it.

"Where the hell did all these bastards come from?" Bufford snarled as he fought with the machinery. "We haven't seen these kinds of concentrations for months, and now all of a bloody sudden they start protesting again? What is it, another fucking miner's strike?"

"Are we clear of the herds?" Larsen's voice cut in sharply. Johnson gave her a quick 'stand by' before spinning the Warrior in a full three-sixty to check.

"Seems clear at the moment," he reported, "I'll wait for more to catch up with us an—" The sound of the rear doors opening cut him off, prompting an outburst from both him and Bufford so that neither of them had their words heard.

"She said," sniffed Kimberley's voice over the vehicle

intercom as the door closed again. "She said to clear them out and come back for her."

Johnson hesitated, feeling the blood rise in his face until he breathed out to stop himself from bursting. As much as he hated it, as much as he couldn't stand not being in control, he had to trust both the young boy and the Norwegian commando to handle their own business.

Selecting reverse again, he set his face and went about handling his own.

———

Astrid Larsen walked fast and smooth away from the rear of the Warrior, which she covered long enough to ensure the occupants were safe behind the closed door. Her gun was up, tucked tightly into her shoulder with her right cheek pressing into the parachute stock and she moved with the grace of a dancer. Everywhere her eyes looked, her upper body pointed. Everything she looked directly at was automatically lined up in the sights of the MP5 so the only decision she needed to make was to shoot or not to shoot.

Three of them fell in rapid succession; their switches were flipped as each emerging Screecher collected a 9mm bullet directly through their open mouths to blow out the brain stem. No other threats emerged, leaving her to make the next decision.

Through the trees or back down the road? she asked herself. The balance was between open space where she could see the threats coming from distance, and simply facing what seemed like fewer of them among the trees. She opted for the off-road route, stalking between the branches faster than anyone watching would expect, without any evidence of noise as her boots weaved her in a wide loop back towards the barn they had slept in.

Twice more, she stopped to dispatch a pair of loping Screechers who were bumping their way awkwardly through the foliage towards the retreating sounds of an engine and the renewed rattle of gunfire. A third, impaled on the low, broken branch of a fir tree through one shoulder, reached for her until the bullet punched through its skull and turned it off.

Buffs got the chain gun working again, she mused over the raucous sound in the distance. Keeping a small portion of her brain tethered to the others wasn't a distraction. She knew *that* for certain as a grey, balding head appeared through a copse of holly leaves with one prickly green addition sprouting comically from its face, and she drilled it through the mouth with a single round from almost a dozen paces away.

That part of her mind, that small percentage of her consciousness that imagined what they would be thinking and saying and doing inside the Warrior, was what kept her mind sharp and focused. If she thought fully about what she had just done, if she logically assessed the facts coldly, she would be tempted to turn and run back to the safety of the armoured fighting vehicle and hammer on the door to be let back in.

As it was, keeping a part of her consciousness with them, what she was doing was just like holding her breath as she ducked underwater. She knew she could go back to safety whenever she wanted, and that knowledge gave her the courage and confidence to do what needed to be done.

Breaking through the foliage onto a wide field of over-grown grass, she scanned her surroundings and detected none of them. Pausing for a handful of seconds, she listened and absorbed every hint of sounds to map the small battlefield better in her mind.

Gunfire and engine behind and to my right, she thought as she marked the position of the others.

Shrieks to my left and behind, the slower-moving Screechers following the destruction wrought by their light tank.

She ran towards the farm, body low and gun still tucked tightly into her shoulder, as fast as she could without winding herself like a racehorse blowing out its lungs. She paused again nearer the collection of low buildings and listened once more.

A heavy sound like meat hitting a butcher's block rang out ahead of her past a line of evergreens, focusing her attention on the nearest farm buildings. Choosing that as the most likely source of something out of the ordinary—or at least *more* out of the ordinary for the situation—she headed towards it.

Nine more wandering corpses went down to her weapon, some requiring more than one shot on the rare occasions she missed. Such misses were due to an unexpected stumble of her moving target, or an unlucky deflection that removed only part of the skull, which the Screecher no longer needed in order to function.

This was no super-human ability, she knew. It was no natural skill that others should be jealous of, but instead was the result of thousands of hours of practice and endless training; like the end result of a knife being sharpened.

The same sound as before, which she now recognised as a body hitting concrete from height, diverted her attention slightly to the right of her approach. Ducking low to shoot a look around the corner of a building, she saw three corpses mangled in a pile underneath a steel ladder. Two others milled about at ground level, reaching upwards and lacking the ability to climb the ladder, which told her that there must be something above her that excited them.

Perhaps a ten-year-old boy defending his position? She thought as she delivered two execution-style deaths to the backs of their heads.

The silent thought was answered by a booming report of a shotgun and the ballistic arrival of another corpse splattering and crunching into the concrete ahead of her, accompanied by a hissed whine of, "Shit!" from up above. Looking at the body still trying to move as the brain wasn't destroyed, she took in the left arm, which was missing from the mid-forearm. With an exaggerated gasp of fear and understanding, Astrid leapt backwards as the thing rounded on her and lashed out its right arm with a speed and accuracy she hadn't seen up close before.

The terror of realising she'd come within arm's reach of a faster one—a Lima—took her breath away momentarily, as the thing began to use one hand and one stump to propel itself towards her along the ground, dragging destroyed legs to scrape the jagged shards of exposed bone noisily along the rough surface.

The mental numbness caused by the realisation evaporated in a flash. Specifically a tiny, suppressed muzzle flash as four single shots spat from the barrel of her gun to punch into the skull and end the grotesque movement. She was panting hard and whipped her head from left to right as she realised her situational awareness had suffered a lapse due to the fear of coming face to face—or boots to face, more accurately—with a Lima.

"More coming 'round the left side!" came a muted shout from above her, Peter trying to keep his voice down and balancing that fear of discovery against the desperate need to warn her of the danger. Larsen looked up, saw the silhouette of the boy's head and shoulders peeking over the edge of the flat roof and looked to her left to raise the gun in preparation for a renewed assault.

"*My* left," Peter hissed. She looked up, saw the direction he was pointing in and glanced down in time to see the front-runners of the wave of rotting meat spill over themselves to get to her. Her mind took less than half a second to calculate speeds and distances, and she knew they would be on her before she could get clear of the building. Without hesitation she dropped the gun on its sling and gripped the cold metal rungs of the galvanised steel ladder to catapult herself upwards.

As she sprinted vertically, arms and legs pumping like a spider monkey in full flight, her brain gave her a quiet admonishment.

Stranding yourself on a roof with a young child isn't the best idea you have ever had...

She told herself to shut up, and climbed.

SEVENTEEN

Downes, wearing fresh military uniform with as much of his old equipment that could be salvaged after a rigorous bleaching, stood when his colleague entered the room. In any other regiment, in many other situations in fact, he would have offered Colonel Kelly a salute.

Even with the obvious brevet rank and field promotion to lieutenant-colonel, Kelly still wore no badge of rank, just as Downes or any of the Special Air Service personnel didn't, but something in him, so far as Downes could see, had changed.

"Downes," he acknowledged almost abruptly with a rapid gesture of one hand to a seat opposite his desk. "How are you feeling now?"

"Much better, Kelly, thank you."

"Heard about the old hypothermia…" Kelly said in a tone that needled Downes for a reason he couldn't quite put his finger on.

"Touch of exposure is all," Downes told him dismissively, internally bridling at the unintended implication of weakness. "The doctor assured me it was a combination of exhaustion and lack of food that made me susceptible. Been rather pushing it on too little food and sleep recently."

Kelly smiled. It was a companionable smile and one that harked back to the start of their acquaintance, if not friendship. The two young parachute regiment lieutenants hadn't known each other before both arrived at Stirling Lines for their first crack at selection. Downes, eager to drink in the full experience, carried his own heavy bags and stepped down onto the platform at Hereford train station to join the milling group of fit-looking young men, reluctant to speak to the other candidates from the off. Kelly, in contrast, bore no shame in his family's wealth and arrived at the gates in a Rolls Royce driven by an employee of his father. He dressed and acted the same as the other men, was just as fit and tough as many and indeed more so than quite a few, but his underlying hint of arrogance put some people on edge.

Both men had performed well in those early days of no sleep and seemingly permanent physical training, often finishing each forced march or run at very close intervals. Where they were pushed harder than the other ranks were before or after the day's physical work was done. It could be anything from having to get up an hour before the men and plan the route for the day, to being pulled aside at a checkpoint to be asked to solve random mathematical equations. All of these additional pressures were designed to ensure the officers' minds were as sharp as their bodies and fit for the task of commanding Her Majesty's Special Forces.

Their physical and mental abilities marked them out in the first two weeks of gruelling, constant competition, as both had shown the unmeasurable quantity which made a man perfect for such endeavours. There was an attitude to each of them, a hidden layer of resilience, which made them both push through barriers and even ignore pain, which allowed them to achieve goals that would be otherwise impossible.

Of the commissioned ranks in their intake, only two men survived until the vaunted escape and evasion phase. This part of their training, at the final stages of their initial selection, was where their mental resolve and strength of character was truly tested. It didn't matter if they'd successfully evaded capture, as at the final checkpoint in the exercise they would be taken, hooded, and subjected to the same treatment that any man taken in the first few days would be. Trying to maintain a watch on the number of hours and days they had been held, deprived of their senses and forced to maintain painful stress positions, both men emerged unscathed to be told that the exercise was over. They weren't told if they had passed it, that torture at least hadn't ended, but both men eventually earned their sand-coloured berets and both performed so well that they were invited to return years later at the rank of major.

"No Guinness and sausage sandwiches this time, eh?" Kelly joked, earning an unforced chuckle as the two men shared a memory from so long ago. The cans of Guinness, poured into tin cups to settle out and be drinkable, had been smuggled into camp illicitly to accompany the fried sausages crammed into the thick slices of bread. Both the sandwiches and the Guinness provided the two young men with their much-needed additional calories.

"No," Downes admitted with a smile which faded when their current business reasserted itself into the forefront of their minds. "My chaps told me a few things that have caused concern, Kelly…" he said, hoping the man would still be in the mindset of their shared past and be forthcoming.

The look on Kelly's face darkened. He leaned back and surveyed the man before him, before taking a sharp breath in and speaking fast as he leaned forwards.

"I've got over four hundred miles of coast to patrol, and I have fewer than two hundred men to do it. Granted, most of that coastline is impassable but that's beside the point. Men need to sleep, men need to eat, civilians need to be kept in check, and quarantine procedures for you ragtag bunch sapped more of my reserves than you could imagine." Downes sat forwards slightly, as if planning to interrupt, but he kept silent, watching the colonel closely as he poured excuses over him.

"I have people making demands of me every day—not least of all the few members of parliament who still believe they are somehow relevant to the current situation—and I still have to keep this island safe from the ever-present threat of an outbreak. So tell me, Major, what *concerns* do you have?"

Downes sat back and kept his face neutral. Although he hadn't worked alongside Kelly for years, he knew the man well enough to recognise the stress behind his words. This was a man who came from wealth and privilege; a man accustomed to success. He chose to engage in a life of hardship to prove himself worthy above all others, and yet...

"And I can see you're doing an admirable job, given the circumstances, Colonel," Downes said carefully. "I doubt many officers I've worked with in my time would have conducted operations so effectively." Kelly gave a small but gracious nod in acceptance of the praise.

"But I have to ask," Downes went on, "who is truly in charge of things here?"

Kelly regarded him with a flash of cold fury for a fleeting moment before he controlled his expression. As much as he tried to mask his anger, his nostrils still flared as he fought to keep his breathing slow and measured.

"Speak your mind, Major," he told Downes.

"Very well. Naval blockades off the coast. The CIA presence on the island. What exactly are we here? Is this a foothold for Britain to regain our home or a foothold for the Americans?" Kelly held his stare for a few seconds before deflating as he released his breath.

"If I'm completely honest with you, I don't know. I'm

assured that the remnants of our civilian government have done some form of deal with the US, which is evidently either 'above my pay grade' as they say, or else they believe the finer points are beyond my limited capability of understanding as a mere soldier."

"So they aren't here to evacuate us, and we can't leave of our own accord?"

"Oh, we're entirely free to go back to the mainland and do as we please, just not free to cross the Atlantic and risk infecting their continent." Downes' lips set in a tight line as his fears were confirmed. They were trapped there, totally at the mercy of a foreign superpower, regardless of their allegiance, and the decisions were being made at a level far above them.

"And the CIA involvement?"

"Ah," Kelly said awkwardly as he leaned back and folded his arms, "there we find ourselves at a technical impasse." Downes took the implication and the information in his stride, reverting to an out-loud train of theoretical monologue.

"So, the CIA are here and seem to be calling the shots. Aircraft have been seen coming in, and they've brought in personnel and equipment which aren't overtly military, according to my information..." He paused to look more closely at Kelly, who kept his features still and listened. "Which could imply to someone that they're conducting tests and require a secure base of operations as near as possible to a steady supply of infected people." Still Kelly stayed silent and motionless.

"Are they conducting tests here, Colonel?"

"Yes," Kelly admitted without hesitation. He seemed to want to say more, as though the force of keeping the information bottled up inside him was causing pain.

"Are there Screechers on this rock right now?"

"Yes," Kelly said again, this time with only a moment of hesitation. "At least I believe so. A team of scientists came in over a week ago with a few CIA agents, a small team of Navy SEALs and a detachment of Army personnel specialising in infectious diseases. They're on the furthest west spit of land possible, and any outbreak faces the Atlantic to the west and a line of guns to the east." Downes nodded slowly, imagining the placement to be Kelly's idea.

"So what do we do?"

"Not much we can do," Kelly answered. "I'm having the others in your little convoy reallocated to patrol sections of coast and replace my boys covering quarantine and guard on the civilians, obviously focusing on the easterly sections of our perimeter." A knock at the door interrupted their discussion. "I'll keep you and your chaps in reserve, if you don't mind?" Downes stood, hearing the tone of dismissal in the colonel's words, to agree and take his leave. Opening the door, he was faced with three people, two men and a woman, who stirred some vague recognition in him, and he crossed their path awkwardly in the confines of the small landing. Fighting the urge to loiter and listen through the door, he returned to the waiting Land Rover and was driven back to his allocated billet in thoughtful silence.

———

Kelly kept his face neutral behind the false smile as the three civilians filed into the room. They all had another person with them; a sort of entourage of one each to ensure than none of them believed themselves superior to the others.

Playing backstop at a meeting with the Under Secretary of State for Agriculture, the Minister for the Arts and the Minister of State for Housing, all very much former titles and positions in his opinion, even though they seemed to cling to them in an attempt to validate their importance, was not a prospect he had been looking forward to.

He smiled to put them at ease, listened and nodded along with their ridiculous ideas for regrowth and repopulation of the British Isles when all the nasty business was over. Just in time before the boredom and annoyance could get to him, before he erupted and told them the truth—that they weren't cowering off the coast with a view to moving back in when the pest control problem magically sorted itself out—Captain Barton knocked politely but urgently on the door before opening it.

Peering around the edge of the door, he smiled and cleared his throat.

"My sincere apologies, Colonel," he lied smoothly as he played his part in the planned interruption. "Urgent military matter, I'm afraid. Can't wait." He flashed his best smile from his strong jawline as Kelly stood and smoothed down his camouflaged shirt, mirroring the smile in falsity, if not quite matching the dazzling charisma of the younger man.

"Duty calls," he told the politicians solemnly, hoping the sheer cheesiness of the line wouldn't betray their deception to end the meeting. "I do hope you'll forgive me. See yourselves out, if you please." He swept from the room to leave the echoing sounds of both officers' boots thundering down the stairs to be followed by the rising pitch of an accelerating engine. Those sounds rose before falling away suddenly, only to rise again as the volume faded away with the next gear, taking the vehicle further away. The politicians, unable to have any kind of meaningful conversation without a referee, lapsed into an awkward silence until they were carried back to the town of Portree.

EIGHTEEN

Strictly speaking, Barton wasn't entirely telling tales about there being a military matter requiring Kelly's attention. The colonel sat in the passenger seat of their vehicle and endured the rough, bumpy roads being negotiated too fast by the captain instead of one of the men under their command.

"I think this will be far enough, Barton," he said, having banged his head once too often on the door frame, forcing him to hang heavily from the handle above the window.

"Not quite, Sir," the captain replied, raising his voice over the noise of the engine and howling wind. "Something has actually cropped up. It seems our colonial cousins have been playing with their toys and have caused something of a stir on the mainland."

Kelly growled low in his throat before asking for an explanation.

"Can't say I'm one hundred percent up to speed on the subject matter, Sir," he said apologetically. "Perhaps we should get it straight from the horse's mouth?"

The horse in question was pacing back and forth as far as the stretched cord of the satellite phone would allow. He was evidently excited as words tumbled from his mouth, barely taking the time to look up and acknowledge the two men as they walked in, other than to raise his eyebrows and smile briefly.

"Yessir," he said into the phone, "yessir, that's right. Uh-huh. Coverage like we never expected... No, Sir drives them crazy. Yessir, I will. Thank you." He replaced the handset into the cradle of the black briefcase and turned to clap his hands together.

"What the bloody hell has you so excited, Fisher?" Kelly demanded.

"Pull up a pew, Colonel, and I'll tell you all about it."

———

The engineer couldn't get away from the place they called 'the facility' quickly enough. Some facility it was, given that it was a farm shed with some hastily welded cages thrown together. What was inside those cages brutalised his senses and would probably stop him sleeping for the rest of the month. Or the rest of his life, he wasn't sure yet.

With that lasting memory fresh in his thoughts, he rushed back to the small hangar he'd been camping out in to be close to his work and began the modifications to prepare the three devices brought from America.

With the precise frequency, courtesy of the radio he'd been told a soldier was trying to tune when the phenomenon was stumbled upon, he was familiar enough with the device to make short work of reprogramming the interior workings. As soon as the first one was ready, he took a break, waving over the single guard sent from the US Air Force to keep watch over the merchandise. Pulling his last pack of Newports from his pocket, he tapped the base twice to shoot two filters free and offered one to the young man, who slung his rifle over his shoulder and smiled as he took it. Producing a lighter, the engineer lit his own and offered the dancing flame over as he sucked in a long pull and closed his eyes to stretch his back. He glanced down at the cigarettes, seeing that the carton was only half full and regretting giving one away, because he was down to his last pack. He'd been around enough military personnel in his time to know that a whole carton of smokes was easier to come by than most things when enough servicemen gathered in one place, but he hoped he wouldn't be forced to switch to an inferior brand before he got home. Perhaps a carton of Lucky Strikes would see him back, he mused.

"Go tell your bosses the first one's ready," he said as he exhaled. "I'll prep the other two and then I can get the heck out of here." He frowned as he took another pull on the cigarette. "Where in the hell are we, anyways?"

"Scotland," the kid replied, as though the vague geographical information made any difference to either of them. The engineer shrugged, taking back his lighter and feeling the unseasonal breeze tighten his skin as he vowed to finish the work as soon as possible so he could go home.

The helicopter crew for the CH-46 Sea Hawk arrived within the hour in a wash of noise and increased wind. They paid the engineer no attention, seeing just a man in coveralls stooped over what looked like a medium sized aircraft munition in the middle of a hangar, and loaded the device they had been sent for.

The pilot spoke in that relaxed tone they always used which, to the uninitiated, sounded like it must have been part of their basic training.

"Roger, proceeding on bearing one-five-one degrees for four-two-zero miles," he reported, signing off as he turned the nose of the noisy helicopter just left of south to drop the device in a large city far away from their safe place off the coast.

Those instructions had come via radio, and the crew had

no idea they originated from a house only a few miles away and came from the Central Intelligence Agency. If they had known, they probably wouldn't have cared because, just like the engineer, they were eager to get their job done and be back where they were more comfortable. In their case, it was the massive aircraft carrier sitting ten miles off the western edge of the Irish coast as part of the blockade to ensure none of the escaping survivors carried the disease to their home.

Their sedate cruising speed of one hundred and forty miles per hour saw them passing over the centre of what their map told them was a place called Bristol, when the pilot slowed and turned a few long, lazy circles to lower their altitude.

"In position," he announced over their link, "drop when ready." In answer, the rear ramp of the helicopter lowered with a mechanical whine to admit a rush of chill air from the abandoned land below them. Unlike a conventional bomb, this one merely had to be ejected into mid-air at a height exceeding one thousand feet for the device to activate on landing. That was as much as they knew—as much as they *needed* to know—and when the seemingly innocuous missile had been shoved clear over the edge of the ramp, they closed it up and began the three-hour flight back.

"Be advised," the pilot reported to their command structure, "package is delivered. RTB."

———

Bristol, a sprawling city on the banks of the busy River Severn, had been devoid of life for some time. Not *all* life, just human life. Or more specifically, it was utterly devoid of all *living* human life.

Trapped inside so many buildings, the thousands of undead woke from their state of hibernation to be whipped into such a frenzy of excitement that many broke free of their prison premises by barging their way through glass windows, and even in some cases breaking down doors in their frenzy to get to the source of whatever it was driving them so animalistically wild with hungry excitement.

Further out, in the suburbs of the city and even into the southern parts of Wales, the same activity was happening and waking up all of those trapped, dormant infected souls and driving them towards the centre of the neighbouring city by way of walking through the wide estuary.

For over a hundred miles, far further still than any of the wildest theories could have predicted, zombies were waking up and forcing their way out of their dry tombs to fulfil their desperate need to reach the source of the low frequency sound that triggered the tiny part of their brains still functioning into believing there was food on offer.

———

"Good God, man," Kelly exploded as he stood from the chair he had been occupying. "We've still got people on the mainland. There are civilians there, have you lost your mind?"

Fisher leaned back in his chair involuntarily in response to the colonel's anger.

"Relax, Kelly," he said. "We have AWACS monitoring and they'll be able to warn anyone nearby if the *swarm* threatens them." Kelly didn't sit, nor did he relax.

"You've just intentionally unleashed hell on those survivors all over again," he said coldly. "And you aren't even willing to evacuate any of them."

"Not true, Colonel," Fisher said as he reached for a piece of paper and waved it towards the officer. "Civilian evacuations are planned to begin at oh-nine-hundred next Wednesday. Your people will get new lives in the US of A."

"And the military personnel?" Fisher shifted in his chair

once, before fixing the hard man in front of him with a stare of pure granite.

"When our job here is done, Kelly, we'll discuss that."

"We'll discuss it now," he said firmly. "You've outright refused to support our efforts in recovering more survivors from the mainland which, until this moment, has been swept aside as inconsequential. I assure you, Sir, it is not. Evacuating the civilians on this island is one thing, but unless we can actively rescue more, then I fail to see the point in us being here at all." He remained standing, chest heaving up and down as he fought to control the many words he left unsaid from tumbling out, after the unwise outburst he had already released.

Fisher stared at him for a few moments, wearing a look somewhere between mild amusement and barely veiled rage.

"Let's get a few more things straight, shall we?" He stood suddenly and leaned over the desk with both fists pressing down hard onto the polished wood. "The United States is not here as an aid mission. The United States is occupying this part of Britain for military and scientific purposes to research, develop and hopefully deploy whatever vaccines or cures or weapons we can to ensure that the disease created here doesn't cross the Atlantic Ocean. There are people on the other side of the globe pondering exactly the same questions to our western borders, and I'm not telling you anything you don't already know when I say they're looking at a hundred Hiroshima-style solutions, so it doesn't matter a good God damn whether the serum we're developing on this island works or not; America *will* defend its borders at whatever cost." He calmed, sitting back in his chair and speaking in a slightly softer tone.

"Colonel, you and your people are backed into a corner with nothing left to barter with. Your price of admission to the promised land when we're done here is your continued service. When the work is done, we're all going home, and you can either come with us or not. But if you don't, then I wouldn't be expecting foreign aid any time soon. So yes, to answer your initial question, I assure you I have most certainly *not* lost my mind and I will continue to order the deployment of weapons both experimental and biological on the mainland until we find a way of killing every last one of those bastards. You can go now, *gentlemen*."

Kelly breathed out, never once having taken his eyes off the man sitting behind the desk holding all the power. With as much dignity and decorum as he could manage, he left the room and kept his face like stone until he was a mile away from the CIA headquarters.

"That *bastard*," he erupted, making Barton flinch and torque the steering wheel alarmingly. He regained his composure before the colonel spoke again, this time in a more equable and thoughtful tone. "But at least he let slip that his show wasn't the only one in town, and he's under pressure to get results or his Washington DC masters will likely pull the plug on him and his little circus here."

NINETEEN

Peter thrust out the spike, punctured a brain through a nostril made more accessible by the fact that the nose was partly torn or bitten away, and risked a glance over the ledge to watch the lifeless corpse bounce down the growing mound of bodies—animated and rendered safe alike—forming against the low building.

He had been running to and fro on the roof, in order to cover both places where his elevation was threatened. Then, behind him, on the other end of roof, the sounds of an approaching body reached his ears. Somehow, they, and he could only assume it was the smarter, faster type of biters, were managing to climb the ladder at the end where Astrid had appeared. On the side he covered now, it was a matter of sheer numbers and extremely bad luck; the misfortune being that the wall was the site where the former farmers had decided to pile enough junk that the hungry crowd below were able to use it as the start of a ramp.

His own efforts to stem the vertical flow of stinking bodies intent on eating him had, paradoxically, made it easier for more of them to climb the growing pile. Turning to his left, he drove the tip of one straight pitchfork prong into the skull of a balding man just behind his ear. The reaching arms stopped reaching for him, but the weapon held fast as the thing's second death had caused it to flop sideways and resist his efforts to tug it back out. He cursed it and began to growl in effort through his gritted teeth, as a scraping noise behind him made him spin to see another one wearing the shredded and filthy remains of a shirt and tie get both arms and half a torso over the ledge. Yanking desperately on the pitchfork, he was forced to reach over his right shoulder to grasp at the smoothed-down handle of his father's shotgun to use the last loaded cartridge at brutally close quarters.

The air in front of his face punched at him with a pressure wave that was confusing, before the sharp cracks he heard tied in with what his eyes were seeing. The zombie shuddered with each cracking noise until the fourth or fifth one snatched his head back and toppled it backwards to fall away and knock a half dozen more of them back to the ground. His mind caught up with his senses and he craned his neck to see Astrid crouching over one knee from a sitting position with her gun tucked into her body tightly and aimed his way. He nodded his thanks automatically, seeing her return the gesture and spin away to reload before she fired more shots over her side and turned to run back to him. Seeing his predicament, she landed one boot hard on top of the bald head and he gripped the shaft of his sticker firmly, straining to pull it free. He fell back-wards as it was released from the gory grip of the skull and rolled back to his feet to begin the routine of thrust and with-draw, this time trying to improve his aim for the soft bits that didn't threaten to steal his tools.

Astrid was firing more intensively then, pausing to fill the temporary quiet with the clicks and scrapes of well-practised hands performing another reload, and she didn't let up until the main assault had been forced back. Peering over the edge again together, Peter saw that only the luckiest or most sure-footed of biters could make it through the mess of farmyard junk and bodies to climb for their position.

Their small breather didn't last long, as a shriek from behind them forced the world to grind down into agonising slow-motion. The shriek, the rasping expulsion of air that conveyed nothing but hatred and malice and hunger, echoed loudly over the low rooftops of the barn louder than anything else in their immediate surroundings. They turned together in time to see the horrifying sight of a young man wearing a blue and white striped shirt marred by dark gore. The terror of being face to face with a Lima, one not horribly damaged and less dangerous, wasn't reduced by the fact that he had either lost his trousers in the months since the outbreak or else had turned in a state of being half dressed. The baggy boxer shorts had remained on, but the socks had worn away at the soles to leave what looked like black ankle warmers banded about his mottled grey calf muscles.

As they stared, neither yet able to bring a weapon to bear, those muscles bunched and tightened in anticipation of the leaping attack they both knew was coming. Both had seen Limas at work before—albeit at a safe distance usually—and both knew what the human body was capable of when free of the constraints binding it to normality.

It launched into the air, limbs flailing as it instinctively thrashed and whirled to correct its aerial course. Mouth open in ready anticipation, both of them could see the wide maw filled with blackened gums and the two flashes of bright metal of the man's gold teeth as a cloud of bright, white smoke obscured their vision, billowing outwards in an expanding cone towards the flying monstrosity.

Peter's hand had reached instinctively over his right shoulder where it landed directly on the grip of the sawn-off shotgun. The web between his finger and thumb, spread wide and taught, hit the smoothed-down wood and triggered his fingers to clamp down and seize it tightly. Pulling it in one smooth movement, he set his stance wide and forced his left palm down on top of the barrels near the breech, as his right index and middle fingers reached for the two triggers.

He couldn't remember which trigger he had pulled when he'd fired the first shot only a minute or two before, but somehow his brain registered that pulling one of those triggers would achieve nothing but a moment of fear before the zombie cut him down in a blur of teeth and pain. Knowing this on a cellular level, even if he couldn't explain it in triple the time it took to act automatically, both fingers squeezed the triggers at once before the gun had even finished the downward arc of his draw, to spit smoke and flame and a deafening noise out ahead of them.

It was only the fourth time he'd ever drawn the weapon to use it, and although each time he had been desperate and facing death just as he did now, he didn't flinch from the noise and violence of the gun going off. He also hadn't expended his supply of ammunition, which he'd tampered with just like his father had done to illegally shoot deer, and the solid ball of lead and wax barely had time to begin breaking apart when it hit the zombie in mid-air. The force of the gunshot spun Peter in spite of his attempts to stay standing, and as his right side was thrown backwards, the body of his attacker-turned-victim fell through the thin skein of gun smoke to land heavily in between Astrid and Peter. It skidded through the rough shale littering the rooftop, just as time seemed to speed up once more when Peter's backside thumped heavily onto the deck.

Peter's shot, fired blindly with nothing to guide it but hope and instinct, had blown away most of the right arm and shoulder to leave a broken and ruined body in which the upper and lower sections seemed unable to communicate with one another. The legs seemed to be furiously pedalling as if the doomed creature dreamed it was in the closing stages of a bicycle race. The upper body, twisted aside at an angle, tried to reach for the ankles of Astrid with each ridiculous and grotesque circuit it thrashed, teeth snapping together as it wheezed, until the Norwegian woman riddled the thing's head with a burst of automatic fire, to leave a sudden stillness and silence to their rooftop.

That silence didn't last long, as the renewed moaning and shrieking from below forced them both to snap back into action again.

"We cannot stay here," she said to him, whipping her head left and right to both keep watch and look for a viable alternative to their current predicament. Peter calmly levered over the catch to break the shotgun in half and up-ended it to allow two spent cartridges to drop to the rooftop. Slipping the bag from one shoulder he thrust a hand into the pouch where he knew the full cartridges would be. He slipped the reloads into the barrels, hearing the satisfying *pop* each side and gripped the chopped-down stock to flick his wrist and snap the breech closed. Restoring the gun to the top of the bag and the bag over both shoulders, he stooped to pick up his pitchfork and nodded at Astrid to signify that he was ready.

As he caught her eye, he saw how hers flickered to her left —his right—and turned to see another two pairs of mottled grey hands breach the high ground.

"Silage," Peter said as he pointed to one of the longer sides of the building. She didn't understand the word or his meaning but followed anyway, seeing as an idea she didn't understand was better than no idea at all. Reaching the edge of the roof with the boy at her side, she saw the twenty foot drop to the tops of low, black plastic covered mounds.

He turned to look at her face, seeing the confusion and scepticism evident.

"It's just grass," he explained in rapid words, "cut and piled up there with plastic over the top. It's to feed cows," he added as though the purpose of the practice would assist her understanding.

"And this is a safe thing to land on?" she asked him. Peter couldn't say yes for certain, but when another shriek behind them from the direction of the ladder added to the chorus of moans from the other side, he guessed they didn't have much in the way of options. With a shrug, he stepped off the rooftop, throwing his legs out ahead of him to fall a few seconds before landing hard on his backside.

The landing was much, *much* harder than he'd expected.

It had been one of the games he played on the farm where he grew up, climbing on the great mountains of cut grass as his father reversed a tractor up and down the steep slope in order to crush it down and squeeze out as much air as possible. When those great slopes of squashed grass filled the slots between the rough concrete walls, they spread huge sheets of thick, black plastic over them to seal in the grass and let it rot just enough to be exactly what the cows wanted over the winter months.

What Peter hadn't taken into consideration was the fact that this grass had been there for months longer than usual, and the added time left to ferment provided a lot less cushioning than his childhood games told him there would be.

He landed hard, knocking the wind out of himself and shooting a pain up through his spine from his tail bone that threatened to make him vomit, on top of losing the ability to breathe temporarily. A thud beside him warned of Astrid's arrival at almost ground level and her melodic voice hissing curses in a language he didn't understand made it obvious that she'd also expected a softer landing.

If their impact was painful, the meeting of running zombie and rough concrete just above them was catastrophic. It had gained the rooftop just as Astrid's blonde ponytail had disappeared from view. Breaking into a run to catch the escaping food, it sailed clear over the ledge of the roof and overtook the woman as she'd dropped vertically downwards. The momentum of the reckless run took it past the small covered mounds to slam it into the hard ground below. As it rose, broken leg bones crunching when it struggled mechanically to regain its feet, the top of its head fountained outwards as the head snapped back to start the slow, spinning descent to the ground. Peter looked to his left to see Astrid lying flat on her back with a pistol in her hand sprouting a fat pipe on the end of the barrel. She scanned that barrel left and right before dragging herself to her feet with a hiss of pain. Peter followed, not waiting for any invitation to move, and the two of them fled across the farmyard to seek higher ground.

"Why are there so many of the fast ones?" Peter gasped quietly to her in between sucking lungsful of air.

"This," Astrid replied, also out of breath, "is what I am thinking also. *There!*" she said, pointing out a tall, steel structure standing forty feet off the ground. Peter saw it, recognised a grain storage silo when he saw one, and also knew that if they were seen going up there they'd never be able to come down again.

"No," he said, tugging her sleeve back while all around them, the shrieks and moans echoed ominously. "We'll be trapped."

"Trust me, Peter," she said. "We just need to stay off the ground long enough for them to come back."

———

"Where the fucking fuck are these fuckers fucking coming from?" Johnson roared in impotent rage as he crunched the Warrior over another group staggering down the single track road.

"There's something going on," Bufford answered from behind him. "This ain't right; not even for the shit-show we live in. And why are they all the fast bastards?"

They had turned around twice now, or at least they'd tried to, and the decision to save ammunition had long ago been made as they faced three or more Screechers for every bullet they carried. Using the heavier 30mm ammunition was even less sensible as they'd probably attract more than they killed with each heavy, percussive shot. Johnson idly wished they still made canister for their guns, or the more modern flechette ammunition, effectively turning their small cannon into a giant shotgun. One shot of that could clear a hundred or more of the bastards, packed tightly as they were on the road, following the noise of their engine.

"Go left here," Buffs interrupted Johnson's daydreaming as bodies still crunched under their tracks. The Warrior slowed and lurched slightly as the junction was taken too fast to be comfortable, not that comfort was their main concern at that point, and Johnson trusted Bufford to read the map to direct him back towards the farm, after their circuitous route to lead as many of the mob away while crushing those in the road as a bonus.

As he drove, fighting away the worry and panic and banishing it from his mind, since that would serve only to reduce his effectiveness, he allowed his mind instead to wander towards other questions that needed answering.

Why has another swarm appeared now? After a winter of seeing very little activity, he had begun to hope that they were dealing with a few stragglers and had turned his attention towards the potential of more living enemies.

And why, he asked himself, angrily echoing his question to Buffs, *is almost every one of these buggers a Lima?*

"Left ahead," Bufford said, interrupting his thoughts, "single track for three miles. Staggered crossroads; left again."

"Roger," Johnson acknowledged, happy that he was effectively driving a box around the area to head back for the boy and female commando he was trying not to think about, in case his guilt overcame him.

"Twenty minutes," Buffs told him in an attempt at reassurance.

"Twenty minutes is a long time," Johnson whispered to himself as he narrowed his eyes and focused on driving as fast as he could without crashing.

TWENTY

"There! I heard it again!" Jessica said excitedly.

"Okay," Daniels told her, "I believe you. Just get your bloody head back inside before something takes a bite out of it." Reluctantly, she lowered her body away from the open hatch, for the spot to be re-occupied by the tall, quiet soldier who carried his weapon like it was a prized possession. Or his first-born child.

"She's right," Enfield said after a few moments. "Towards our ten o'clock. That's seven-six-two if it's anything." Daniels, having seen the marine for what he was, took that assessment as pure fact without question. Instructing Duncan to look for roads branching off in the direction of their ten o'clock, he fought with the map until he was looking at the right section for their general area.

There were far too many zombies around for his liking, and more than one person had voiced an opinion that something was going on, because there was no reason for every dead person in the county to suddenly up and decide to head in one direction. He didn't know anything about that, but he did know that he was much happier heading back into a fight with the two royal marines on his side.

"Mortars?" The marine sergeant, Hampton, pondered aloud. Daniels, the sound so familiar to him as to be ingrained in his psyche, answered before Enfield's mouth could even form a word of response. "That," he announced confidently, "is the sound of Mrs Rarden birthing six of her most troublesome daughters..." When silence greeted his poetic musings, he sighed, "I'm wasted on this audience. That's 30mm on full auto. One of ours. The SSM's over there."

It took them over half an hour to battle their half-blind way through the country lanes towards the last place they could guess the sounds were coming from. No more gunfire sounded, which made the task of hunting down the original source difficult, but eventually they rounded a bend in the lane and saw a small crowd of dead clambering over one another to form a rising mound of once-human bodies, all of them reaching upwards for what looked like two small shapes clinging onto the fragile frame of a metal silo.

"Sarge," Enfield said urgently. He didn't raise his voice, merely spoke with an increased intensity that cut into everyone crammed inside the small space of the armoured vehicle.

"What do you see, lad?" Hampton asked with mirrored urgency.

"Need you on that gun. Two friendlies up high, and two metric fuck-tonnes of Screechers underneath. My nine o'clock."

Hampton didn't hesitate. He wouldn't describe himself as a brave man; that self-awarded description was for people who craved recognition for the things they did. Bill Hampton was simply the personification of a no-bullshit attitude that allowed him to get the job done. He didn't act how he did to get his men to like him; instead, he just did his job to the best of his ability and the men loved him for it, just as they didn't perform to avoid his punishments, but out of a need for the sergeant to like them; to tell them they did well.

Without questioning the matter of his personal safety, he undid the hatch and squeezed his wide shoulders out of the gap to swing the big machine gun in the general direction of the things he didn't like and started blasting away.

He fired in short, controlled bursts like he had always been taught. In fact, the only time he had ever fired one of these beasts on fully automatic for an entire belt was eight years prior when he'd lain on his back on the high ground at San Carlos bay and fired a full belt at an Argentine fighter plane wreaking havoc on the vulnerable ships at anchor. He hadn't told anyone the story, and those who had seen him do it weren't encouraged to repeat the tale, because it wasn't necessarily something he was proud of.

He was proud now, he realised, but he knew that he didn't need anyone else to be proud of him. He felt no remorse for the dead because they had no souls. They fought for no cause and had no regard for anything. Their war would rage until the end of humanity and beyond. The dead weren't the sons and daughters of people any longer. They weren't just like him, only on the other side of the battle lines, and he unleashed hell on them with a stony expression.

Two hundred rounds of ammunition, to the uninitiated, sounds like a lot of bullets. In truth, two hundred rounds is not nearly enough to get many jobs done. Hampton stopped to attach another box of ammunition and feed it through, before yanking back the warm metal of the charging handle to resume his one-man onslaught.

The growing mountain of dead became a sea of twice-dead, and the reaching hands stopped reaching upwards and began reaching towards him. The gunfire paused long enough for him to lean back and shout down through the gap that perhaps their driver would kindly reverse for roughly fifty paces. At least that was what Steve Duncan chose to hear and not the actual words used, which could only politely be described as 'salty'.

The incessant, percussive rattling of the machine gun started up again until the remainder of the zombies were spread out in a reducing cone towards their vehicle.

"What in the hell are you doing here?" a voice Hampton recognised shouted at him. Looking up again and recognising the shape of Astrid Larson with her shock of bright blonde hair, he realised he was obviously just as noteworthy to her, although he imagined himself to be significantly less attractive.

"Saving your arse," he yelled back. Enfield chose that moment to emerge from the other hatch and bring his small rifle to bear on anything in their immediate surroundings still moving. A sharp bark of laughter drifted back to him in answer.

"Where's everyone else?" he yelled.

"How about I tell you when you get us off this thing?"

"Fair point," Hampton grumbled to himself as he leaned inside again to give instructions. The Sultan crept forwards, crunching over the bumpy obstructions, which were mostly physically immobilised and not actually dead again. As soon as they reached the foot of the metal grain silo, the two refugees clambered down to drop onto the hull of the vehicle. Hampton's big gun stayed silent but Enfield continued to spit small bullets into skulls whenever anything threatened their perimeter.

"We've got more coming," he warned them as they obviously weren't getting inside quickly enough for his liking.

"Are they the fast ones?" Larsen asked breathlessly.

"Don't look like it."

"Good. Time to get out of here." Hampton dropped down and helped Astrid inside the Sultan, where she immediately banged her head and her elbow on exposed metal, providing enough of a distraction that the others didn't notice the smaller of the rescued people enter. The hatch was closed, plunging them into a darker setting until Enfield closed down his hatch too, to remove the last of the daylight.

"Where are the others?" Hampton asked.

"We got separated," Peter said. "I was... I was left behind when we were attacked. Astrid came back for me..."

"Johnson took the others to lead away the swarm," Astrid explained, taking up the recounting. "There seems to be an unnatural number of what you call the Li—"

"Peter," a voice said from nearer the front. The word was muffled as though the name had been uttered from behind the speaker's hands, which they had.

"J... Jessica?" Peter asked, but he already knew it was her. He broke down and sobbed like the young boy he was deep inside, pushing his way through the press of bodies as the tears started to flow more freely than they ever had. He clawed his way the short distance to his sister and threw himself against her, until she wrapped her arms around him and cried just as hard and freely as he did.

The two children, reunited against all odds, would not let one another go in the gloomy interior of an overloaded armoured vehicle, and the only other sound to fill the space was the quiet sob of another occupant.

"Where's my Amber?"

———

Johnson's concentration had never been more focused than it had been on that drive. He pushed twenty-five tonnes of armoured fighting vehicle through the overgrown lanes. At the staggered crossroads Bufford had warned him about, he had to throttle back and decide the best way to navigate the obstacle of three cars which had collided so many months ago.

From twenty feet away, he saw the dried-up remains of the driver of a Vauxhall Carlton turn to face his approach.

"Hold on," he said unnecessarily as he ran the left side tracks over the front of the car with much less discomfort than he expected. Accelerating away, he looked out for signs of the upcoming left turn Bufford had called out to him. Overgrown road signs were barely visible but the faded white lines in the road gave subtle clues to the presence of adjoining roads, if a person knew what to look for. When the centre line turned a solid white, he slowed, looking for the tunnel created by the trees hanging down where the branches hadn't been forced back by the passage of people in vehicles.

Those branches snapped away as the Warrior forced its way through like they were nothing. The close confines of the narrow road made the going much slower as he fought with the huge machine to keep it out of the ditches either side of them, driving their speed down even more and increasing Johnson's stress levels. The hull scraped and banged with the noise of their aggressive progress until they emerged from the wooded tunnel into the harsh light of the full dawn. Before them, the edge of the farm opened up with the sprawl of low buildings seeming to grow outwards organically. Everywhere before them lay the crushed and broken remains of so many former people they had destroyed.

Only they weren't. These had been cut down by gunfire moving in the other direction and couldn't have been from their escape. Just as Johnson opened his mouth to call this information out to the others, with fears of another Nevin incident surging to the front of his mind, Bufford beat him to it.

"Armoured vehicle," he snapped as the turret hummed to swing towards the unexpected intruder, "nine o'clock, fifty yards." Johnson stopped the Warrior and immediately threw it into reverse out of habit. His conscious mind caught up with the subconscious in time to tell him that the likelihood of him having been drawn into an ambush was slim to non-existent. But training born of repetition took just as long to undo as it did to become second nature in the first place. He stopped, realising that he was highly unlikely to get an instant profile recognition, as the man in the turret wasn't a cavalryman. He hesitated, experiencing a rare moment when he didn't know the right thing to do; and then the radio came to life.

"Foxtrot-Three-Three-Alpha, please tell me that's you…"

———

Rushed radio traffic was exchanged between the two armoured hulks and the route for extraction was agreed. The Sultan followed in the wake of the larger Warrior, which was the obvious choice to take the lead, and they all listened with wet eyes and breaking hearts to hear the shaking voice of a young woman talking through her tears incoherently to hear the sweetest of rare sounds when Amber spoke a single word into the radio in the rear section of the Warrior.

"Mummy?" she asked in a small voice before bursting out in tears for Kimberley to hug her tightly.

"We need to get clear of whatever the hell is going on here," Johnson said to Daniels over their link.

"Agreed," he said. "We've seen concentrations of Limas at the front, with a strong force of Screechers behind, then miles of stragglers lagging behind them. They're all heading north by north-northwest, from what we can tell."

"What's north-northwest of here?" Johnson asked back.

"Bristol," Bufford interjected dourly, leaving a moment of silence hanging afterwards.

"Jesus," Johnson muttered, "I thought even the Screechers would have better taste than to go to bloody Bristol." The joke was a weak one, but for the few people who had visited the city recently, the words held more than a little merit.

"Something's off about it all," Daniels offered pensively. "Can't quite put my finger on it yet, but it's got to have something to do with the Americans... Let me think about it and we'll talk when we find somewhere safe to stop."

That was their current priority—finding a place beyond the reach of the steady flow of slow-moving zombies to stop and reunite the stricken mother and daughter who were crying inside the two respective vehicles with inconsolable happiness. They headed directly east, an agreed compromise between turning directly away from the flow of dead back towards the coast, which would hinder their overall goal of heading to the far north west of Scotland, and trying to avoid said flow of dead.

"Is it me...?" Daniels asked over the radio after almost twenty miles of relatively flat A-roads.

"No," Johnson answered, "they're definitely thinning out." Another ten minutes showed no signs of any Screechers on the move, so they took a turn north and stopped at the nearest patch of raised ground. Emerging carefully with weapons raised, they inspected the tracks and undersides of their vehicles to ensure they weren't carrying any biting hitchhikers.

As soon as the all-clear was announced, a young woman with the same fair hair as little Amber dragged herself clear of the Sultan's hatch desperately. Dropping to her knees and sobbing, she reached out to beckon her little girl to her and held her so tightly, like she'd never let go again.

"Oh my baby, my baby," she said over and over as she showered the girl with kisses all over her head and face. "My baby. Who found you? Who looked after you?"

Wordlessly Amber leaned around her mother and smiled with her right index finger pointing at the unlikeliest of rescuers. Picking Amber up and carrying her, she threw her free arm around Peter's neck and pulled him tight to her.

She whispered fast in his ear, and although Johnson

couldn't hear the words, he was sure it was her thanks for saving the girl. He'd done more than that, the SSM knew. He'd not only saved her life but had cared for her with a patience he was sure many adults couldn't muster even under normal circumstances. When Ellie released the boy, he was grabbed roughly by the big man's hands. Johnson eyed him for a second with a mixture of ingrained fear and relief, before hugging him close just as the woman had done.

"You frightened the shit out of me," he berated the boy as his eyes lifted to take in the bedraggled appearance of Larsen and nodding his heartfelt thanks to her for risking her life. Peter stayed close to him, not quite hugging him but not withdrawing either. A girl cleared her throat to get the attention of both of them, and Peter pulled away from the hug he was returning, not able to tell Johnson just how much it meant to him.

"And who's this?" the SSM asked.

"This is my sister," Peter said, his words choking on the tears he was holding back, "Jessica." Just the simple act of speaking her name triggered the pent-up emotion hidden away for so long, and Peter collapsed into Johnson, who wrapped him up tightly in an embrace that made him feel safer and more secure than he had ever felt in his entire life.

TWENTY-ONE

The testing of the device had been a success and had elevated Fisher's standing greatly. The applications for the adapted technology were huge, and he had received the reports from their AWACS early warning aircraft that the effective radius of the device was roughly forty miles, which gave them the ability to cover about five thousand square miles with each device.

He was no fool. He knew that the plan would be to attract as many of the infected into single locations for the air force to wipe them out, and that was how they would reclaim Britain, if it was deemed viable. But now, he had given them a way to do it with minimal expense. Already the reports had upwards of ten thousand infected gathering in the city they'd chosen far to the south of their remote, offshore location. He knew that back at Langley, their technical people would be figuring out the distances and times required, based on the information they were gathering now on how to use a ripple effect to drop the devices and pied-piper the infected all into one location, where they could be hit with napalm, or whatever, and be wiped out.

Obviously, they would still need to deploy ground troops to check every room in every house and building in the whole country, because there still had to be plenty of people who had been infected and turned after shutting themselves away at home.

He looked again at the brief report received by fax on the effects of the device. As anyone would expect, the first to reach the location of the device were the faster ones, and calculating how many of them used their superior—or at least less impaired—physical abilities to get to the city first gave an indication of how many would follow. That swarm, that migrating herd, that infected singularity merged and grew from all directions, all heading for the same spot, like iron filaments in water with the introduction of a magnet. The sheer numbers on the thin printout in his hand didn't fully reflect the gravity of the situation; either how many had died or how many had turned and still needed to be dealt with.

What he wanted, and what he proposed in the report he was trying to formulate, was for *his* idea to be used as the method for purging Britain of the dangerous infected. He would sell it as the most cost effective way. Not cheaper in terms of dropping bombs, because he knew better than most people just how many his country had stockpiled ready for all-out war; but in terms of not destroying the infrastructure, buildings and resources that such a devastating bombardment would cause, and hence minimising the future rebuilding costs. His way would mean that the infected simply bled themselves to death and would be just a pile of bones and puddle to clean up by the time US forces arrived to put boots on the ground.

The UK was a perfect foothold to reclaim Europe and beyond, and if the American forces could develop the fastest way to clear an area of infected and kill them off by the thousands, then the riches of half the world would be theirs for the taking.

They could emerge as the dominant power on the entire planet.

Fisher's personal ambition wasn't quite so grand, but he would be a fool not to seize the opportunity on offer. The least he expected when the business was done was a position as section chief somewhere.

His reverie was interrupted by the mechanical sounds of the fax machine chirping and chuntering as another vital piece of information was received, and as he watched the printer arm shoot back and forth over the roll of paper, he jumped slightly, startled by the sudden noise of the satellite phone's shrill ring.

"Fisher," he said in economical answer to take the incoming call.

"This is Jacobs," came the slightly delayed and detached voice, "pickup by chopper at twenty-one-fifty your time for briefing."

"Understood," Fisher answered, hearing the call cut from the other end.

He slowly replaced the receiver into the case and rested the fingertips of his right hand there, smiling. If Jacobs was involved, then he knew Langley and, in turn, the White House, would be investing in his plan.

A glance at his watch told him he had a little under thirty minutes to be at the nearby airfield, so he threw on the heavy coat he was sure he'd die of exposure without in the harsh landscape and drove himself.

———

The ride to the carrier stationed thirty miles to the west was short but uncomfortable as the helicopter bucked and dropped, thanks to the icy crosswind it flew through. Fisher could only imagine how harsh it had been there in the middle of winter and was thankful he'd arrived as the worst of the weather was beginning to break. He was amazed how the conditions could so drastically switch from a fresh covering of perfect dry snow to a diagonal downpour of stinging rain like a million needles aimed for any gap in a man's clothing where skin was exposed.

Those musings killed the time until the engine note changed and their airspeed slowed for the pilot to begin clawing his careful way sideways to land the skids on the rolling deck. The rotors powered down and Fisher unstrapped to reach for the door as it was opened from outside. Another agent greeted him. Fisher didn't recognise him, but the appearance of a man in a suit was so out of place on a navy warship that it made his agent status obvious. The man shouted over the noise to confirm he was who he was and led him inside.

"Briefing room is this way, Sir," the man said, offering nothing more but leading the way to what counted as a large room aboard the floating fortress.

"Fisher," Jacobs called out to him as he walked in, "take a seat." Jacobs didn't introduce any of the dozen other men sitting at the chairs arrayed before a raised dais and Fisher saw a mixture of uniforms which were primarily naval. Others not in uniform were just as obvious, but the briefing started before he could get a bead on them.

"Okay then, I'll get right to it. Aerial surveillance reports indicate that the use of the device was far more effective than expected, with a confirmed radius of roughly forty miles give or take, depending on the terrain," Jacobs explained, telling Fisher that everyone in the room was just as read-in on the situation as he was, if not probably more so. "Other devices are either being retrofitted in theatre or are in transit from the US and expected to be fully operational for deployment within seventy-two hours. Mister Robertson will fill you in on the method."

Robertson, tall and built like a sportsman but appearing

oddly timid in the company he was presently keeping, stood and adjusted his spectacles. The man was clearly *with* the agency and not an agent, so Fisher marked him down as one of their eggheads immediately.

"Gentlemen," Robertson began with more confidence in his voice than Fisher expected from his demeanour. He nodded towards the back of the room and the lights dimmed in response. A projector started up to flicker a bright display against the solid wall to their front. A map of the UK appeared, quickly followed by another acetate sheet laid over the top, showing a red circle.

"The plan is to drop a series of devices in sequence over a period of nineteen days." Another three sheets were laid over the displayed image with more red circles appearing and over-lapping. "These devices will bring out any of the infected people and cause them to congregate in a single area, ready for the deployment of a cure." Murmurs rippled around the briefing room and Fisher shifted in his seat uncomfortably. "Estimated time before we are able to begin operations there is eight to twelve days." Robertson nodded at Jacobs and sat again. Jacobs' eyes found Fisher and his expression invited him to chime in. With a long intake of breath, Fisher steadied himself and stood, proceeding to walk to the front of the room to be able to turn and see everyone's faces.

"Are you planning to drop this special ordnance and congregate every possible infected being into the same location as the test area?" a man in a naval uniform asked.

"Negative, the area…" Jacobs looked to another suit, who consulted a stack of papers for a frustrating handful of seconds.

"Bristol."

"Bristol is being used as a secondary test area to deploy serum and also test the most effective munitions against the infected. The other devices will be dropped ranging north to south and will cover most of Britain, eventually leading every-thing to…" He once again snapped his fingers impatiently at the man with the papers, who desperately rifled through them to find another place name.

"Hastings," the agent said eventually.

"So the infected all end up at Hasti—" Jacobs shot a quizzical look at the agent, who froze with no idea why that had caused the man any confusion. "Seriously? We're having another Battle of Hastings? Anyway… it's been calculated that this is the best area that won't damage any real infrastructure or impede deep-water ports for the eventual repopulation efforts." He scanned the room to make sure there were no little hands raised in the air and wrapped things up.

"First off, gentlemen," he said confidently, "let's be clear on what we mean by the word 'cure'…" He paused to take in the expressions on those faces. "The 'cure' being developed is a serum that prevents any of the infected from representing a danger to any living person or animal. It kills the infected person by causing massive haemorrhaging. It is not pretty, but it does work. I've seen it."

"Seen it how?" asked a voice from the front row. Fisher opened his mouth to respond but Jacobs cut him off.

"The how and the why and the where are classified," he said abruptly. "What's important is that the serum is in produc-tion, the first batch of which will be delivered very soon."

Fisher's eyes went wide for a second before he got himself under control. Professor Grewal had been adamant that further testing was required, but Fisher's eagerness to provide results had forced his own hand in reporting the success back to Langley. Both Grewal and Chambers—who he found far more amenable than the Brit—were in agreement that the 'cure' as they all liked to call it, wasn't ready for use without more testing. As Jacobs went on explaining more of the logis-tics of how it would all happen, Fisher leaned back against the edge of a desk and tried to sum up the courage to interrupt the more senior man.

That courage never materialised, or at least his career aspirations stopped the words from forming in his mouth, but either way he stayed silent, as the plans to bring troops over the Atlantic in time for spring were discussed.

"What about the evacuation of anyone left there?" a voice asked from nearer the back, unaware or simply unconcerned that 'there' was more accurately 'here'.

"Quarantine and evacuation protocols will be dealt with by the military," Jacobs answered, "and the President has agreed to expedite all applications for asylum from British citizens, but this is *not* our primary concern. Our primary concern is developing the most effective method for corralling and destroying those infected."

"What's the method for deployment of the cure?" a man asked, the wings on his US navy uniform indicating that he was a pilot.

"Airburst munitions," was all Jacobs said.

"Specifically?" the aviator asked, unperturbed at the attempted stonewalling. Jacobs sighed.

"As of oh-eight-hundred tomorrow, three AC-one-thirty Spectres will be stationed in *Las Palmas*. They will have the necessary munitions supplied to them and the delivery will be by forty-mike-mike and one-oh-five-mike-mike airburst. Any other questions?"

"What about a BLU-eighty-two with a daisy cutter?" one man asked.

"Too much serum to waste in one go if it fails. Next?"

"Las Palmas?" asked another voice uncertainly, sure they were asking a stupid question but going ahead with it anyway.

"The Canary Islands," Jacobs explained, reciting information he'd recently learned by the sound of his voice. "The outermost region of Europe, a little off the western coast of north Africa in the Atlantic, owned and controlled by the Spanish government. We entered into an agreement with that government some months ago but since then contact with their continental base of operations has been lost, with obvious assumptions for what that means. There is a contingent of government on those islands who are effectively trading new lives in the US for all their surviving citizens for use of the island chain by our forces indefinitely."

"In-flight refuelling?" the pilot asked.

"KC-one-thirty-fives," Jacobs told him, the information meaning nothing to many in the room but evidently satisfying the man asking.

"When do we start?" asked a new speaker.

"In forty-eight hours," Jacobs said. "As I said, deployment of the sonic lure devices will begin in the north and head progressively south, providing the fastest time on target for our planes when the party starts."

The briefing was dismissed, leaving Jacobs and Fisher at the front of the room. The two men's eyes met and Jacobs must have detected the trepidation in Fisher's.

"Forty-eight hours," he said again, waiting for Fisher's acknowledgement.

"Forty-eight hours. Understood."

TWENTY-TWO

Finding somewhere to safely park two armoured vehicles under cover was no simple task, given their size. The sudden and oddly concerning lack of wandering zombies made the task infinitely safer and more simple, and while that conundrum was pushed temporarily aside, they settled on a large industrial garage unit.

Bufford and Larson got out first, the former having been cooped up inside the Warrior for too long and the latter insisting that she was fine, in spite of having expended almost all of the ammunition she'd been carrying only a few hours previously. They entered the unit via a small pedestrian door, before emerging a full ten minutes later as Bufford hauled on a chain to roll up the big shutter and admit the two vehicles reversing inside. The roller shutter came down behind them and Duncan immediately set about searching the large work-shop for fuel stores.

As they all congregated and stretched their cramped muscles, sounds of a trapped animal, hissing and yowling, drifted out of the hatch to them, followed shortly afterwards by a small projectile of brown and black exiting the vehicle and seeking the nearest piece of low cover too small for a human to fit. Everyone but the royal marines looked shocked. Peter had already learned of the survival of the cat who had followed him and Amber so long ago. He smiled at Johnson, who just seemed speechless.

"Bloody thing has to be down to two lives maximum," he muttered, digging in his pack and handing a tin of something to Peter. He fished in a pouch on his webbing to produce a tin opener, offering it to the boy, who was already proudly holding his own and grinning at the SSM.

Kimberley hovered behind Peter and smiled nervously at Johnson as she fussed over the boy and earned suspicious glances from his sister. Ever since he had been left behind at the farm, she had blamed herself and expected criticism from others, but when none came, she seemed to act harder on herself than even before. Johnson smiled back, forcing his facial muscles to move into some semblance of an expression designed to reassure her that she wasn't to blame. Privately he blamed himself, even taking Peter aside when he could pry his sister from him for just a minute, to apologise to him. Peter had been the one to offer the reassurances then, taking responsibility for sneaking away from the group without telling anyone.

Johnson, a man accustomed to large industrial garages, returned the conversation to the subject of diesel and brought Duncan's attention to the grubby metal tank standing in the yard.

"Better to get it now than risk having company later," he said. The logic was sound, but it was a hassle to drive the two big wagons back outside and crank the heavy hand pump up and down to brim their tanks, while the others formed a loose cordon with their guns trained outwards. The task all but drained the remains of their strength. When both wagons were full, Johnson encouraged them to fill the three metal jerrycans they found with diesel, seeing as they were already there.

Safely back inside, they set a guard and began a debrief on what had happened since they had last seen one another.

Daniels, finally stood down from the need to do things immediately, filled Johnson in on what he'd missed.

"It was bad, Sarn't Major," he admitted. "We lost half the boys when they went back to the base for more wagons and gear. Only Povey made it back and that was because the Regiment boys found him being chased by a pack of the bastards. It was Nevin." At the mention of the squadron sergeant major's nemesis, the big man scoffed in derisive anger before a smile crept across his bearded face and he recounted his last sight of Nevin—undead and trapped inside a shattered body halfway down a cliff—to the radio operator. Daniels' smile grew to mirror the SSM's.

"Good," he spat vehemently. "Less than the fucker deserved after what he did."

"That's not the half of it," Johnson went on. "Seems like our missing troop sergeant set himself up as lord of the hill and was running a bloody protection racket, which Nevin found himself a part of. It was those two bastards who wrecked our little winter headquarters with a Ferret."

Daniels nodded towards the two royal marines. "But they did for him?" Johnson sucked in a breath as he fought down the physical response the recalled emotions threatened to overwhelm him with.

"Yeah," he answered. "Saved our lives by being prepared to give up their own. It's bloody good to see them in one piece…"

"The others, the Mister Palmers and Mister Lloyd, went to Scotland with the SAS blokes and the helicopter crew." Johnson nodded along as Daniels gave him the details on that, listening as he described the brutal winter with too many mouths to feed and not anywhere near enough food to go around.

"Funny," Daniels said, "when they all left, there was more than enough food left. I think that's the way, you know? Small groups…"

"Probably right," Johnson agreed distractedly, his thoughts evidently going elsewhere.

"We going to talk about this or ignore it?" a voice asked from behind them. Daniels turned, hearing the hostility in the tone and misunderstanding it. He found himself facing the wild-bearded SBS sergeant whose abrupt manner he had taken as angry. Johnson, accustomed to his directness, answered him.

"Can't say it hasn't been on my mind," he agreed. "Charlie? Fetch me a map of the area."

The map was laid out flat with most of them huddling over it.

"We're here," Johnson said, indicating a small town outside Salisbury, "and the Screechers stopped coming round about here," he said, tapping the sharp tip of the bayonet he was using as a pointer on the map a few miles to the west.

"The house was back here," Daniels said as he tapped a finger on the map, "and AWACS reported the swarm down here." Again, another tap on the map some twenty miles to the south.

"All of them heading in the same directions…" Larsen said thoughtfully.

"So why do you think this has something to do with the Yanks?" Johnson asked Daniels.

"They were on to me straight away," he said, brow furrowed as though he was trying to find the source of the paranoia in his own words. "I'd been broadcasting regularly, seeing if I could get them to make contact back."

"Them?" Bufford asked gruffly.

"The Americans, mainly. There's at least one French frigate and some supply boats from other European countries. Our navy's there too, but they're not running the show, by any stretch of the imagination."

"And you know this how?" Johnson asked, suspecting he knew the answer but not comprehending that anyone had the patience he suspected Daniels possessed.

"Spent all winter going through every NATO frequency on the list," he answered flatly. His tone gave away the fact that it had been tedious work, to say the least.

"I got a response in the beginning," he went on, "and they wanted to know our location and strength and all that. Said they were cataloguing survivors for future extraction when the situation was under control. I asked what that looked like and they didn't say anything. Anyway, they took my emergency hailing channel and just stopped answering. Gave up after a while; I was more interested in finding yo—in finding any more of our boys who'd made it off the island and were at a loose end."

"And we appreciate it, Charlie," Johnson said, seeing through the young man's pretence. "But that still doesn't answer the question..." Daniels looked down for a moment, probably deciding on the best way to phrase his thoughts, before raising a single finger and wagging it slowly as he spoke; almost as though it were connected to his mind with an invisible string that teased out the conclusions from the mess of suspicion.

"They were already up in the air and had eyes on this swarm not long after it formed—my guess is that there were a lot of Screechers still hanging around after the island—and this is after months of the Yanks not making contact."

"So, you think they knew about the swarm *before* it happened?" Bufford grilled him, leaning in to see the man's face and gauge the answers his expression would give when his words would not.

"Something like that," Daniels answered, still frowning

pensively. "What if they weren't looking for a swarm specifically? What if they were monitoring the county to see if the
Screechers responded to something?"

"All you can eat buffet?" Bufford asked sarcastically. "One
of those raves for Screechers?"

"Weapons test?" Johnson asked, unable to keep the hint of
trepidation from his voice.

"What?" interrupted a small voice from behind them. They
turned or craned their necks to see Peter approaching, his older
sister following close behind almost uncertainly now that she
was no longer the protector of a frightened, naïve young boy.
"Some kind of thing that calls them all to one place?"

They all stared at him for a second before exchanging silent
looks with one another.

"Well, they were all heading in one direction, weren't
they?" Peter went on, not put off by their attention or fearing
adults like he used to. "And the faster ones were all at the front
with the slower ones behind, so that makes sense…"

"It does make good sense," Astrid said, having wandered in
to join the impromptu pow-wow. "Do any of you have an
alternative suggestion?"

"I get that we're all interested in this and all… *aargh*,"
Hampton said with a groan as he put his stiff leg up on a low
stack of car batteries. "But what difference does it make really?
So what if someone's fucking abou—"

"Ahem," Ellie cut in, having been the last to join the
group's congregation.

"—if someone's playing silly buggers with the Screechers
and sending them all to one place, as long as that place isn't
where we're going, I present the case that we accept that fact
and carry on about our business."

"What the sergeant's trying to say," Enfield said in his calm
and controlled voice, "is that we're wasting braincells on a
problem we don't need to deal with. Not yet, anyway."

"Exactly," Hampton agreed. "Thank you, Marine Enfield. Next time I need you to speak for me, I'll shove my hand up your jacksie and use you like a puppet." Hampton was joking, although only those who'd spent the last winter with them would know that the marines never needed to exchange harsh words or fall back on the rank structure to get anything done.

Enfield held Hampton's gaze, even when the sergeant waggled his eyebrows once and muttered, "all the way to the elbo—"

"But they were heading north," Kimberley asked. "Scotland's north. Who's to say they aren't all heading for where the others are?" Johnson opened his mouth to softly explain what she'd missed, hoping that nobody else beat him to it, as the thought of her feeling embarrassed or shamed in any way stung him. He *was* beaten to it, but in such a kindly and commanding way that he found his feelings move from protective fear to something resembling immense pride. And a healthy dose of protectiveness.

"Because we went east," Peter told her, beckoning her towards the table where he looked at the map for a moment, trying to get his bearings. He'd evidently been watching earlier as the soldiers had discussed it, because his eyes were lingering on roughly the correct grid squares before Johnson tapped a gnarled fingertip on an area to the east and slightly south of the place he'd identified as their current location. "Since the..." he swallowed and shook himself like a twitch overtook him. "Since the farm, we went this way. Corporal Daniels told Mister Johnson that they were going south to north to begin with, and the Screechers we saw were going east to west." With each directional description, the young boy ran his finger in the relevant compass point flow. Johnson saw Kimberley hiding a smile that he knew would not be out of amusement at the boy playing grown-up, but would be from genuine pride.

"So they're all heading to a single point which is west from here and northwest of where the others started off?" Kimberley asked him, having leapt far ahead of his explanation logically but taking a brief moment to let him develop his confidence.

"So, it would make sense that if we went north we'd see them heading southwest," Peter concluded.

"Only they've stopped," Johnson said. "About eight miles back. No obvious reason why."

"Could be the range of whatever's attracting them. Like blood in the ocean attracting sharks over a certain distance." A few faces grimaced at the analogy.

"That's Hollywood rubbish," Bufford chimed in, sounding almost bored as though he'd had the conversation before. "I've been in the water all over the world and sharks don't go into a frenzy just because someone cut themselves shaving or got stabbed multiple times." He added an unapologetic shrug which raised more questions than it dismissed about his history of underwater activities.

"Regardless," Johnson said, rolling up the map and raising his voice a little to change the subject and take charge. With more civilians and two more soldiers, he felt as though order needed to be restored. Him taking charge wasn't an arrogance —if anyone more capable who he trusted to guide their choices was there, he'd happily take instruction rather than give it—but things needed to be done.

"We've got maybe two days of water on our wagon. What about your lot, Charlie?" Daniels looked abashed as though he'd failed his sergeant major.

"A day. And food. We left in a bit of a hurry…"

"We were the same," Hampton added as he idly picked at a piece of hard skin by a fingernail with the small blade of a folding knife. He saw the attention his actions were receiving and mumbled a reassurance that he hadn't stabbed any Screechers with the knife before. "We had two canteens full and are down to half that now. We also didn't get any food on the way out the door on account of not having been there long and some cock-jockey of a civvy trying to tell us what to do."

Priorities needed addressing, and for once, Johnson missed how simple that small matter had been over winter. There had been weeks at a time when fresh snowfall could be collected and allowed to defrost, and that didn't take into account their comfortable home—before the village had been destroyed—that still enjoyed running water.

"First things first," Johnson said, looking to Enfield, who was already lifting the small rifle and bending to pick up the large, padded gun slip. He held out the smaller weapon to Peter, who hadn't held it since he helped the marine sight it for the first time so long, and yet *not* so long ago. Enfield headed for the steel staircase leading up to the half-mezzanine floor but Peter hesitated and glanced behind him. He smiled at his sister, who seemed to give a small nod of permission before he turned back to follow and swallowed down his recent memories of steel ladders and mezzanine floors.

Sentry duties covered, Johnson then recruited Bufford to lead a small recce and see what the immediate area offered. He would ordinarily have asked Astrid to go too, but she was displaying a post-adrenaline exhaustion that would make her reactions sloppy. Coupled with the fact that her weapon was filthy through firing and her ammunition count was incredibly low, he tactfully left her out of any plans.

"I'll come with you, Buffs," he said, picking up his gifted MP5 from the table and walking away. "Bill?" he shot back to Hampton, who smiled sweetly in comical response. "Square everything away in here and set about seeing if there's anything we can use?"

TWENTY-THREE

"*Yo*'s in place," Jackson said to Miller in a quiet voice. The team was looking forward to this fetch and carry mission, because it required the liberal application of bullets to the heads of infected monsters. They weren't bloodthirsty or callous, not overtly at any rate, but the SEALs were becoming frustrated by being in sight and smell—oh dear *God,* the smell —of the enemy. Miller nodded and took up position, wishing for the third time in the last half hour that he'd brought the Colt rifles from the ship's armoury in addition to the loadout he had opted for, to keep their noise profile as small as possible.

He reassured himself that these things didn't wear any kind of protection, and a five-five-six round went through a skull or a face just as well as the 9mm they carried did.

"Okay," he said, after checking the action on his weapon again, "light it up."

Flares were activated and tossed ahead of them, and the briefcase device—their new, non-human *yo*—was set a little way behind the cargo net. Even before the device was switched on, the flares revealed two shadowy figures shambling awkwardly, drunkenly down the hill towards them. They'd elected a new spot for trapping, as they had every time they'd been sent to the mainland for test subjects, only this time they would get to end the suffering of more than a few before they hopefully got what they came for.

"They're slow ones," Shepherd said in a low voice, asking permission with his tone.

"Okay," Miller told them, "nice and slow. Take your time and mark your shots."

It took a few seconds for the suppressed snapping sounds to start coughing from the barrels of their guns. The first wave of shambling enemy fell quickly, the sudden absence of their moans swelling those coming on from behind, much in the way bees would respond if you swatted one too close to their hive. It was like a pheromone was released when one died, which made the others coming behind even angrier, and when a commotion at the back of the slow advance cut the air with a spine-chilling shriek, they knew their target was in play.

"We got one incoming," Miller barked to his men. "Hernandez, you get ready to hit the gas. Daves, fall back and keep shooting. Jackson, Kid? Cover and move. Go!"

Slick and professional, the two Daves—Coleman and Shepherd—stopped firing and fell back, keeping their profiles low so as not to interfere with the shots of Jackson and Wilson. Miller was already behind the slung net, standing tall in plain view as the two moving men stopped, turned, and began lining up headshots at the advance so the other two could fall back under cover of their fire.

It was a natural thing to maintain their fire discipline and training, even if this enemy didn't fire back, because to learn something different now would mean to lose the years of muscle memory, of ingrained training, and would run the risk of them not knowing instinctively what to do when the shit hit the fan.

Too many of them were approaching now, so Miller gave

orders to start slowing them down instead of wasting time with a careful headshot which required a good aim.

"Kneecaps," he called out. "Drop the bastards and slow them down. We need the fast one to reach the net first." He raised his own weapon and began rattling bullets ahead of them in controlled three-round bursts, by flicking the safety catch down two notches.

To his left and right, he heard the rattle of near-continuous gunfire interspersed with his team calling out their magazine changes. Cycling his own weapon like he'd fired a hundred thousand rounds through one—which he guessed he probably had—he removed the pressure from the trigger as another shriek sounded close to the leading edge of the advance. It burst through the front rank and stopped, bone-thin arms held low and away from its skeletal body with fingers splayed out like claws, staring directly at him.

In the half-second it did that—the half second that felt like an excruciating minute to Miller—he stole a fleeting glance down at the case at his feet. He didn't have time to marvel at how effective the device was, and yet it was its very success that had contracted his life and the lives of his men into that tiny warzone on the edge of the icy cold water off the western coast of Scotland.

"Get rea—" he began saying, just as it crouched down and burst towards him, lumbering fast like an animal charging him head-on.

"Break, break, break!" Jackson yelled, telling all of them to get clear of the net. "Hernandez, now!"

The SEALs scattered, running and rolling and yelling as the sound of the outboard motor of their boat gunned it to maximum with no preamble. Miller moved, feeling that familiar bullet-time phenomenon as his mind and senses operated at a level that cycled information faster that the rest of him. His legs seemed to take an age to respond. When they did, his boots moved so slowly over the sandy shale of the beach that he might just as well have been in the water up to his waist. Slowly, desperately, he ran to his left as the rope connecting the left side of the net to the boat accelerating away to sea began to go taut and lift from the wet ground so fast that it left the water soaked into its fibres behind. He threw himself over it, sailing through the dark, cold air at waist height just as the shriek off to his right sounded both impossibly close and impossibly loud.

He hit the wet sand with a thud and spun to bring his weapon up. All around him, the gunfire had started again as he stared at the living, shrieking whirlwind of limbs that was the faster one fighting against the heavy, wet fibres of the net trapping it.

"We need to get the fuck outta here, Miller!" Jackson barked at him as he stopped firing long enough to click in a replacement magazine and charge the weapon. "Last mag!" he added.

Miller snapped out of it, jumping up and raising his weapon once more to empty the magazine in bursts aimed at head height into the ranks of the infected backlit by the red flare, still advancing on them. They retreated back towards the water before Miller spun and jogged back towards the thrashing net, calling for the others to cover him. Reaching down for the handle of the case that was just a little too effective at riling up the infected, a bony hand with broken and ragged fingernails shot out of a gap in the net to claw at his left calf muscle. Even through the thick trouser leg, he felt the sharpness of the attempt to drag him into the snapping teeth he could hear but not see. He tugged his leg away hard, hearing a snap that could easily have been bone, and reached down again for the case.

The thing trapped inside reared up on its knees and lunged. Miller reacted on instinct, applying force with the nearest weapon on his body to the closest target on his enemy.

His right knee crunched cruelly into the face of his attacker in the dying light and freed him to scramble away. The team, still firing and moving, splashed into the black water where Hernandez had brought their small boat back in to collect them, before opening up the throttle again and dragging the writhing bundle out to sea.

———

Professor Grewal waited eagerly, fighting the urge to administer doses of serum to the remaining three test subjects to satisfy his anxiety that it would randomly be ineffective against them.

Every test conducted so far, through every means of exposure, had resulted in the catastrophic haemorrhaging of the infected subject and resulted in death. Or at least permanent death.

He paced, unable to stay still with nervous anticipation of what the unsmiling, bearded soldiers were bringing back. They had been deployed specifically to bring back one of the faster ones, and *only* one of the faster ones. They seemed pleased to be given the green light to start executing the infected people, and the report via radio that they had succeeded caused the makeshift lab to erupt in fist-clenching, high-fiving celebration.

The wait for them to return had been agonising, and more than a few false starts had deflated the excitement when people claimed to have heard a boat engine. The last false alarm had been a female lab technician who pointed inland with her claim, and her beratement was still ongoing when a voice called out from the seaward entrance to the large outbuilding.

"Here's your goddamned fast one, asshole," Miller snarled, dropping the rope he was holding, with the rest of his team following suit to leave a soaked, writhing, shrieking bundle.

Grewal had no time to respond to their arrival or the insult as Yates barked orders at his team to suit up and secure the subject.

Subject, Grewal scoffed to himself internally. *It's much easier to call them that than acknowledge what they really are.*

This one had been a young woman. Tall and probably thin to begin with, given that the remnants of clothing she wore didn't seem baggy on her. It was obvious to anyone who had observed the behaviour of the infected for any amount of time that she was different; her movements were faster, sharper, and her blind eyes above a viciously broken nose that still oozed dark gore zeroed in with a terrifying speed and accuracy on anyone who spoke.

In spite of Yates' strict instructions, his team struggled to loop the thick wires on poles over the matted strands of lank hair and had hit her in the skull hard enough to knock off chunks of grey skin and expose the bone beneath.

"Be careful of the head, we need her alive!" Chambers shouted at them, earning a salvo of savage looks which all spoke of an invitation to pick up a pole and show them all how it was done. He got the message loud and clear but still flinched every time the skull was impacted. Grewal ignored the 'alive' part of his warning and prepared a dose of serum in the same aerosol dispenser he'd used the first time.

A shout of alarm behind him made him spin. No words reached his ears; only the guttural yell of primal fear as though a Neanderthal was being attacked by a predator.

Grewal decided that what he could see actually matched that description perfectly, as the subject had thrown off one of her captors and grabbed the heavy pole attached to her neck to swing it around savagely. Yates was standing directly in front of her—*it*—and ducked to save himself but ultimately doomed the soldier on the other side, who took the full ballistic force of the swinging pole in the side of the head to be knocked out.

Untethered on both flanks, the thing snapped its gaze to lock onto Yates and advanced on him, forcing him backwards. It writhed and thrashed as it moved, like a feral cat wearing a collar, until the force of its efforts dislodged the coil of wire from around its neck.

Grewal, standing fifteen feet away from the unshackled monstrosity, froze and let out the slightest involuntary whimper of terror.

Yates, however, didn't freeze. He let the pole drop in his left hand as his right instinctively reached for the heavy forty-five, realising with crippling panic that in his haste to get a suit on, he'd left the weapon holstered under the thick, baggy rubber suit where it was useless to him. Looking back up to his attacker in time to see her mouth open wide enough to rend a fresh tear in the mottled grey skin of her cheek and fighting down the urge to coat the inside of his protective visor with the MRE he'd recently consumed cold, he did the only thing he could and brought the pole up desperately to defend himself.

The thing bit down at him, teeth breaking on the rough surface of the pole's grip as the full bite force was deployed without the breaker fuse of pain feedback. Yates was treated to an up-close, an *extremely* up-close, view of two teeth being forced out of the dark flesh of a gum and drop onto his visor. He screamed. Bellowing incoherent rage and fear, the sound formed an ululating, keening war cry as he pushed back on the pole with every ounce of strength he possessed.

A crack sounded. Not a clear, sharp snap like the clean breaking of a bone, but the sinewy crunch of something being forced out of joint.

None of them knew that Miller's knee had come close to breaking the neck cleanly and had driven shards of shattered nose into the brain. It had done damage that would have been irreversible, had she still been fully alive. The pain such an injury would have caused would have been crippling and debilitating, but without that circuit feeding back to the brain to cease all activity, the ruined body carried on attacking until the force exerted on the spinal injury was too much and the joint gave way.

The broken neck alone wouldn't have been enough to kill the creature, not fully, but the movement shifted those shards of bone to puncture that part of the brain that drove the infected to keep fighting. With a last limp expulsion of dark gore from the mouth, she slid off Yates to land face down amid shouts of alarm. Two men of the SEAL team burst back in, weapons up and eyes scanning until they took in the scene and advanced on the still body of the thing they had gone through so much to capture. Yates was hauled to his feet and had multiple weapons trained on him. He was so dazed that he didn't even spit back an insult when ordered to strip off the suit and prove he wasn't bitten. When they were satisfied he wasn't infected, the atmosphere in the room turned from fear and shock to anger.

Arguments raged around Yates as he sat with his face in his hands and took a series of long, deep breaths. The SEALs were unhappy that they would have to go back out, an understatement to end all understatements.

The scientists were unhappy in their turn that Yates had killed the one test subject they needed to give the green light to the operation. Yates reached a shaking hand down to his right hip to run his fingers over the wood inlay of the gun's grip, reassuring himself that it was still there and telling himself that he would never be out of reach of it until they were off that cursed island.

Loitering in the shadows, a man in a heavy black coat sighed and slipped away. Successful confirmation test or not, Fisher would damn well give that green light to start deploying the serum, because the timeframe he had been granted had almost expired. He didn't see their delays as relevant or in any way likely to affect the overall mission.

Fisher smiled to himself in reassurance as he climbed back inside the vehicle to be driven back to the CIA base of operations, telling himself that he'd soon be settling into his new office as a section chief, if it all went as well as he hoped it would.

TWENTY-FOUR

Fisher was once again picked up by helicopter and ferried back to the floating fortress out in the eastern edge of the Atlantic. It was a great expense to go to, only to have a single spectator involved, but he hoped it was an indication of how his stock was rising.

In truth, Jacobs wanted him there ready to be sent back to the US, should anything go wrong. If it did then Fisher, as the sacrificial lamb, wouldn't be afforded time to find a replacement for his own neck on the chopping block.

Fisher strode in, confidence exuding from his body like a scent, nodded greetings to the faces he recognised and shook hands briefly with Jacobs.

"Time on target?" he asked the senior man.

"A little under twenty mikes," Jacobs told him, gesturing behind them at the coffee pot and paper cups. Fisher didn't want a coffee but poured himself one anyway, in case a refusal would be seen as nervousness. Twenty minutes was a long time to wait when your career aspirations were riding on the outcome of what was about to happen.

"Sir," a uniformed technician called out. Fisher stood

upright from where he had been leaning against a wall, incorrectly thinking that he was being called over, but hesitated when Jacobs answered and stepped up to the console. "Gunship approaching target area."

"Put the channel on," Jacobs instructed, leaning back and producing a packet of cigarettes to add to the already thick, smoky atmosphere in the darkened room. Fisher stepped forward, listening intently to the sounds coming from the speaker beside the radio and fighting to make out the words over the continuous droning hum and whine of the engines.

"Affirmative, Zeus-one-one. Conduct reconnaissance circuit and report," the speaker announced.

"Acknowledged," came the reply from the pilot as the background noise shifted almost imperceptibly. Hundreds of miles away, in the dark skies over a city teeming with inexplicably agitated undead, a large cargo plane similar to the one which had brought Fisher to Scotland banked forty degrees to its left and began flying a long, seemingly lazy loop of the area.

Their infrared detection package, state of the art in any of the world's former militaries, was rendered useless as the massed bodies gave off no heat to identify them as bright white outlines in a sea of abandoned black and grey. They adjusted the contrast of their imaging displays, until the black outlines of human figures could be made out at the edges of the densely packed crowd.

"Jesus 'aitch…" one of the crew muttered as he finally understood what the enormous mound was in an open area adjacent to the wide river. The writhing pyramid of dead meat rose from ground level like a molehill, only instead of fresh earth, it was the animated bodies of the former inhabitants of the UK.

"Zeus-one-one. Confirm concentration of infected, Control. Advise are we cleared to engage, over?"

"Zeus-one-one, Control," came back the clipped tones of

the operator in the control room on board the carrier. "Confirm you are cleared to engage. Repeat, clear to engage."

The crew of the AC-130 went to work. The pilot kept the steady banking manoeuvre at the same angle to maintain the even platform for the gunners to do their gruesome work.

Their commands were short and clipped, their drills slick and well-practised as they poured round after 40mm round screaming down through the night sky, to detonate in violent air bursts and fill the air with the weaponised aerosol serum.

Almost immediately, the mound of infected piled high over the device, which was humming and radiating its almost-silent rallying call out for miles in every direction, began to fall away. A minute after their brutal aerial bombardment began, a hundred and twenty small bombs had exploded just above ground level. The infected—the zombies—fell in uncomprehending physical failure, as their sallow skin blackened from every cell in the remains of their broken bodies, as the minute tissue walls degraded, the fluids left inside their bodies haemorrhaged with catastrophic results.

As the serum spread through the massed crowd, they began to fall and lie on the ground to twitch and leak black gore into the concrete, moving for the last time. When the treated ammunition was spent, the crew switched to their standard load and began destroying everything outside the test zone, paying careful attention to and recording the most effective means of destruction.

The armed cargo plane stayed on station for almost an hour, pouring every piece of serum-treated and standard munition they carried into anything moving. With a brief radio report, the pilot levelled out the long wings of the aircraft and headed south to rendezvous with their mid-air refuelling appointment and back to Aeroporto de Gran Canaria.

"Rewind the tapes," the crew chief said into their intercom. "There'll be a jet standing by to take it off our hands."

———

Before they had landed, another aircraft had taken off to head over Britain at high altitude. The crew had flown that same route so often that it was second nature to them. But this time, their brief sent in the night gave them specific co-ordinates to concentrate on, instead of a general patrol searching for infected activity.

Their last mission had sent them to the same area, and their discussions went on, back and forth for hours as they flew, debating why they had been sent to that specific location again. The only person on board not to involve himself in the speculation was the overall mission commander, a lieutenant colonel. The idle chatter died down and the crew lapsed into relative silence, until the pilot's voice broke the stillness in their earphones.

"Approaching target co-ordinates," he said, receiving no reply but knowing that the crew would be readying to carry out their individual tasks.

"Confirmed infected singularity still occupying the city," one of the men with his eyes pressed into the viewfinder reported. "Estimate numbers to be… hold the phone… hold the goddamned phone!"

"What is it?" another muffled voice asked over the intercom.

"That answers the question," the man staring down through the strong magnification told them. "Something… something *killed* all of them."

"Repeat that," growled the voice of the mission commander.

"Confirm no movement, repeat no movement in any of the infected," the operator, a lieutenant, replied. "They appear…"

"Take your time," the mission commander said slowly,

though not to be misinterpreted as kindly, "and give me a report."

"Sir, they appear to have… melted, or something."

The mission commander closed his eyes and relaxed. He knew without looking through the scope or viewing the footage from far below them that the serum had been deployed and the results had been everything they had hoped for.

"Confirm no movement of infected?" he asked, waiting a handful of seconds for a response.

"Sir, I'm getting some residual movement but… but nothing I can see for certain. I see none of them still alive. Or whatever it is they are."

The mission commander switched his headset over to a radio channel only he was tuned to, hailing the same small command and information centre in the bowels of a US navy aircraft carrier. He hailed them with their callsign and waited for the response.

"Confirm mission successful," he said clearly. "I repeat, mission was successful. Some residual movement at ground level but confirmed deaths of infected are believed to be as close to one hundred percent as possible."

He listened to the response, given with whoops and the sounds of enthusiastic backslapping in the background, then ordered the flight crew to fly a pattern over the target site for a full video to be taken, and to head back home.

TWENTY-FIVE

In typical fashion, the Sultan broke down after two days. The Warrior pushed ahead of it to be able to sweep a large section of their perimeter, should they be threatened by any Screechers, as the other armed members of their small group fanned out with their eyes alert and their personal weapons made ready.

"How is it, Charlie?" Johnson called out from the commander's hatch of the Warrior.

"Fucked!" came the terse reply. "Gearbox is shot. We can crawl in first or stall in sixth with fuck all in between. Second line job at least. Got a REME FMA in your pocket?" Johnson ignored the rhetorical question.

Hampton, up on the top of the stranded tracked vehicle with both hands on the big GPMG, huffed in annoyance. They stripped everything they could from the wagon, down to the last bit of diesel they could siphon out, using the length of yellow rubber garden hose to fill the jerry cans they'd decanted into the Warrior's fuel tank. Hampton, remaining in place behind the machine gun until the job was done, unclipped it from the pintle mount and handed it down to Enfield who had, in turn, made his own small rifle safe and handed it to Peter to hold.

The boy swelled with pride as he turned outwards to keep a watchful eye on their surroundings, eager to demonstrate that he didn't negligently point the barrel at any of their own people, with all the enthusiasm of a child seeking praise. His sister, loitering near the open rear section of the Warrior that would become a very cramped and uncomfortable place in the near future, watched him with a curious expression on her face.

"Let's get this buffet moving then, *aah–shit!*" Hampton cursed as his damaged knee took the shockwave of him jumping back down to the roadway. He hobbled for a few paces, muttering more colourful phrases to himself like Popeye reciting an angry monologue, and shot a narrow-eyed look at the girl trying not to smile at his misfortune.

With a forlorn last look at the uncomfortable metal box that had been his only permanent residence since everything went to hell, Charlie Daniels climbed into the driver's section of the much newer metal box, this new home making him feel as capricious as the cat, who had been corralled into a more permanent mobile detention centre than the taped-up cardboard box it had previously been trapped in.

He was grateful for once that the men he was slightly envious of and whom he held in very high regard didn't possess his skills. Johnson took up his appropriate role in the commander's spot with Bufford at his side, who had already been partly instructed in the use of the Warrior's weapons systems, and the rear section was packed with people and equipment.

Their 'shopping' yielded perhaps three days' supplies for them, which meant that they would be stopping for another supply run within two days. Johnson reckoned that they had maybe four hundred miles of range. He was guessing from what he could recall, as he hadn't had much in the way of familiarisation with the vehicle and the one he had played with at the proving grounds had admittedly been a test chassis. What they found, however, was that their progress was often halted by blocked roads and their average speed suffered massively as a result.

"Corporal Daniels," Johnson asked conversationally as they slowed to approach yet another blockage of rusting vehicles.

"Sarn't Major?"

"Remind me why we're going around cars and not over them?"

"Erm…"

"Bugger me, Charlie," Johnson sighed. "I know it's a Volvo but we *are* driving a sodding tank, Son."

Johnson couldn't see the look on his corporal's face in response to his words. Why it hadn't dawned on Daniels to be more bullish with their progress until then was a mystery, but receiving such an epiphany through the medium of permission caused a smile to slowly creep across his face.

"Hold on tight," he warned over the vehicle intercom. "Bit of turbulence ahead…"

He went slowly, running one side of the tracks over the front of the large estate vehicle, then tipped them over to one side until the other tracks crunched over a smaller car which flattened with much greater ease. They travelled that way for hours on end until the occupants of the cramped rear section could take no more discomfort and they found somewhere appropriate to stop.

Three days went by like that, each day sapping their strength and morale until Johnson was pulled aside by Hampton when they had stopped to rest.

"We need to dig in for a day at least," he said. "Everyone needs some rest and the supplies are dwindling." Johnson nodded, appreciating the straight talking approach from a man he suspected was even less inclined towards bullshit than Johnson was himself.

"Town ahead," he told the marine sergeant and nodded in a general direction to their front. "We'll find somewhere and range out again for food and water." Hampton nodded back, less inclined to waste his breath on words than many people, and went back to where the others were stretching their legs and their backs and generally blinking at the alien display of sunlight, after being cooped up inside the back of the Warrior for days.

Of Peter, Johnson had seen less than usual as he was relegated to the rear section and had his sister's undivided attention. She fussed over him, but Peter seemed oddly resistant to her. Amber had gone the other way, it seemed, and had understandably regressed to the extent that her mother was unable to put her down without the girl bursting into panicked tears and making an uncharacteristic amount of noise. Johnson felt sorry for her, not because of the fear and loss they had all experienced, but for the fact that she couldn't understand what was happening. Being so young, she had understood that her mother was gone—lost to her—but now that she had inexplicably come back, the girl had become overwhelmed by everything. He didn't blame her, simply felt a sadness that he could do nothing to salve.

He stayed on watch in spite of the tiredness he felt behind his eyes after hours of peering intently through the observation window in the Warrior, and noticed how the tall, quiet marine had found himself a piece of high ground to occupy and was scanning the horizon with his weapon. Johnson had thought both men lost, sure that they had died in defence of the village they had been living in, and that he—*they*—owed their lives to the two men. But then he found out so unexpectedly that they had survived, and this whole experience made him understand a little better how Amber must be feeling now.

They had travelled north west, bypassing Birmingham and the densely packed sprawling suburbs that all major cities sprouted outwards from their cores like weeds, continuing straight on past Stoke-On-Trent and went to ground in a large industrial unit a day's drive north west, near the banks of a wide river.

Travel weary, if not downright bedraggled, they spilled from the vehicle like they'd crashed and were trying to walk off their minor injuries. The area they had stopped in was open enough that there was little to no threat of any immediate attack, but that didn't prevent them from having their weapons ready, even if their cramped-up bodies didn't move with the slick alacrity they could demonstrate on better days.

"Buffs?" Johnson said quietly. The SBS man turned to look at him, silently following the direction of his outstretched hand with his eyes until he saw the side of the building he was pointing at. He looked back to Johnson, seeing him first point to himself then snake his hand around in an exaggerated movement to the left to signify that they would meet around the back. Johnson looked back towards the others, to see Hampton settling himself into a position of relative comfort near the driver's hatch on the lower hull of the Warrior, just as Enfield adopted a position of overwatch with his small rifle, his backside nestled on the cold armour of the turret. Hampton gave him a nod, signalling that they had this area covered and that the two men could do what they needed to.

Johnson moved, knowing after so long together that Bufford would already be ahead of him as his drills were slicker and more intense than his own. He saw no competition between them, just a maturity and an understanding that his professional soldiering had taken him down a different path. They all had their roles to play in the current game plan—or at least what had been the plan for Her Majesty's armed forces before the world turned upside down—and that game plan was transitioning from all-out nuclear war with the Soviet Union to a somewhat sandier climate. Bufford's role would be to insert himself into enemy territory, most likely by water, but he was also capable of dropping by parachute, walking or driving over any terrain; the aim being either to destroy something vital to the enemy, or to feed back intelligence and targeting information.

Astrid Larsen, as innocent as she looked to the untrained eye, was a hardened woman whose role would be to insert herself far behind enemy lines, as Bufford would, only she was also able to blend in as a native of their enemy's motherland and would be trained to sneak in and collapse local infrastructure; transport, power and communications. Everything about the woman made Johnson and the others question why their own armed forces still refused to allow women to conduct frontline fighting roles.

Johnson, along with Daniels for that matter, was the one who could use his light and mobile armoured vehicles to lure the T-55s of the USSR into chasing them down, only to find themselves swamped by the combined firepower of the rest of the squadron. It was Johnson who had been trained to set such an ambush; to look for the perfect geography and encourage the men to be patient until that trap could be sprung.

What he wasn't, and he knew this instinctively, was a Special Forces operator.

He made more noise than was strictly acceptable, given their circumstances, as he pushed through the overgrown foliage pressing up against the building, and to add insult to injury, he had only covered a third of the circumference before Bufford called out softly from his front to minimise the risk of getting shot over a simple misunderstanding.

"Anything your side?" Johnson murmured as Bufford appeared through the leaves.

"Side door on the far side. Doesn't look like it's been

opened for years. You?"

"Nothing. Try the side door or move to the next building?"

"Next building," Bufford said. "I don't much like the alter-native exit strategy for this one, if you catch my drift." Johnson did. One of the cardinal rules for surviving the death of the world by flesh-eating monstrosities was never to paint yourself into a corner.

They moved to the adjacent building, exchanging some brief hand signals with the two royal marines before they ducked out of sight once more. Johnson worked thoroughly, careful not to make too much noise and finding the going easier than the previous building's exterior had been to navi-gate. It took him precious seconds to understand why, until his brain caught up with his instincts and he noticed small tell-tale signs of human presence. He froze, not yet sure if that human presence was alive or dead. Tightening the grip on his weapon, he pressed on, turning the corner after a quick glance around it showed Bufford on one knee covering the side door to the unit. He joined him, seeing the intensity in the man's eyes as he pointed to the apex of the roof above them, indicating the three small windmills stuck to the structure, with wires snaking down to the door they knelt beside. Bufford's eyebrows went up as if asking for Johnson's opinion. Johnson shrugged, reaching up with his left hand to touch the door handle and gently pull the handle down. It gave, creaking only slightly as the door opened a crack. Bufford readied himself, nodding to Johnson to signify that he was ready.

The door was wrenched open and they burst inside, guns up and fingers ready to move onto triggers, with no idea what they expected to find.

"Fucking *hell!*" Bufford swore. Johnson glanced over his left shoulder to where the SBS man had moved to. In terms of expectations, Johnson wouldn't have been surprised to find a ravenous horde of undead. Wouldn't have been shocked to find other living humans pointing weapons at them. He was, however, very surprised to see neat rows of dark soil in troughs with lengths of hosepipe running along them, jury-rigged lamps hanging above them and green plants sprouting upwards to creep towards the source of the light and heat along intricate networks of wire and sticks.

Johnson lowered his weapon, reaching out with his left hand to grasp the most unlikely of items and one that he realised he had given up all hope of ever seeing again.

Pulling gently as his fingers squeezed, the vine pulled with him until the ripe tomato popped off to shake the whole row. He held it up in front of his face, turning it around and inspecting it like it was a chunk of moon rock. He focused his eyes on the incredulous face of Bufford behind the juicy item and spun slowly on the spot to take in the multiple rows of dirt-filled troughs all sprouting different forms of sustenance. He saw potatoes and carrots to accompany the two rows of tomatoes, dreaming of adding a couple of rabbits and some salt and pepper to it.

Then the truth dawned on him. He was trespassing on some other survivor's farm, stealing their supplies and threatening their livelihood. A glance at his friend told him that the other man knew it too. A noise from behind them made them both turn and raise their weapons; Johnson standing tall and Bufford dropping to one knee, to train their weapons on a tall, muscled black man with a tangle of dark beard and wide, wild eyes staring at them over a tight-lipped mouth and who was seething with anger. His right hand wasn't empty, although his heavy metal spike was held low, which somehow made both him and the weapon more menacing, like he knew how to use it and was so confident that he didn't need to threaten them.

"Calm down, JP," a strong Liverpudlian male voice echoed around the inside of the empty factory unit. "I'm pretty sure they aren't here to pinch our carrots."

TWENTY-SIX

"You did what?" Professor Grewal shouted, slamming down the clipboard he was holding so hard that it bounced back up off the desk.

"Keep your hair on, Doc," Fisher replied so casually that the scientist was ready to start throwing punches in an attempt to knock the reckless stupidity out of him. "The test was a complete success. Every one of them dead. You should be proud of your achieveme—"

"Do they teach you this kind of ignorance in the CIA or simply recruit people who naturally possess it?" Fisher's face dropped the false smile it was maintaining.

"You were given a job to do. You did it. Don't think for a second that this was a pet project of yours, that you had any control over the timeli—"

"They just recruit the arrogance then," Grewal snarled with angry sarcasm, "understood." Fisher took a step towards him and swelled up his size, but Grewal matched his movements and bested him in both height and the intensity of his anger.

"You deployed an untested serum on thousands—*hundreds*

of thousands—of infected subjects with no idea what it would do to them. That kind of stupidity is… is…" he shook his hands beside his ears as there simply wasn't a word in the English language strong enough to accurately describe what they had done.

"It *has* been tested," Fisher shot back with a retreating step. "You tested it here and it was successful in one hundred percent of the trials. You want more time to repeat that test? You want to be responsible for *more* deaths when we could be wiping out these assholes with the serum we *know* works?"

"It's *unfathomable*. We *don't* know it works," Grewal answered him angrily, "that's the whole point." Fisher's face screwed up in total incomprehension. Grewal looked fit to burst, like a kettle boiling water with no steam vent. Seeing this, professor Chambers stepped in between the two men.

"I believe we were quite clear," he explained. "We needed to test the serum on one of the anomalous infected before we could guarantee with any kind of certainty that it would work fully."

"What are you saying?" Fisher asked, doubt infecting him like the viruses they were discussing could so easily. Chambers rubbed tiredly at his face, turning to see if Grewal wanted to jump back into the conversation, but only seeing him walking away and kicking the large plastic boxes that had contained their lab equipment. He sighed and looked back at the CIA man.

"Viruses produce different responses based on the physical response of the host. That's where you get unexplained strains of immunity to certain illnesses." He paused to check if the slightly shocked agent was keeping up. "The reports—*confirmed* reports— tell us of a faster type of infected which retains a significant portion of motor function and some higher cognitive ability. This means that the initial infection causes a low-percentage response which, unfortunately for us, actually increases their lethality."

"In English, Doc," Fisher said as he had done so long ago when the current events were little more than a spark of an idea.

"Simply put, Agent Fisher, the virus has already created mutations. The genetic makeup of those infected who are… *different*, could have as yet unknown side-effects when combined with the serum."

It finally dawned on Fisher. "Why the hell didn't you test it on one of them?" he half yelled.

"Because you shot your bloody load early and went to war before we said it was ready," Grewal hissed through his teeth as he returned to the conversation. "And I can only hope for your sake that it kills them just the same as it does the others."

Fisher paced back and forth for a few seconds, evidently deep in thought.

"Okay," he said finally, "here's how we're going to play it. We get one of the faster ones back here and test it right away."

"And if it doesn't work?" Chambers asked.

"Then we update the threat package that a tiny percentage of the infected are still in play. We'll have to go in with ground teams—whole armies—if we want to take the UK back."

"Ahem," said a voice in mimicry of clearing the throat. Grewal turned to see Staff Sergeant Yates stepping towards them. "I think you're kinda missing the point; these faster ones aren't just a bit quicker on their feet than your average schmuck. They *think*. They actually *hunt* us, like we're prey. That updated threat assessment better be accurate if you don't want more lives at risk."

"It doesn't matter, anyway," Grewal interrupted before Fisher could respond. "It'll take weeks for them to corral the remaining infected into one place and deploy the serum again.

I imagine it'll also take a while to manufacture the sonic devices and create more of the serum."

All eyes turned to Fisher, who had the decency to look embarrassed.

"Yeah, that's, uh… that's not exactly *accurate*."

"What are you saying?" Yates asked.

"I'm saying the planes are already flying the devices in and the serum's loaded into munitions. They're ready to rock."

"Unless we can tell them otherwise," Chambers said, trying to get the conversation back on track.

"Sure," Fisher agreed, silently telling himself that there was no way he would put his neck on the line to pull the plug on a billion-dollar operation, based on a few infected with the magical ability to jog and open a door surviving the fire. Surely the military would be capable of mopping up a few grasshoppers when they got there?

"Good," Chambers said, raising his voice to encompass the whole makeshift lab and get everyone back to work. "In the meantime, we'll prep for the arrival of the anomalous infected."

"Assuming we *do* get one and it survives long enough to be injected with serum," Grewal added with a fleeting, sideways glance at the staff sergeant.

TWENTY-SEVEN

Two agonising hours later, a wet and angry SEAL team returned. They dragged behind them the same cargo net with a thrashing, shrieking detainee trapped inside and Miller's words to them before the net was unfurled made it clear that triggers would be pulled if they screwed up a second time. He glowered at everyone in the room before spinning on his wet boot heel and ordering his men back to secure the boat.

Yates took control, instructing everyone to either suit up and get a pole or else get the hell off his lab floor. The once-living occupant of the sea-soaked net was dragged into the mouth of the nearest open cage door and locked inside, for the net to be teased off the subject with difficulty until a bony limb broke free and everyone jumped backwards with shouts of fear and alarm.

It thrashed its way out of the bonds, wailing and shrieking as though made even angrier by the kidnapping and the warm bodies so close to it, yet at the same time finding the way to them blocked by steel mesh. It rammed itself into the metal barrier over and over again, gouging chunks of flesh from its body and losing a front tooth with a snap as it tried to bite its way through.

"We need tissue samples," Chambers said loudly, looking around and waiting for a volunteer to present themselves. Normally this would be a simple thing; approach the cage door and allow the subject to reach out with a hand through the gap, then grab the limb and cut away some cold flesh. Yates turned his head in an exaggerated move left and right to see that none of them—neither the scientists nor his own people— had the balls to get the job done.

He stepped up, no doubt uttering choice opinions inside his protective visor, and waited for the arm to come out of the aperture towards him. It did, striking like a viper as he grabbed the wrist hard. Just as he was about to shout for someone to take the sample, he found himself dragged clean off his feet to impact the cage, the unbelievable strength of the disgusting creature taking him by surprise.

It was superhuman. Incomprehensible how someone not overtly muscled like a prize-winning bodybuilder could exert such brute force, and for the second time in his life, Staff Sergeant Yates came face to face with one of the faster ones, with nothing but desperation and crippling fear driving him to escape.

Hands pulled at him, making him become the rope in a panicked game of tug of war, as the savage, snarling creature threatened to drag him back towards it and pull his whole body through the small hole if it could. Yates roared incoherently with rage as his gloved right hand found the grip of his pistol.

He ignored the screams of protest, of fear that he would kill another precious test subject and send them all back to square one, because he knew what he planned wouldn't leave the thing double-dead, but would free him and obtain the tissue samples in one unorthodox move.

He pressed the barrel of the forty-five-calibre pistol against the slender forearm of the thing, angling it upwards as he braced his body with every ounce of remaining strength and leaned away before pulling the trigger three times.

The sound of the gun going off in close quarters amid the pack of bodies was deafening; not just the sound of the three small explosions but the concussive wave of pressure that accompanied each pull of the trigger.

The flesh burned where the muzzle flashes had scorched it, but the fat bullets punched their way through flesh, bone and sinew to make the grip fail. Yates fell away, conscious to keep a firm grip on the wrist of the hand still digging its nails into the thick rubber of his suit. He tried to ignore the image of the grey skin stretching before it tore away to leave him lying on his back, holding the violently severed hand.

"Stand back," Grewal shouted, his command muffled by the protective suit. "Back!" They moved aside as he stepped close, an aerosol machine held in both hands, looking like an oversized vintage perfume dispenser.

He pumped it, covering the grotesque face of the creature with a fine mist that it aspirated simply through the effort of shrieking and trying to get to so many fresh victims. It gave no reaction at first, but that was to be expected as the other, non-anomalous infected didn't exactly fall down choking and clutching their throats like comedy villains on the big screen.

It faltered, staggering slightly as though drunk, and blinked its milky eyes at them.

"Here's your goddamned tissue sample," Yates gasped as he stood, holding out the dead hand for Chambers to take, before walking off unsteadily.

The anomalous infected, the thing they had heard being called a Leader or *Lima* in the intelligence reports, blinked its eyelids again and slumped back in the cage to land heavily against the cargo net, where it raised the ruined, ragged stump of its left forearm to inspect it.

A low hiss sounded; not like the hiss they emitted before they shrieked the air back out so hideously, but a noise that sounded far more pensive than they had ever heard one of them make.

Chambers crouched down to meet the creature's eye level, pulling off the large hood of his suit, despite the warnings from others.

"Look at the eyes," he said, lifting a tentative finger towards the sitting subject. They did. The eyes, the milky orbs from their infected dreams that they'd expected to see, were fading, allowing a dark iris colour to return and lend the hideous beast an air of humanity.

Before any elation could spread, it exhibited a kind of seizure and shuddered as if in agony or racked by a sudden bout of epilepsy. It stopped, going still as they all stood and stared, before it relaxed finally to be at peace. Chambers stayed crouched down, still staring at the face, which had regained a hint of emotion before it went slack.

"Dick?" Grewal said gently from beside and above him. Chambers looked up at him, seeing him offer a sterile steel tray to take the severed hand he was still clutching like a prized possession. Chambers held it out for him, dropping the hand just as the tray fell away to clatter onto the hard ground. Time moved slowly for him, while the others in the room seemed to move fast to throw their bodies away from him. Then he turned his head back to face the cage.

Those eyes, no longer milky but bloodshot white with a jet black iris, were wide open and fixed on him. The creature flew forwards, its remaining hand shooting out of the gap with perfect accuracy to grab him by the sleeve, hauling him forwards. Chambers screamed. He screamed with the terror of what was happening, even if he didn't fully understand it, and he screamed with the pain of his index finger being bitten clean off between the first and second knuckles with a bite force the rational part of his brain couldn't believe belonged to a human body.

A gunshot erupted again, loud and close, and Chambers scrambled away from the cage, clamping his left hand hard around his right wrist, with speckles of dark gore patterned over his face. He blinked it away but felt the sting of the sticky fluid on his eyeball as strong hands hauled him upwards.

A tourniquet was lashed around his right forearm and twisted to be painfully tight as voices fought for space in his brain. One shushed him, telling him in an American accent that everything was going to be okay. Another screamed repeatedly in a deep voice, which only paused briefly for the man making the awful sound to refill his lungs and start again.

"Too late," a gruff voice said over him. "It's all over his face. Can't guarantee there's no infection." He recognised the army sergeant's harsh tone and connected it with the sound of a gun's hammer being cocked.

"No," another voice—Grewal's voice—snapped. "Wait, please."

Grewal ran to the sample fridge, knocking aside a panicked lab assistant in his desperate haste to fetch a fresh vial of serum. Opting for the direct application method, he stabbed a syringe into the rubber section in the lid and tipped it up to draw out an unmeasured amount of the clear fluid before squeezing the plunger to force the air from it. Not bothering to find a vein, he jabbed it hard into Chambers' shoulder and depressed the plunger to fill the muscle with the cold liquid.

"It's his only chance," Grewal's voice drifted to him as the fever began to burn him up faster than he expected.

Professor Richard Chambers had precisely zero percent chance of surviving from the moment the infected thing bit into his flesh. The metaphysical changes alone that the subject had undergone in a matter of seconds were unprecedented, and now with its head blown half off, it would never reveal the secrets of what made it especially lethal to living humans.

Chambers, by the cruellest twist of fate, was also one of those few people, one of the tiny percentage of human beings that possessed a certain genetic trait which combined with the virus in a way that left them just as violent and ravenous, but still in possession of enough cognitive ability as to be truly, horrifyingly dangerous.

The addition of the serum to his body before he died simply accelerated the process and bonded with the original virus to create the freshest version of hell mankind could conjure.

All over the south west region of central England, there were almost five thousand like him, all spreading out with murderous intent and a newly unlocked ability to stalk and hunt their prey—living people—with renewed energy and lethality.

Chambers sat upright, tensed the muscles of his right forearm and snapped the tourniquet off his limb. Pulling at the heavy, cumbersome protective suit, he tore it away from himself with startling ease and turned his head to face professor Grewal.

Grewal had seen that look in his eye once before—had seen it just before the scientist had punched him in the face—only now the eyes weren't light blue and on the verge of tears but jet black amid a sea of red lightning bolts running through the white sclera. It drove a cold dagger of terror into Grewal's chest.

Before Grewal could move, Chambers' hand shot out impossibly fast and gripped his neck so hard that his hands and arms went painfully numb instantly. He tried to speak, at least his mind formed the words but his mouth couldn't respond, due to the pressure around his neck.

Chambers leaned forwards, sniffed him once as he growled

low in his chest, then bit him on the cheek hard enough to scrape his front teeth down Grewal's cheekbone before the burn of the fever started to take him.

Chambers dropped the other scientist, the two of them finding themselves once more on the same side, regardless of how they'd felt about one another. He set about hunting down the other living people. Impacts hit his body, but as none of them blew apart his skull, they barely slowed him as he leapt and climbed and tore at them; never stopping to eat but just dealing debilitating blows before his attention was caught by another living enemy.

———

"Okay, that was definitely a forty-five," Dave Shepherd said to the other SEALs, who had all stopped their work to stare back up the hill at the building they had just come from. The answer to the statement came in the form of an explosive rattle of automatic fire which had to be from a squad gun. If that was being used inside a building, then the day had almost certainly gone to shit, Miller knew.

They began to ready their weapons again, stacking up and waiting for the word to advance back up the hill just as screams filled the black sky.

"No," Miller said. "It's loose, and that means an outbreak. You know our orders."

They did.

Wordlessly, they climbed into the boat and pushed off, taking a compass bearing to direct them out to sea where they would find the naval flotilla and hope to be done with the scourge.

TWENTY-EIGHT

The men of the British Special Forces elite took their role seriously.

Acting as the cut-off between what was obviously some kind of viral testing facility hastily thrown together by the Americans in a secluded farm on the west coast of the island, and the rest of the population to their backs in the east. They had never officially been told that there were scientists there testing the sickness that caused the dead to become ambulatory and tear the flesh from others unthinkingly. However, their strict orders to destroy anything coming from that direction that didn't give the correct codeword response to their challenge—with a heavy inference to shoot first if they weren't speaking at all—made it clear that they were facing the potential of infected people seeking a way through them.

They had made a small town of tents in the lee of a raised hillock which sheltered them just a little from the harsh weather the island experienced. But since they'd all successfully completed SAS selection and training, and had all spent time living in harsh environments where the power of the elements alone might kill them, this hardship barely even registered as one.

They rotated their turns on the road barricade, just as they took turns sleeping and patrolling the impassable ground either side of the only stretch of flat ground which the road ran through. That road was covered by two interlocking firing arcs of belt-fed general purpose machine guns capable of destroying any vehicle moving towards the farm.

"I still don't like it, Tip," a trooper complained to the man beside him as he lit his cigarette and tucked both hands back under his armpits to leave the smoke dangling from between his lips as he spoke. "There was more bloody gunfire earlier, so the boys said."

The man he spoke to sighed, as though bored of hearing the same arguments come from him. "There's always gunfire from there. It's the easiest way to kill one of them."

"Well, I still don't like it."

"What don't you like, Ed?" corporal Tipuric asked trooper Jenkins.

"Well," the man said, voice still muffled by the cigarette and his Welsh accent, "they could be doing all sorts of things down there, and we don't know anything about it."

"What are you worried about?" Tipuric snapped, the cold taking the edge off his usually long patience. "Expecting a BTR-Eighty to come plodding up the hill? Howay, man. Bloody cold's got to your brain."

"Well, if one does come up, it can bloody well have one of these bastards," the reply came as one hand was taken from the warm armpit it resided in and tapped a dull, green tube standing vertically.

"Take more than one," Tipuric answered absent-mindedly, annoyed with himself for even being drawn into the idle conversation. He was saved any further retort by a sharp sound from the darkness ahead of their position. Both men froze, hearing the sudden absence of low chatter from either side of their roadblock. For ten long seconds nobody said a word, waiting to see if the noise repeated itself. Tipuric didn't move, other than to tighten his grip on the Colt rifle he cradled and run his thumb up towards the safety catch.

"Fox," he said confidently. Before anyone could disagree, the sound came again, only much further to the left of where it had originally sounded, to give the impression that there were more than one of the animals out there. That sharp cry was answered by a low chorus of hisses in various tones.

Tipuric stood, flicking off the safety catch and pointing his rifle front as he shouted.

"Stand to! Stand to! Attack front!"

Muzzle flashes from the medium machine guns lit up the dark night, showing hideous snapshots of men and women wearing a mixture of camouflage uniforms and white coats, all smeared with dark patches of blood, approaching at a run up the slope towards them.

Behind them, a mortar was sent up to pop high over their heads where a small parachute deployed to gently lower the fired projectile back to earth as it burned brightly and provided illumination to the battlefield.

That illumination did not make them happy. Tipuric's mind counted just over twenty, which wasn't an insurmountable number by any stretch of the imagination for such well-trained and well-armed men, but something nagged at the back of his mind as he lined up heads between the iron sights of the rifle and clattered off bursts of fire.

He should have listened to that nagging doubt. If he had, they might have won. Might have survived. As it happened, the noises they had ignored had originated with two former people—one in a pale shirt with a missing finger and another wearing the uniform and insignia of a US army staff sergeant —who had flanked the roadblock from the impassable high ground to each side and fallen upon the men firing the GPMGs.

As the guns went silent in unison, Tipuric instinctively turned to his left and began triggering shots off at the shape of a crouching man in a once light blue shirt with the collar undone and the sleeves rolled up as though he was still working after a long day. The shape crouched further, like it was powering up, then leapt clear of the aim of his rifle like a human-sized grasshopper, which left the SAS man momentarily stunned. Spinning and searching for a target, he looked back at the trooper who had been beside him, in time to see the man's boots fly through the air as his rifle flashed with automatic fire when his trigger finger spasmed. As trooper Jenkins sailed backwards out of their defensive position, one of the bullets he inadvertently and negligently fired ricocheted from something and thumped into Tipuric's side with just enough force to punch its way an inch into his flesh. Immediately, the wound welled with hot blood and took his breath away, but he was instinctively certain nothing vital was hit. Staggering back to his feet, he hefted the rifle with the heavy attachment under the barrel for firing small grenades, only to find the space before him empty.

A feeling. A creeping sensation. A cellular knowledge made him turn around, as the absence of sound and wind from behind him told his brain that there was a person there.

Rotating his head slowly, he saw the shirted man standing with such horrible and unnerving stillness that his presence was the absolute portent of the violent end he always expected to meet in battle one day.

He had expected it by an Argentine bomb or bayonet in the Falklands and he had expected it from a sniper in an attic room in Derry or Belfast, but he never, not once, expected to die as he did on a freezing roadside on a Scottish island.

He began to raise the gun but it was knocked violently

aside by an arm much stronger than his own. He retreated a step to whip the Browning pistol up and trigger two fast shots into the chest right where the heart was, in the classic double-tap he had trained to deliver for so many years.

The muscle-memory of the fatal shots—fatal in almost any other scenario—cost him his life. Had he acted less instinctively, had his brain pulled the trigger and not his subconscious, as he had trained his body to do, he might have aimed for the head and scored a lucky hit.

The two bullets did nothing. They didn't even delay his death for a second as the hideous thing before him snatched a hand out and dug the fingernails of its right hand into the flesh above his collar bone, tearing through the three layers of clothing to break the skin and snap the bone as it dragged him towards its open mouth.

The last thing Tipuric saw, before he was blinded by the sheet of blood flowing from the bite to his head, was the bright reflection of the illuminating mortar in the black eyes of the thing that killed him.

———

Fisher, unable to sleep in his bed, went downstairs in the house he and the other CIA men had adopted as their own and sat in a threadbare, wing-backed chair that he guessed was older than he was. He poured himself something from a bottle bearing a name on the label he couldn't pronounce and held it up to the small light that the lamp bulb emitted to bathe the room in a soft, dull yellow. The colour and clarity of the drink was to his liking, and he allowed himself the small fantasy that he was a connoisseur of such things before taking a hit of the drink and tossing it back without tasting it.

He coughed hard, spluttering as if the harsh whisky had fought back and insisted that he treat it with more respect than to just swallow it like it was prescribed medication, instead of something that took years to mature.

He wiped his eyes and stood to pour another, still coughing intermittently, and took a tentative sip this time. He allowed the drink to coat his mouth and burn his gums before taking a swallow and feeling the liquid pass down his throat to where it warmed his stomach and tempted him to take another sip.

When that glass was finished, he allowed himself another, arguing internally that he was unlikely to hear anything important until the morning when the tapes of the air bombardment and the reconnaissance fly-over were delivered to the carrier.

That footage would vindicate him, he was certain. It would show that the infected were made inert, were bleeding out to pose no threat to the lives of American servicemen who would be arriving by boat the following summer to begin cleansing the nation, ready for clean-up and repopulation.

After that, they would move into the European states that could be easily defended, and from there the pattern he had devised would be repeated. They would again use the devices to attract the infected into concentrated areas before destroying them with the anti-virus developed under his direction. This simple, and most importantly cost-effective, strategy he was sure would earn him an elevated position when the deck was shuffled, which it surely would be soon.

There were other states in the world still alive, still independent, but their survival was largely down to luck and geography, whereas the United States remained whole through strict quarantine procedures and a hard line of dedicated defence. He'd heard the scuttlebutt that so many ships had been sunk and so many aircraft shot out of the skies to prevent even the slightest chance that the virus would land on their home soil. All of those refugees who had followed procedure and been taken in would one day be repatriated to run what would effectively be a client state of their own administration.

He knew that if the boot were on the other foot, the Brits or the French would do precisely as they had done. He doubted the might hiding behind the Iron Curtain would have been much different, for that matter.

Fisher's tumbling thoughts of the world's politics and his own ambitions swirled in his head until, ironically, the sleep that eluded him in bed took him quickly as his head slumped against one of the high wings of the armchair.

A hammering noise woke him, reminding him of a jack-hammer ripping up the road to make way for more roads, more cars, more people. The world had too many people in it already.

The hammering sounded again, reaching his brain fully this time and setting off the alarm bells. The bangs on the wooden door sounded as if the person on the other side were fleeing the very hounds of hell.

He woke with a gasp, the empty glass falling from his lap to land on the thick hearth rug with a heavy thump of the crystal tumbler's base. A strangled noise escaped his throat as he stood, unsteady through tiredness more than the few glasses of scotch, and he made his way to the door to slide across the heavy bolt and admit a red-faced, terrified man in American military uniform.

"Sir!" he gasped, "We have to get the hell outta here!"

"Calm down, soldier," Fisher ordered him. "What's going on?"

"Outbreak," the soldier panted, "at the lab."

Fisher stared at him for a second with a blank expression on his face. He rejected the urges to ask if he was sure, or to state the idiotic belief that there had to be a mistake. He swallowed, nodded to himself, then turned to face up the stairs and bawl out that they were leaving. The other two agents had already been woken up by the banging and both appeared at the top of the stairs to exchange terrified glances with one another.

"Take the other vehicle and meet us at the airfield," Fisher told them as he shoved his feet into his boots and pulled open the door under the stairs where they had stowed their emergency gear. Fisher took a spare magazine for the Beretta he carried to augment the two full ones, then picked up a Colt sub machine gun, similar to the larger versions so easily recognised the world over but firing the smaller ammunition like his sidearm. Two spare magazines for that went into a pocket of the coat and he turned to see the uniformed man almost dancing on the spot as he glanced behind him into the darkness, clutching his own service weapon.

Fisher prompted him to move, climbing into the left side of the vehicle as the panicked soldier drove a little too fast for the narrow roads.

"Calm it down a little," he said after one too many close calls with the rocky edge of the road, "we ain't getting out of here if you kill us in a car wreck now, are we?"

"No, Sir," came the reply in a voice that sounded almost tearful.

"Tell me what you know," Fisher instructed him.

"We had watch on the quarantine barricade, like you said," he blurted out. "All of a sudden they just lit up the night; full auto and flares. Then they went quiet and the noises started in…"

"What noises?"

"The screams, like, *animal* screams…"

"Like a screech?"

"Yeah, only… only worse than I ever heard…"

"Did you call it in?" Fisher asked, trying to get him back on track.

"The Lieutenant was trying to. He sent me to get you back to the airfield so you could call in reinforcements or whatever…" Fisher chuckled darkly.

"Sir?"

"Son, why would the United States military throw reinforcements at this place? We were only here to test the serum against *them* and now we know that works, well…"

"So, everyone will…"

"LOOK OUT," Fisher snarled as the soldier snatched the wheel over to narrowly avoid a gatepost they were heading directly for. "Eyes on the goddamned road!"

They arrived at the airfield after a few more miles of tense silence and Fisher slid from the vehicle to start shouting orders for the helicopter to be made ready to fly. The air crews seemed surprised to be roused in the night, but the news of a suspected outbreak encouraged them to get into the air as soon as possible.

The rotors were turning, and Fisher was standing at the rear ramp when one of the crew tapped him on the shoulder and beckoned him to the bulkhead, where he was handed a headset. The pilot was on the other end, asking when they were taking off. He looked back out into the darkness, wondering how the other two agents could have taken close to half an hour just to get dressed and drive the few miles to follow him, and he made a judgement call.

"Go now," he said, "if they aren't here by now, I don't think they're coming."

The helicopter took off, rotating in the air to point the nose west before dipping it and surging through the dark sky. Their path took them over the house that Fisher had been in so recently, and when he heard the reports of a fire there through his headset, he couldn't understand how the idyllic farmhouse, with its surprisingly comfortable chair and potent scotch, was burning. He knew, or at least he strongly suspected, that the other two agents with him had run into the infected shortly after he'd escaped the house, and his thoughts tortured him, wondering if they might still be alive if he'd stayed long enough for them to get dressed and get in the vehicle with him.

Cold, hard, good sense reasserted itself and he knew that if he had stayed, it wouldn't mean the addition of two more lives on the aircraft now, but would spell the death of everyone. That guilt hit him immediately as his conscience forced him to give everyone still on the island as much of a fighting chance to survive as possible.

"Call up the base," he instructed the crew. "Tell them there's been an outbreak. Tell them... tell them to do whatever they can."

TWENTY-NINE

The door to the room Downes had adopted as his own burst open as if the big Scotsman occupying the doorway was clearing the room of terrorists.

"On your fucking feet, Boss," Mac barked. "Bastards are on the island." If any words would bring a man into full alertness under any circumstances, it would be the report that Screechers had boots on the ground in their safe haven.

"Where?"

"East coast."

Downes was dressed before the brief exchange was complete, sitting on the bed again to lace his boots, as Mac picked up the major's webbing and checked it for magazines before holding it ready for the man to shrug into.

"The boys ready?"

"Smiffy's on the door," Mac told him. "Dez has gone to rouse the others."

That made sense to Downes. Smiffy was still limping from the sprained ankle he'd given himself kicking the head half off a Screecher, so Dez being the runner was the sensible choice.

"Major?" snapped a crisp voice from the lower floor of the

small house. "Major?"

"Here!" Downes answered in a clipped voice that was all business. He appeared at the top of the stairs to see Captain Palmer at the foot of them, similarly dressed for battle. He saw the anger and concern in the younger man's eyes and felt for him; they'd been through hell enough already, and the responsibilities heaped on the man who should, by rights, be in command of a section of main battle tanks, had so often threatened to be too much for him to bear. "Your men?"

"Half on patrol on the north coast, half in town," Palmer answered, hesitating before he anticipated the next question. "No way to get word to them, I'm afraid."

"Has anyone sent word to Colonel Kelly yet?"

"The Colonel was the one who sent word to *us*, Major." Before Downes could respond, a knock on the open door grabbed their attention. Maxwell was there, eyes wide with the same fear and indignant rage that his captain mirrored.

"Men are forming now, Sir," he reported. "What's our orders?" Palmer looked to Downes, as though admitting that he hadn't thought that far ahead. Dez reappeared at that point with steam emanating from his exposed head and face into the cold night air.

"Locals are awake and getting out. I've told everyone to form up in the little town square thing by the pubs." Downes nodded to acknowledge the report but Dez wasn't finished.

"Couple of the local boys are fishermen," he went on, "reckon we can get to St Kilda through the Outer Hebrides if we can get enough people into boats."

"Where?" Palmer asked, confused.

"You've heard of the Deep Sea Range?" Downes asked. Swirling information about missile ranges in their remote northern areas.

"We… we have people there?"

"Unmanned base," Mac explained as he dragged the bags

of spare equipment and ammunition from the corner of the room. Dez slung his MP5 and hefted the GPMG taken so long ago from one of Maxwell's abandoned Spartan wagons.

"Defensive position?" Palmer asked.

"We can line everyone up at the docks with our backs to the sea," Dez answered. "Other than that, there are multiple approaches. If it was armour or vehicles, we'd stand a chance, but…" he shrugged to indicate that the Screechers could come at them any way they liked.

"Do it," Downes said before turning back to Palmer. "Is there anyone we can send in a vehicle to fetch your men back?" Palmer looked at Maxwell, knowing that he couldn't afford to lose him, if he wanted the men and the civilians kept in check. He turned back to the major and drew himself up.

"Yes, there is."

"What the bloody hell is all this noise about?" Oliver Simpkins-Palmer complained as he yanked open the door to investigate the shouting and banging which had woken him. Everywhere he looked, he saw people running, carrying children and possessions in a state of panic.

"We have a deployment, eh?" croaked an elderly voice as a private from a Scottish infantry regiment led the mostly senile old man down the stairs.

"That's right, Colonel," he said reassuringly, "we need to get you in the fight. Show the lads how it's done."

"Splendid!" Colonel Tim crowed from inside the multiple layers of knitted clothing he was wearing to counter the ill-health that had afflicted him since arriving on Skye. He saw the second lieutenant and tried to wave his family claymore towards him. "Blighters want another crack at us, Palmer!" he cackled. "Get your hat on and grab a revolver."

Oliver Palmer didn't bother answering, having lost all patience with the old man shortly after arriving on the island and realising he held no power there. He'd spent the subsequent time doing very little, as his brother had removed even the small amount of responsibility bestowed on him, preferring instead to trust the royal marine lieutenant in his place.

"Olly," the voice of his brother snapped. He turned to see him dressed for battle and wearing a hard look of resolve.

"Julian," he answered, one lip curling in jealous derision. "Come to mock the unemployed?"

"Olly, I need your help." The words shocked the young man into forgetting his arrogance.

"What's happening?"

"There's been an outbreak on the west coast of the island," Palmer Senior told him quietly, "our American friends are either dead or have abandoned us. We have to make a stand and consider fleeing the island."

"What? And go where? Are you sure?" he bombarded his brother with questions, all of which were ignored.

"Can you find Lloyd and the others? They're patrolling the north coast." Younger brother fixed elder with a hard look, as if suggesting his brother only wanted him when the officer he rated as a better soldier wasn't available. The fact that he was being sent to fetch his preferred replacement only added insult to the injury he felt he had been dealt. Before he could say anything, his older brother recognised the look on his face and grabbed his shirt with both fists. He took three hard paces forwards to slam the second lieutenant into the interior wall.

"This is no time for your childish jealousy," he snarled. "How many times have we come through the fire against the odds? How many? The *one* time you were asked to do any real soldiering, you did well. So why the hell can't you just do what I'm asking of you without the bile?" Oliver shoved his brother back to break the grip and stepped up with the same savage look in his eyes.

"*Real* soldiering? Like seeing to the civilians and keeping the mad old bat of a Colonel out of your way? Like managing the lists of supplies while you send sergeants out in charge of patrols?"

"Yes," Julian answered with the same vehemence. "All of those activities you think are boring, that you think are beneath your lofty station"—he sneered those words at him—"*that* is real soldiering; doing the hard work that doesn't win you a blasted medal."

The two brothers stared at one another for a few seconds until their anger began to abate.

"Please, Olly, go and get our men back and let's save as many people as we can." Oliver drew himself up, adding a very military bearing to his stance, and he accepted his brother's orders.

———

"Keep the civilians moving," Maxwell shouted, waving his arms frantically to force the flow of people towards the handful of fishing boats that illuminated the docks with their harsh deck lights. Even such a small number of people—no more than two hundred in Captain Palmer's estimation—packed into a confined area like the small dock in the town, seemed like a stampede trying to pass through a funnel. He feared that the gunfire would start soon, that the time to get as many people as possible safely off the island would be over.

With each minute that went by, with each boat that filled up and pushed off to safety, the sense of dread grew heavier in his stomach. He looked at his watch, counting the minutes since his brother had left and hoping that he would have found the detachment of marines and yeomanry and would have turned them around to bolster their armed defences.

As that thought struck him, the concern of having enough space on boats to evacuate them all dragged him back down into frightened depression.

Then the shooting started. One rifle fired, then it was joined by half a dozen others, like a contagious infection, but any other noises were drowned out by the screams of the terrified civilians who crowded onto the boats, unheeding of the warnings not to overload them.

Palmer heard clear voices ring out above the din; voices of Maxwell and Foster, the marine that Lloyd had placed trust in. Those voices called for order, for calm, for action without panic and they were like rocks on the shallows that the fear broke upon.

Palmer saw them then, coming from the higher ground, shadows flitting between the buildings as the last of the civilians pushed out to sea. The firing had stopped as no more targets were spotted, and in the lull in noise, Palmer heard a sound that cut through his flesh to chill the very marrow of his bones.

The shrill, barking cry of an animal pierced the air. It froze the men, too, and more than one frightened face turned to look at the captain as though he could save them, could reassure them somehow. He knew they wanted that from him, knew that he could tell them that it was just a Lima, and hadn't they killed plenty of Limas before?

He tried, but he couldn't force the words from his mouth.

The sound came again, undulating and yowling like a wolf's cry. It was undeniably an animalistic attempt to communicate, and his fear rose as high as he had ever known when he realised, with utter horror, that this was something altogether new.

"Make ready," he called, shouting the only thing he knew to say. It had the effect he wanted in that it did indeed steady the men. They all leaned into their weapons and waited for a fresh hell to fall from the shadows.

———

Fisher's arrival on the windswept deck of the carrier in the middle of the night was met with little reaction. The report that they had lost most of their forces based on the island was met with less reaction than he expected, and his seniors were only interested in the results from the deployment of the serum.

Residual movement, that was the term they used. Residual movement was a good day as far as they were concerned. Jacobs asked him outright if there was any reason *not* to go ahead with the full-scale deployment of the sonic lure devices and end all of the infected with the serum.

He kept his mouth shut, not wanting to add a feather of failure to his cap and delay the plan to start saving the world because some dead scientist wanted to try it out on a redhead or something, to make sure it worked on all of them. Residual movement, that was the terminology that stuck in his head. If the combined military might of the United States Armed Forces couldn't handle a few infected left, then who was he to throw fear into the mix?

He said no, and Jacobs snatched up a telephone handset to mutter into, before replacing it a few seconds later.

"You need a break," he told Fisher. "Get a hot shower and some chow; the show's about to start."

————

Before the first of the sixteen devices planned so precisely to land on UK soil dropped, before the cargo planes full of serum-filled munitions landed in The Canary Islands, ready to be loaded onto three AC-one-thirty-H gunships, a lone, small cargo ship fought through the choppy sea around the north west tip of the Isle of Skye.

The man at the helm, a reclusive Scot who was less than impressed to be roused by twenty armed men demanding his assistance, piloted his craft recklessly in order to satisfy the two officers who shouted encouragement to him.

The decision to abandon their vehicles and head directly to the evacuation site was driven by the young second lieutenant who appeared to his royal marine counterpart to be far more enthused than was his usual languid style.

In short, he imagined the younger man had received a rocket directly up his arse.

They heard the gunfire as soon as they rounded a headland against a choppy tide, before the flow of the water pulled them faster towards the Portree dock hidden from sight by the dark rocks.

"I say!" Palmer yelled at the semi-toothless man spinning the wheel to keep them steady. "Can you turn around," he shouted clearly and slowly as though he was conversing with a foreign waiter and was ignorant to how offensive he came across as, "and bring us into the dock stern first?" The old man looked at him like he was insane for a few beats, before shrugging and muttering something only he could hear.

"Look alive, boys," Palmer cried as he checked the magazine in his own weapon and charged it, ready to forge a path through the huddled men of the yeomanry and marines. When he reached the rear railing, what would soon become the very front rank of the fight, he turned a full circle and treated them all to his best bloodthirsty smile. The men all knew him, so none were convinced as to what the spoiled aristocrat was up to.

"It's about to get rather busy here," he went on, "so any man not willing to get his hands dirty should make his way to the rear and give us all a little more space." His roguish smirk, visible to all of them under the harsh, bright deck lights, lent him an air of being a little unhinged.

As much as the men mistrusted him, given their previous experience, they recognised his bravado for what it was.

"You buying the drinks afterwards, Mister Palmer?" shouted a voice from half a dozen paces away. Palmer, blessed with outstandingly good fortune, recognised the speaker and could even marry the wet, windswept face with a name.

"Help me get the others out of this steaming pile of shit, Sergeant Cooper, and I'll share a brandy with you all."

"Yeah," Cooper added, pushing his luck, "but are *you* buying the bottle, Sir?"

Palmer checked his weapon once more and pulled a spare magazine from his webbing to hold it alongside the gun as a statement of intent. "Cooper, I'll buy a whole bloody barrel of the finest stuff if we see the dawn."

As he delivered the line, thinking—*hoping*—for once that he had managed what he had seen so many officers achieve and made the men want to follow him into danger, the boat's engine note changed pitch and ramped up to bubble the water at the stern.

"You heard the Lieutenant," Lloyd said as he shouldered his way through the men to occupy the same spot on the railing as Palmer did, yanking back the charging handle of his rifle as he spoke. "Look alive!"

The boat swung around, revealing the raging battle that their own side was most definitely losing.

———

"Keep firing!" Captain Palmer roared, just as his own gun ran dry and he fumbled to replace the spent magazine. The area immediately to his front filled up with ragged bodies of former inhabitants of the island, mostly soldiers in various forms of torn and bloodied uniform, with civilians added in here and there for flavour. They flowed like water into the void that his reload caused, and the closer the enemy got to him, the more he struggled to seat the fresh magazine.

"Shit, shit, shit," he hissed to himself as he couldn't force his hands to work. He almost threw himself down in fright as a massive, clattering noise erupted to his right.

"Fuck off!" Dezzy, one of the SAS men, yelled at the Screechers he threw down as he fired the GPMG from the hip. He flashed a toothy smile at the captain and followed it up with a wink before opening up again with another long burst of heavy, rattling gunfire. Palmer seated the magazine and fed a round into the chamber as he stole a glance around their shrinking battlefield.

"They're retreating," Downes yelled over to him. He looked again and saw it was true; the enemy were falling back into the shadows. As welcome as the reprieve was, the connotations of what it meant chilled the cavalry officer to the bone.

Then he heard it again. The yelping noise, like a screech but speaking a language he couldn't understand. It was animalistic, but it was clearly heeded as the wave of freshly turned undead slunk away into the darkness.

"Reload," Palmer yelled. "They won't stay gone for long." The remaining men followed his instructions as voices called out names of their friends who they had lost in the confusion. Some lay bleeding on the wet ground of the docks, whereas others had been dragged away. Palmer kicked over the body of the thing that had caused all the commotion; a slim female with one missing hand from what he guessed was a recently earned gunshot wound at close range. There was something odd about her appearance, something *different*, other than the fact that she'd sailed twenty feet through the air from the nearest rooftop to land behind their front rank and bring chaos to the fight.

Bayonets had brought her down eventually, but her slashing nails and ripping teeth had done enough damage to open the gates to the surging attack from the darkness ahead.

That was when it hit Palmer. It was a concerted attack; not

the kind they had seen from the swarms in the past but an infinitely more *human* attack.

It was deliberate. Planned. Orchestrated and executed well, and when it failed, the enemy commander had sounded the retreat. He sought out Downes in the huddle of surviving men and fixed the man's eyes with his own. Something passed between them in that moment; some understanding of what had just happened. What they were facing was new, and far more frightening than just a mindless horde marching heedlessly into their bullets.

A noise behind them made them turn. A ragged, rolling cheer that swelled into a war cry of massed men ramping themselves up into a frenzy, ready to join the fight. Palmer couldn't understand where these men had come from until he recognised the sharp profile of his younger brother's face at the very front of the men, and his eyes zeroed in on his brother.

While their backs were turned, the next attack came.

The barking, shrieking yelp came from up high, revealing the position of a blooded man in a torn blue shirt with the sleeves rolled up above the elbows. He shrieked again just as a targeted mass of Screechers piled into the right side of their position and overwhelmed the men there.

Downes was their target. The bloody and blackened fingernails reached for him, ignoring the other potential victims within range, dragging him backwards and making him drop the weapon he was holding. Palmer didn't hesitate; just slung his own gun and stooped low on the move, as he fast-paced forwards to scoop up the automatic shotgun and reverse it to point the dangerous end at things he wanted to render immobile.

He triggered off a burst of rounds, feeling the savage, violent recoil of the gun and not even blinking at the gore and destruction it wrought.

The heavy gunfire of the GPMG added to Palmer's

onslaught to ruin the attack, then as the major was left on the ground, Dez switched his aim back to where the enemy commander had showed himself.

He—*it*—ducked away before the bullets could walk their way up the wall towards its position, but the damage was done. The renewed attack on all fronts was met by a hail of bullets from the rear of the boat as the reinforcements came into range. Smiffy helped Dez, crouching beside their officer to defend him and pour fire at the Screechers, even though they must surely have known he was done for.

Palmer stepped up beside them, adding measured shots from the shotgun to blow away limbs and remove heads. He fired until the gun ran dry, slinging it diagonally over his body to retrieve the sterling and start rattling off more shots. A hand grabbed his shoulder, pulling him back slightly. He tried to shrug it away, thinking that someone was attempting to force him to retreat but instead he found his younger brother pushing in beside him to add his own fire to the desperate defence.

The attack failed again, and only a few shadows rippled in the middle distance. The barking noise sounded once more; so like a Lima and yet infinitely more terrifying, considering what they had just witnessed.

"Onto the boat," Palmer Junior yelled, repeating the order as the men fell back without turning their vulnerable backs to the face of the enemy.

"Onto the boat, Julian," he added in a low voice.

"We must help Major Downes," the captain answered, just as Mac burst through the men to fall beside his teammates.

"Oh, no, Boss," he crooned with more sadness and emotion than anyone thought him capable of, "what the fuck have they done to you?"

Downes choked, bubbling blood out of his mouth as he looked down to see the puncture wounds caused by fingernails in his ruined abdomen. He turned his head and pointed with a shaking hand, unable to speak as he fought down the convulsions the pain caused him.

Mac saw it. Saw the neat row of teeth marks in his neck and knew it was over for the officer. Setting his face in a grim line he nodded, trying to convey his feelings and coming up woefully short.

"I'll… I'll stay with him," Smiffy said, handing up his weapons and shaking them until they were taken. His hands fumbled for the pistol and the spare ammunition before he was asked by the dour Scot just what in the hell he was doing.

"Bastards…" Smiffy said between gasps of breath, "bastards got me too," he admitted, rolling up his right sleeve to expose the raged chunk torn from his forearm. "I can already feel the burn," he said as he turned to Dez and gave him a wan smile. "Look after that Ruski rifle," he said, pointing a bloody finger at the stolen VAL from a lifetime ago.

"Time to go," Lloyd said, turning to shout more orders. Palmer looked up to see the shadows moving again, no doubt swelled with slower reinforcements in preparation for another wave of attack.

"Go on," Smiffy said, cradling his boss' head in his lap, "fuck off now."

"No," Dezzy snapped, "I'm not leaving you like this."

In answer, Smiffy took back his pistol and gestured with his head for them to leave.

They left before the next attack came, leaving the docks empty but for dead and turning soldiers, and two dying SAS men.

As the boat followed the reverse course out of the shielded bay, two small calibre shots echoed out to sea after them.

EPILOGUE

The handful of fishing boats eventually sailed through the choppy water to slide into the small bay on the uninhabited island of Hirta in the Outer Hebrides. They were freezing cold, frightened and so uncertain of any future that the numbness they felt was just as likely to be from the emotions coursing through them as from the exposure to the elements.

Palmer jumped down first, paddling through knee-deep water until he stepped clear onto the sandy beach. The dawn hadn't fully broken yet, providing the steely grey ambience that made the whole situation even more surreal.

"Where to now, Captain?" asked a rich voice he knew well, only now it carried an edge to it that only battle could muster.

"Up the hill," he answered, "to the military base, I presume?"

"And hope to find a roaring fire and a hot bath?"

"Indeed," Palmer said, before bowing his head and regarding his bloodstained hands holding two weapons. He looked at the shotgun, staring at it for a moment until snapping himself out of the numb reverie.

"Olly," he said quietly, "I... I owe you an apology. What

you did saved the lives of the men—saved *my* life—and you have my gratitude." As soon as he said the words, he felt as if they hadn't been enough to convey his true feelings. They felt too formal, too wooden and not believable enough.

"Orders, Captain?" Lloyd asked, arriving with a squad of marines looking ready for work.

"Press on ahead, if you please, Mister Lloyd, recce the base and see if you can't find a way inside." Lloyd nodded and urged his men onwards with some kindly insults to get them moving. Behind them trooped the rest of the survivors, some of whom had been with them since even before the captain had arrived in the commander's seat of his *Annabelle* so many months before. They had saved none of the Germans who had saved their lives, and of the special air service patrol, the surviving fifty percent stopped beside the two brothers.

"That answers the question of what the bloody scientists were doing on Skye," Mac stated flatly. "They've taken the Limas and made the bastards even faster and smarter."

"Did you notice how none of the ones attacking us were the Screecher type?" Julian Palmer asked quietly.

"Like life couldn't get any fucking worse?" Dezzy asked rhetorically. "So what? They've made the virus or whatever *worse?*"

"Perhaps," Captain Palmer opined. "Perhaps it's just nature. Perhaps the Screechers have adapted and evolved. Which begs the question of what our next move is."

"We do the same as they've done," his younger brother answered with strength and more than a little vehemence. "We survive. We fight back. *We* adapt."

FROM THE PUBLISHER

Thank you for reading *Adaptation*, the fifth of six books in Toy Soldiers.

We hope you enjoyed it as much as we enjoyed bringing it to you. We just wanted to take a moment to encourage you to review the book on Amazon and Goodreads. Every review helps further the author's reach and, ultimately, helps them continue writing fantastic books for us all to enjoy.

If you liked this book, check out the rest of our catalogue at www.aethonbooks.com. To sign up to receive a FREE collection from some of our best authors as well as updates regarding all new releases, visit www.aethonbooks.com/sign-up.

JOIN THE STREET TEAM! Get advanced copies of all our books, plus other free stuff and help us put out hit after hit.

SEARCH ON FACEBOOK:
AETHON STREET TEAM

ALSO IN THE SERIES

SPECIAL THANKS TO:

ADAWIA E. ASAD
JENNY AVERY
BARDE PRESS
CALUM BEAULIEU
BEN
BECKY BEWERSDORF
BHAM
TANNER BLOTTER
ALFRED JOSEPH BOHNE IV
CHAD BOWDEN
ERREL BRAUDE
DAMIEN BROUSSARD
CATHERINE BULLINER
JUSTIN BURGESS
MATT BURNS
BERNIE CINKOSKE
MARTIN COOK
ALISTAIR DILWORTH
JAN DRAKE
BRET DULEY
RAY DUNN
ROB EDWARDS
RICHARD EYRES
MARK FERNANDEZ
CHARLES T FINCHER
SYLVIA FOIL
GAZELLE OF CAERBANNOG
DAVID GEARY
MICHEAL GREEN
BRIAN GRIFFIN

EDDIE HALLAHAN
JOSH HAYES
PAT HAYES
BILL HENDERSON
JEFF HOFFMAN
GODFREY HUEN
JOAN QUERALTÓ IBÁÑEZ
JONATHAN JOHNSON
MARCEL DE JONG
KABRINA
PETRI KANERVA
ROBERT KARALASH
VIKTOR KASPERSSON
TESLAN KIERINHAWK
ALEXANDER KIMBALL
JIM KOSMICKI
FRANKLIN KUZENSKI
MEENAZ LODHI
DAVID MACFARLANE
JAMIE MCFARLANE
HENRY MARIN
CRAIG MARTELLE
THOMAS MARTIN
ALAN D. MCDONALD
JAMES MCGLINCHEY
MICHAEL MCMURRAY
CHRISTIAN MEYER
SEBASTIAN MÜLLER
MARK NEWMAN
JULIAN NORTH

KYLE OATHOUT
LILY OMIDI
TROY OSGOOD
GEOFF PARKER
NICHOLAS (BUZ) PENNEY
JASON PENNOCK
THOMAS PETSCHAUER
JENNIFER PRIESTER
RHEL
JODY ROBERTS
JOHN BEAR ROSS
DONNA SANDERS
FABIAN SARAVIA
TERRY SCHOTT
SCOTT
ALLEN SIMMONS
KEVIN MICHAEL STEPHENS
MICHAEL J. SULLIVAN
PAUL SUMMERHAYES
JOHN TREADWELL
CHRISTOPHER J. VALIN
PHILIP VAN ITALLIE
JAAP VAN POELGEEST
FRANCK VAQUIER
VORTEX
DAVID WALTERS JR
MIKE A. WEBER
PAMELA WICKERT
JON WOODALL
BRUCE YOUNG

9 781949 890518